Cover Licence provided by selfpubbookcovers.com; Copyright © Shardel 2017.

Paperback First Edition 2017

Published By:
Alternative Fiction,
Waterford, Ireland.
Publisher's ISBN: 978-0-9934247

Printed & Bound By:
IngramSpark,
Lightning Source,
Chapter House,
Pitfield, Kiln Farm,
Milton Keynes MK11 3LW, Britain.

ISBN-13: 978-0-9934247-2-4

In memory of my parents

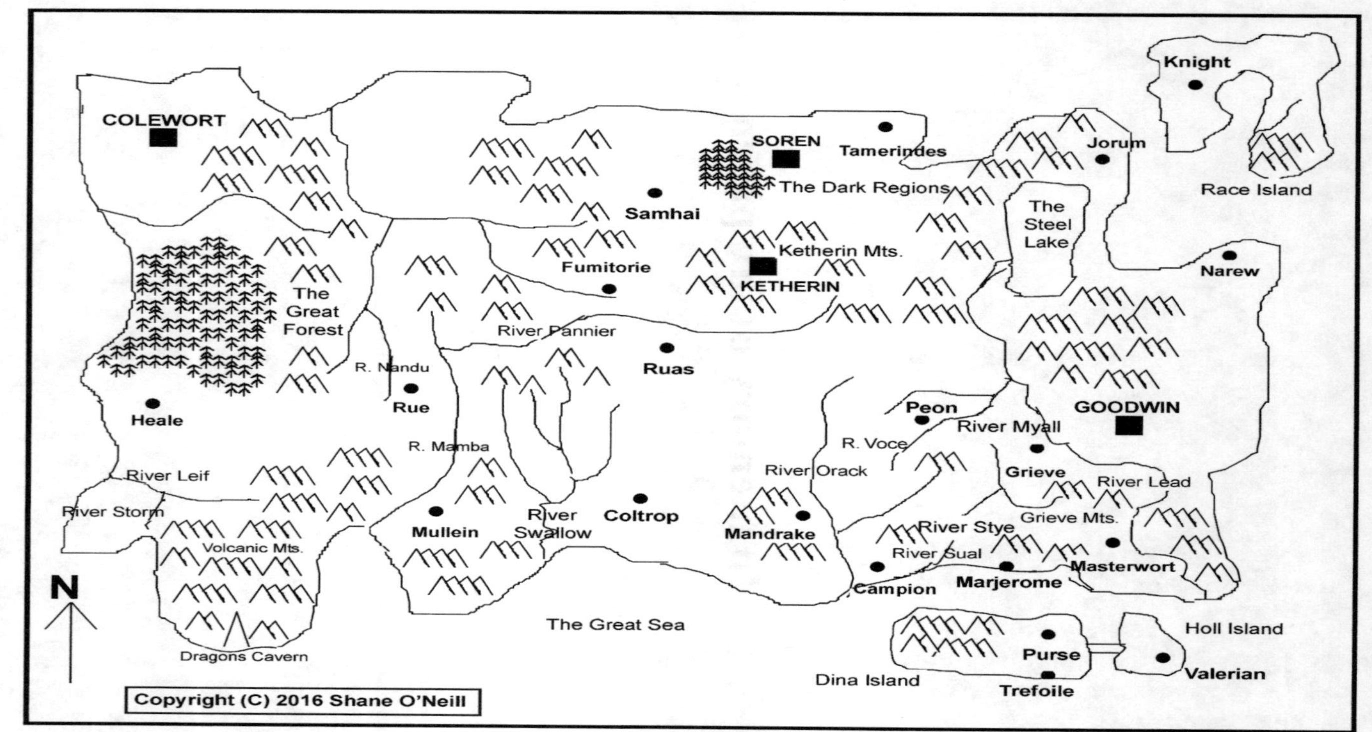
COLEWORT
Knight
SOREN
Tamerindes
Jorum
The Dark Regions
Race Island
The Steel Lake
Samhai
Ketherin Mts.
Fumitorie
Narew
The Great Forest
KETHERIN
River Pannier
R. Nandu
Ruas
Rue
Peon
GOODWIN
Heale
R. Mamba
River Myall
R. Voce
River Orack
Grieve
River Lead
River Leif
Grieve Mts.
River Storm
Mullein
River Swallow
Coltrop
Mandrake
River Stye
River Sual
Masterwort
Volcanic Mts.
Campion
Marjerome
N
The Great Sea
Holl Island
Dragons Cavern
Purse
Dina Island
Trefoile
Valerian
Copyright (C) 2016 Shane O'Neill

PROLOGUE

Parents often make it easy for their children to despise them. One might expect being the daughter and only child of the supreme ruler of the nation would grant you dispensation from this cursed norm, but rather this predicament bestows upon you a singular viewpoint; money does indeed not purchase happiness, but a life of privilege and wealth simply makes your misery more comfortable.

I always hated my father; Segal Goodwin, the High-Lord and second only surviving member of the destroyed Wizards Council, an accolade he shares with his arch-enemy Soren who was the orchestrator of the committee's destruction; the obliteration of which he gleefully enjoyed by butchering its members. They had conspired to formulate a plan to strip Soren of his magickal powers, an agenda he naturally found not to his liking.

I never cared for their politics or the bitter feud Soren shares with my father, never having to entertain the responsibility of those decisions. But I was totally unprepared for the tragedy and madness which unfolded.

It was nearing nightfall when a lone rider came down from the highlands upon the gates of Goodwin City. The populace of the capital quickly gathered around the mysterious stranger, excited and eager for any news of the outside world. Yet the message he brought was not for their ears. The guards did not bar entry, but escorted him directly through the crowded streets to the castle situated in the very centre of the city. He entered the huge structure via massive darkly-polished wooden double-doors and was momentarily taken aback by the sheer size of the hall which greeted him; stretching into black infinity, its full length obscured by seemingly unconquerable darkness. Doors lay at either side, barred; revealing no obvious sign of habitation. No statues or busts of kings or queens or any other indication of past royal rule lined the walls of the bleak hall; neither had governed this vast land for decades. Yet the castle nevertheless in their absence managed all of the necessary financial and political affairs of the country.

The one man in whose honour the structure was built was not of blue blood, but was a person who possessed just as much power and induced just as much terror as if he were. He was a man feared by all, except the few as powerful as he, or the foolish.

Nervousness gripped the messenger as he finally approached a door to the study and knocked hesitantly. The escort left as a gruff reply was heard beyond. The soldier forced his shaking hand to turn the handle and entered. Rows of books on shelves which seemed to decorate every conceivable part of the walls greeted him suddenly, and he hesitated once again before approaching the apparently only piece of furniture present in the room, a large oak table laden with further volumes and manuscripts.

A single shadow was standing behind it. The figure slowly stepped into the light and the messenger took a moment to study the fearsome individual before him. The wizard stood at a proud six foot possessing curly dark hair and beard and was at a rough guess barely half a century in age. He boasted a robust frame, accompanying thick muscular arms and had piercing blue eyes. The Magus showed annoyance at the sudden disturbance.

"Yes, what is it?" He growled.

"A message from the explorer Patrius Turbith." The rider stuttered nervously, placing the scroll on the table.

He raised an eyebrow in interest. "You may leave now."

The messenger let out an audible sigh of relief and quickly left. The mage waited until he was absolutely sure the soldier had truly departed before he opened the letter.

To the High-Wizard, and High-Lord, in the city of Goodwin.
Greetings from Patrius Turbith, explorer, the town Mullein.

I trust my message reaches you in good health, for sadly I am not. I at last proved the existence of the mythical Dragons' Cavern and found it as I always believed to be at the very edge of the Volcanic Mountains. I found both to my joy and disbelief approximately one hundred dragons in total, more than enough to finally defeat your great rival Soren. I ask humbly for only two things: one, that you cure me of my malady, for I fear I am dying. I had the misfortune to fall into a cooling pool of lava on the return journey and lost an arm in the process with the rest of my body also heavily burnt.

I trust you not to ignore my plight and travel directly to the Cavern since the route is enclosed

*with this letter. Secondly, I ask for half the treasure
at the mountain.*

> *It is mine after all by right.*

    Segal Goodwin let the scroll fall from his
fingers into the blazing fire and turned towards the
window to gaze out into the night. The path to the
Cavern burned in his mind like a fever. He smiled.
"Let the game begin."

CHAPTER ONE

A chill breeze blew through the dark tunnel causing the small figure to hesitate and tremble. The intruder waited patiently for the wind to lose some of its bitter strength before crawling on again slowly through the tight space. Despite the constrictive nature of the shaft, the little girl moved quite quickly, fearful lest she be discovered. She knew such a crime as spying on the master of the castle would be treated very seriously. But it was irresistible curiosity that drove the child down the dark secret passage on this cold day. She cast her mind back to only a few nights previous where with awe she witnessed the incredible spectacle carried out by the master in his private study. It was to her utter amazement she saw the mage open a giant pit in the floor of the chamber and an enormous grotesque creature, black of skin, crawl from it, vomiting fire and obscenities from a mouth lined with razor-sharp fangs. The monster had stood at a massive twelve feet, displaying a robust body of bulging muscles and sinews, and dark white-less eyes.

The demon and the master then conversed for several long minutes in a coarse language the child could not understand. Yet she could not avert her eyes from the scene before her even though she was terrified what might happen if the sorcerer or the creature saw her. She hoped that she might witness such a similar spectacle this night. She began to increase her movement through the tunnel, shoving her small seven year-old body through the dark passage.

The company she gladly deserted was yet again on its seasonal-excursion to the castle. It was the only daughter and child of the master of the city who voluntarily took the group of orphaned children here. The girl took a sudden turn in the shaft, moving more slowly and more quietly now, for she was close to her destination; the chamber of the High-Lord. She halted altogether upon hearing loud talking. The intruder crawled forward a few inches and glanced through the gaps in the bars of the grille, the sealed entrance to the vast room beyond.

The Magus stood motionless, gazing out through the pane-less window into the night. Suddenly he turned and left the chamber. The child glanced around the room in boredom, disappointed the wizard had left and was not going to raise another monster. Then something caught her eye. What appeared to be a crumpled piece of parchment was smouldering on the edge of the blazing fire. Even as she looked on, the flames began to renew the consuming of the partly-devoured paper. She contemplated entering the study and snatching the dying manuscript, yet fear of the sorcerer's return held her back. But curiosity gripped her and in an instant, she clutched onto the bars of the grille and pushed with all of her young strength. To her relief, it began to slowly shift out of place and crashed heavily onto the floor. The small intruder held her breath, thinking the master might have heard the noise. But from the door came no reply. She quickly ran across the room and snatched the burning parchment from the clutches of the hungry fire. She threw it to the floor and began to stamp on the paper violently, expunging the life of the flame and creating black smoke in its wake. She opened the manuscript and began to glance at its contents, but stopped upon hearing the approach of the mage. The girl rapidly folded the parchment and pushed it into one of the many pockets of her jerkin. She then ran back to the entrance of the shaft and crawled in quickly, replacing the heavy grate behind her.

She arrived soon after at the other end of the tunnel, out of breath in her haste. The small thief however noticed that she had been gone from the company for almost an hour and her absence had been noted.

The master's daughter had sent the other children off to search and was now close to anger. The adult immediately spotted the girl. "Where have you been?" The guardian shouted down to the child. "We've been looking everywhere for you!"

Yet from the girl came no reply. She instead reached deep into a pocket and handed the dark-haired woman the blackened paper. Sasha, daughter of the High-Lord gingerly took the document and instantly saw to her surprise the name of her father. She opened her mouth to scold the child, but then noticed it was partly burnt. She opened the frail paper and quickly read.

Sasha gasped in shock and put a hand to her mouth. She stared down at the girl. "Where did you get this?"

Yet the child did not answer. Sasha saw she was on the verge of tears because of what she had done.

"It's all right. I won't harm you," Sasha soothed. "Where did you get it?"

The girl hesitated before answering. "In the...master's book-room."

The other children returned just then and Sasha was quick to order them all back to the orphanage, ignoring the cries of protest. A sudden tap on the shoulder made her jump and she let out a scream. Before her was her lifelong friend and companion Ace, a handsome swordsman in his mid-twenties, standing at six foot having short blonde hair. Ace was the name he had given himself at a young age after the sudden death of his parents. Sasha had never dared enquire as to his true identity, for she knew only too well it was painful for him to speak of his past, however she was always naturally curious.

"My, you're jumpy today." The young man remarked, smiling.

"Listen, Ace, something has happened..."

But he did not hear and was quick to interrupt. "There's a pretty wild wedding festival going on at Procel's." He grinned, hoping to attract some interest.

The woman instead in silent reply opened his hand and placed the blackened letter on the palm, forcing him into a curious silence. He looked at her blankly.

"Read it." She declared, her arms folded.

The young man carefully opened the manuscript and read silently. His smile slowly dissolved and his face betrayed a frown as he began to absorb the contents. He moved back a step and the large broadsword strapped to his left hip swayed with the sudden movement. It was a blade revealed quite often, more often than Sasha would have liked due to his habit of mocking every second passer-by that might cross his daily path. Not that Ace could not handle himself. On the contrary, he was considered by many as one of the finest swordsmen in the land. She just wished he could evade most of the skirmishes by simple debate rather than killing the unfortunate opponent who was simply defending his honour.

He finally finished reading and stared at her in wonder and astonishment.

"You realise what this means?" She said aloud. "If my father claims those extra beasts, he will finally win the war against Soren. Yet in the process, he could very well destroy this entire land. We have to stop him!"

He gave an audible sigh in reply. "That is easier said than done. How?" This was a story he had heard many times before. Sasha's hatred of her father was well known, and to Ace this seemed like another such goose-chase, even though this time, it appeared a bit more serious.

"We could go to this Cavern and stop him using the dragons." She replied flatly.

Ace groaned. "Do you have any idea of how dangerous such a journey would be? You've never in your life set foot outside this city. But I have; I'm a traveller. I've seen some things I would not want to meet again. Besides, I have never gone out that far. Who knows what lies out there?"

"We have to stop him!" She repeated.

Ace saw that she was determined as ever to see this through and he knew how stubborn she could be in holding to a decision. He sighed. "All right, I'll do it." He knew he was going to regret this. He felt as if he was already regretting it.

She finally smiled and suddenly hugged him fiercely, forcing the breath from his lungs.

"Hey, don't get carried away. We'll need a special guide and more people for such a trip."

With that, he led her out of the castle and they disappeared into the crowd, leaving behind her home and her father.

*   *   *   *   *

Ace stood at the corner of a derelict house located down a filthy back-street. Sasha had been in this building many a time, but never could get over the size of it. How anybody could possibly live in such appalling conditions was beyond her. The difference between one of the large chambers in her home and Ace's whole house always seemed to strike her like a physical blow. The dwelling in fact was only one room with two windows looking out into the dirty alley. In the right corner of the chamber adjacent to the entrance was a hearth accompanied by a dusty crude fireplace of wood and stone. Approximately two metres from the fireless hearth was a small uncovered beech table and two worm-ridden chairs. The left corner as if in contest betrayed a single bed possessing dusty torn covers. No decoration or hangings of any description covered the bare walls matching the cold, but surprisingly clean stone floor. The roof's construction was of straw and dried mud, requiring repair quite frequently, especially in time of storm.

"Can I offer you wine?" Ace asked, reaching for one of the many flasks hidden under the bed.

She nodded, knowing Ace drank habitually, but would be embarrassed to drink while she did not. He reached up and took two goblets from above the fireplace and placed them both on the frail wooden table and began to pour. Sasha sat down, first brushing the dirt and dust from the chair while he fetched the maps out from under the bed. She took pity on his poor existence for he only inherited this meagre house and the blade he carried from his parents, but still he refused any help because of his pride. He himself then sat and spread the largest of the maps in his possession along the length of the table.

"The best guide known is a man called Amon Rusheus in Valerian on Holl Island. Also, on the neighbouring Dina Island is the town Purse where resides the School of Mages. A wizard on our travels to the Cavern would be welcome considering the dangers on such a journey. With luck, we can get one to join us," he stated gingerly, for he knew well Sasha's hatred for sorcery. He stared at her. "We need a magick-user." He expected an angry refusal, but from Sasha to his surprise came only silence. "I believe I can get Procel to lead us as far as there," he said, smiling. Then his voice took on a more serious tone. "When does your father plan to leave for the Cavern?"

"He will have to prepare himself first in order to control the foul beasts, so he will probably depart before the next full moon."

"And how long will it actually take him to reach the mountain?"

"He will travel by his strongest dragon, so it will take him only about one day in all to travel the distance."

Ace gasped. "Then we must leave with the next dawn. Go back to the castle and pack, and especially don't forget your weapons."

*   *   *   *   *

Ace himself packed little. Into his makeshift bag went some food, clothes, rope, the charts and his mountain-climbing tools. While he waited for Sasha's return, he sharpened his sword before strapping the blade to his waist.

Sasha arrived shortly and sighed upon seeing Ace swiftly drain the last of the open wine-flask before they left for the open street. He did not bother to bolt the door behind them, but Sasha guessed that he really didn't possess anything worth stealing.

An hour had passed before they sighted the house of the guide. From outside they could clearly hear the sounds of cheering and shouting.

"It seems Procel is enjoying the wedding celebrations without me," he laughed. "He's probably drunk." With that, Ace opened the door of the building and Sasha was shocked by what she saw before her.

Both men and women alike of various descriptions lay sprawled in odd positions on the floor while their more active comrades proceeded to empty flasks of wine and ale in wanton fashion. Those less intoxicated cheered and applauded the bride and groom before they too collapsed to the floor in a heap. Stretching her gaze across the 'battle scene', she saw Ace crawl over strewn bodies to the centre of the floor where a young man was the focus of attention. The individual in question was balancing a giant mug of ale on his head while simultaneously drinking from another. Ace swiped a flask from the hand of a nearby man who was too drunk to really care for its disappearance. The swordsman then threw the liquid back into his throat before approaching the man in the centre of the chamber. He lightly tapped the balancer on the shoulder, making him turn suddenly and causing the beer to fall down over the man's chest and legs, drenching him.

The victim let out a loud growl, but laughed when he saw his attacker. "Ace! I knew you couldn't resist the drink. Join us!" he shouted, spilling drink from the mug in his hand over several nearby people.

"Maybe later. Listen Procel, I need to talk to you about a journey I'm making." Ace shouted above the noise, and then looked around. "Where's Myru?"

Procel turned and pointed across the room to the sleeping female sprawled over a seat.

"Come on, let's get out of here." Ace interjected and began to drag Procel out of the drunken mess.

Ace called across the chamber to Sasha to grab hold of Myru while he began to carry Procel out of the house. Sasha arrived outside with the still-unconscious female just in time to see Ace drop the guide into a nearby fountain.

Procel duly surfaced and spat water out onto the path. "Hey Ace, what did you do that for?" he choked in a hurt voice.

Ace sat down on the edge of the fountain and gazed down at the soaked guide. "Listen Procel," he repeated. "I need you and Myru both if need be, to lead us to Holl. So, how about it?"

"Perhaps you should tell me what this is all about?" Procel said and began to shake his head vigorously and painfully to bring back his senses.

Ace reached over and offered a hand which Procel gladly accepted and began to cough with sudden feelings of nausea. The company then left the vicinity of the house and the noise of celebrations which carried on into the early hours of the following morning and which never noticed their absence.

CHAPTER TWO

Procel passed the blackened letter back across the table to Ace. "You realise that madman Soren will soon find out about this?" Procel said, his face stern. "This is way over my head."

"Look Procel, I would not have asked if it wasn't you we needed."

"I'm flattered," the guide replied. "But I just don't know Ace, it's maybe too dangerous."

Ace snapped. "When has that ever stopped you? Come on Procel, this chance won't ever come again. And besides," Ace said, smiling. "Think of the treasure to be found in that mountain."

At this, Procel's face lit up and he fell into a silence before he finally spoke, cancelling the tension between them. "All right, we'll do it," he said and all present sighed with relief. "Stay here while we get our things." Procel added as both he and Myru left Ace's house.

Ace looked across the table at Sasha. "How exactly do you intend to keep the dragons from your father?" he asked.

"I don't know." She sighed.

"You realise we'll most probably have to try somehow to destroy the beasts?"

"Yes, I know." She answered, sighing again.

"Then we can only hope that the guide on Holl or the School of Mages know of something that will help us," he stated and glanced at the window. "Finally, they're back." Ace said and stood up to open the door for the two friends.

"Are you sure we have to leave immediately? There's still all that drink back at the house!" Procel protested.

Sasha laughed in reply and nodded, much to his disappointment.

*   *   *   *   *

Fresh horses were fetched and within the hour they were beyond the city boundaries.

"Did you leave a message for your father as to where you might be going, say to throw him on a goose-chase?" Asked Myru.

"There was no need," Sasha replied sharply. "He won't notice my absence with his head buried in those damn books. He was so engrossed in his magick that he even missed my mother's funeral."

None of the others could find voice to reply. It was Ace who finally broke the uncomfortable silence after several moments. "We've come to the River Lead." He said and pointed to the long and winding waterway before them.

"Will the horses be able to cross it?" Asked Sasha.

"Yes," Procel answered. "It's shallow here and the current is not strong."

The beasts crossed easily and Procel drew close to the others and produced a torn map from a pocket of his jerkin. "We will stop at the town Grieve next. Our journey from here to Valerian on Holl Island and to Purse on Dina Island should take about six days."

"Six days." Echoed Sasha with a groan.

"There is no great danger from here to Dina, but from there to the Cavern, expect the worst." Procel said and pocketed the map.

Sasha gave Ace a nervous glance, but the swordsman did not look at her. His eyes were firmly fixed to the ground and the road ahead.

*   *   *   *   *

Shadows on the wall of the chamber receded as the sun's power cast light, banishing the darkness until it finally came to rest on the face of a man clothed all in black. The mage instinctively put up an arm to shield the painful radiance and pushed the chair backwards until it reached a gloomier part of the room. The wizard rose and walked to a distant corner of the chamber and began to pull a square wooden plank off an enormous oblong object.

Once he had removed the wooden obstruction, the light revealed a huge cauldron, waist high and appeared to be made of a foreign dark metal. It was filled to the brim with water. He glanced down at the liquid and reached out a hand to caress the surface. The black-robed mage instantly felt piercing cold enter his fingers and he drew his hand back.

The surface of the water swirled at the foreign contact, but within a few moments resumed its usual placid state. The wizard did not touch a second time, but instead observed his reflection. The calm surface betrayed his greying brown hair, yet clean hairless face. To his many sighs and annoyance, it also disclosed the wrinkles and age-lines which infested his forehead and cheeks; the result of many years of stress and worry. He frowned and stroked his forehead and sighed. He was after all not an old man. Barely forty, he stood at a proud height of six foot and considered his body still firm and strong for his age.

The sorcerer cast his mind back to others of the art who had failed because they were weak. But Soren considered himself different. He had not succumbed to incompetence and so passed onto the higher levels of the art, and with that, came more strength. Power and magick were the only things that mattered. That was why he had never married. He did not wish to pass on that skill and wisdom that took him so long to accumulate to a son or daughter. He believed such people only did this because they knew one day they would die and the knowledge would be lost. But Soren was determined this was not to be his fate. He intended to reach the highest level attainable in the art, and so become immortal. That, surely, was the meaning of magick.

He returned his attention to the cauldron. From a nearby table he grabbed a fistful of herbs and dropped them onto the surface of the water. Several minutes went by before an image began to form on the calm liquid. Fuzzy at first, but slowly became more distinct. The picture of four people on horseback became clear; two men and two women. Only one of the group did he recognise. The company appeared to be approaching the elf-populated town Grieve. He sprinkled a further assortment of spices so he might get a closer look at Sasha. But still the image was not distinct enough. He began to throw in handful after handful of the herbs until he could actually see right through her bag of possessions. It was then he noticed the letter bearing the name of her father within the bag. He concentrated, hoping he might be able to read the parchment, but in vain. He would need to have the paper in his very hand to read the entire contents.

The mage cursed and went to the open window. From out of his cloak he revealed a thin silver whistle and blew, yet no sound from the object came. However, almost immediately, an enormous golden eagle appeared at the window and rested on the ledge, its sharp claws digging into the stone. The wizard then spoke words of the art containing directions and orders for the beast. The eagle shrieked in reply and rose up off the ledge. It then flew towards the sun and soon disappeared from view.

The wizard turned away from the open window and rubbed his hairless chin in contemplation. Goodwin's brat would never leave the city unless it was something of grave importance.

He had to have that letter, at all costs.

*   *   *   *   *

A flourish of dust rose up from the hooves of the four riders' horses as they approached the town Grieve. Smoke could be seen to rise from almost every cottage chimney as they came to the town entrance. Two elfin guards dressed in rough bronze chainmail confronted them at the settlement gates. At their sides were broadswords which they brandished and used to bar the company's entrance by crossing the path.

"State your business." Demanded one of the elves.

Ace moved to the front of the group. "We seek only shelter for the night."

"Names." Ordered the second guard.

Ace sighed in annoyance. "Ace, Procel Sanicle, Myru Woodrose," he paused, "and Sasha Woodrose; her sister."

Sasha frowned and glanced at the swordsman. But Ace said nothing further. The larger of the two guards revealed a notepad into which he quickly wrote. The elves then lifted their blades and permitted entry into the town. The four strong company were quick to enter and leave the vicinity of the guards.

The settlement before them was protected by a fortified wall surrounding the entire town bearing a turret at each corner and two at the north and south gates. The open gate they had just left was so rust-eaten that it probably would not budge even if the need arose. There was one main path which ran straight from one gate to the other. Winding out of this were an enormous number of side streets and alleys. In the centre of the community was a giant fountain rising twelve feet into the air, the water spouting out of its tip to come crashing down onto its basin and the pavement around. Several of the populace were gathered around the fountain with pots and flasks for the water.

Procel turned to the rest of the party. "By my memory, we should find an inn down a side-street across from the fountain."

Ace took the lead, the others following close behind.

Sasha drew up alongside him. "Why did you say I was Myru's sister back there?"

"I had to. If they knew who you were, they might have asked too many questions."

Sasha did not reply. She looked at the elves taking water from the fountain. She did not blame them for their mistrust of magick and their operators. The battles between her father and Soren were the cause of many of the disasters that had befallen the world such as the droughts and the plagues as they sucked more power from the land for their war. This was all because her father had provoked him, leading the Wizards' Council's crusade against Soren; for which she had never forgiven him, yet he seemed oblivious to her anger. It seemed all compassion had disappeared from her father upon beginning this war with Soren.

The company dismounted and entered the side-alley to the tavern. The community at the fountain did not look up. There was indeed an inn present, but certainly not the best they had ever seen. The two-storey tavern before them presented only three windows in all; two on the bottom floor and one on the second floor. It appeared to all intents and purposes, that there was only one sleeping-room in the entire inn. But the travellers were too exhausted to look for a better one. Procel grabbed the reins of the horses and led them to the stables adjoining the tavern while the rest entered via a weather-beaten door. Upon entering, all eyes present turned towards them. To the left was a welcoming fire, its heat felt all around the room. Dead ahead of them was a waist-high semi-circular table upon which were an uncountable number of empty mugs. The barmaid behind this structure glanced up and snatched three mugs up off the surface of the table and proceeded to fill them.

The only other people present in the room were two shield-maidens talking continuously in the right corner and a large soldier, his back to the fire. The women kept talking while they both stared at the travellers fixedly. The soldier glanced up once and then shrugged.

Sasha was intrigued by the man. He bore a fine chainmail-coat under thick armour and a splendid red robe which flowed over his shoulders and back to touch the ground. This was no ordinary man-at-arms. The individual's boots and leg-armour betrayed splotches of blood. He was almost bald, and what he had was greying. He was in the process of cleaning a massive two-handed broadsword of blood before it permanently stained the blade. The sword appeared to be his only weapon. Sasha also noticed clothes which were strewn on the floor, once obviously white, now marked by dark splashes of blood.

The barmaid who was also the owner of the inn strolled over to the company and snarled. "What'll it be?" She leaned over them, impatiently.

Many was the insult the barmaid had received concerning her weight, yet she persisted in protesting she was just a bit plump. But Ace could clearly see that this was not the case. He could not look up to answer because of his disgust. If she slipped, he would surely be crushed to death. He guessed that the rumours about how her late husband was found swinging from the rafters of this inn might have some truth in them when he took a close look at her. Her long auburn hair was dripping with grease and dirt which she often scratched to prove the theory that it was home to nits and fleas. She frequently brushed this hair off her face with filthy hands and nails caked with dirt. If all this was not bad enough, she also possessed a violent and quick temper. Nobody would dare start a fight in her tavern. Ace wished they had found somewhere else.

Sasha was the one to respond finally and what she ordered made Ace sigh with relief. "No food, just ale, thanks," she said, answering for all of them. "And one more for our companion arriving shortly."

"Right." The woman replied and left them.

As if called, Procel then entered, glancing around briefly, before sitting at the remaining vacant place at the table. The barmaid instantly snatched up a fourth tankard and began to fill it. She then placed all four on the table and Sasha paid both for the drinks and bed and board for the night. They quickly drank and retired early to the one room they all shared.

The plain room had three beds on either side. One was without covers and the one adjacent to this was occupied by the sleeping form of the large soldier Sasha had seen earlier. His huge blade lay across the chair next to the bed, its handle turned towards the man. Was he running away from someone or something? pondered Sasha. But she thought no further on the subject, for she was exhausted. She unbuckled the shortsword she wore and shed the light chainmail before getting into bed and was soon asleep. The rest of the group were asleep almost as quickly, their thoughts far away from any danger.

Out in the distance, the sharp cry of an eagle could be heard.

CHAPTER THREE

The chill breeze that entered via the open window awoke Sasha with a start. She yawned and reached over for her clothes placed on the chair adjacent to the bed. She had shed the remaining garments during the night because of the heat. Yet her dreary sleepy eyes opened fully when her hand touched not cloth, but hard, cold wood. The clothes were gone. She sat up and glanced over the side of the bed. Sasha frowned when she noticed that her garments were strewn all over the floor around the area of the bed. Sudden fear gripped her when she saw her jerkin. It was ripped to shreds. In panic she snatched up the torn remains and frantically searched for the note. To her dismay she found it to be gone.

Nothing could have prepared her for what she saw at the end of the bed. She could only gasp speechlessly in fear and shock upon seeing a giant golden eagle sitting motionless on the bedpost. Its dark eyes stared unblinking back at her in hatred. Pinned under its hooked beak was the letter addressed to her father which also contained the route to the Cavern.

Sasha could only stare back in amazement. The creature contemplated the reward it would get when it returned to its master with the parchment. But first, it would make sure that Goodwin's daughter would never read another note, or anything else for that matter. The bird flexed its enormous wings and swooped towards the young woman, its talons spread out in front, ready to strike at Sasha's eyes. Instinctively, she put her arms up to her face, waiting for the blow.

Yet it never came. A large strong gloved hand appeared seemingly out of nowhere and grabbed onto one of the bird's outstretched wings and halted its flight. The eagle screeched in pain and terror as feathers were torn from its wing. It would have dropped the letter from its mouth but for it being pinned firmly onto the hooked part of its beak. The creature changed its course and flew out of the grip of its attacker and made for the open window. A knife flew from the hand of its assailant towards the escaping beast, but narrowly missed and lodged instead into the wood of the window-frame. The man cursed as the eagle made good its escape. He approached the window and with a grunt, removed the blade from the wood, before replacing the knife to the bedside of Procel.

"Sorry, I missed." The man said.

"That bird was going to blind me." Sasha stuttered in reply.

"I've seen you before," he said and approached the bed. "What is your name?"

"Sasha." She answered apprehensively.

"Where from?" He inquired. "Of whose family are you?"

Sasha hesitated before speaking again. She wondered if she should continue the charade of being Myru's sister. But this mysterious soldier had just saved her sight, perhaps even her life. Surely she could trust him. The man-at-arms waited, pondering on why she would not speak.

"Daughter of Segal Goodwin," she said finally, with a tremor in her voice. "My name is Sasha Goodwin."

He stared at her fixedly. "The daughter of the High-Mage Goodwin, head of the destroyed Society of Mages?"

She hesitated again before answering. "Yes."

"You have his eyes," he responded, "no offence, but I bear no love for your father."

"We have something in common there." Sasha declared.

"I am Jual Dittany, ex-Chief of Guards from Ketherin." The soldier stated.

"Ex? What happened?" Sasha asked as she began to dress.

"The Alderman of Ketherin had become a tyrant, killing people to stay in power. I led a revolt and forced him out. But now I have no position. I was travelling to Goodwin City to find work there."

"I could certainly get you employment there." Sasha said, relieved she could repay the debt.

"What are you doing out here, anyway?"

"That's a long story." She sighed.

"I'm in no hurry." He smiled.

*   *   *   *   *

A crumpled piece of parchment fell to the stone floor, and for the second time it burst into flames. But on this occasion there was to be no salvation, only oblivion. A fist crashed onto the nearby table and swung, sending books onto the floor with a thud. Before the dust could settle however, another blow sent several more volumes crashing to the floor.

"If he gets to the Cavern before I do, I'm finished! It's obvious his brat is travelling there first before him to check the explorer's story and prepare the Cavern for him. She has to be stopped, at all costs!" He screamed and turned to the window-ledge to the eagle. "Fly, my servant! Find Goodwin's child and inform me of her progress. Do not fail me. Now, fly!"

The beast took flight, not waiting for a reward for its previous service. The man in black rose from the chair and approached a rectangular-shaped steel chest. From around his neck he removed a small gold key which he inserted into the lock. There was an audible click and it opened to reveal only one article; a square bundle wrapped in dark cloth. The mage ripped the garment off the object and sighed in pride and remembrance. The item was a large book bound in black leather and embossed in fine gold. The volume was the possession of one of the most powerful demons from the Netherworlds; a creature the mage had tricked into giving. He had promised the beast freedom from the Abyss in exchange for the book, but cancelled the spell when it was about to enter the portal into this world.

The entire book contained only one spell he was interested in however. The incantation was to be used upon a force equal to your own or greater. The operator and the victim would have to be close together, but it would enable the caster to drain his opponent's magickal power, strength, and finally the lifeforce. It required little or no waste of energy on the spell-caster's part for you would be using the person's power against himself.

The wizard remembered the demon well, very well. A nasty piece of work, he pondered. The demon had stood at an impressive eight feet, bearing a ram's head with eyes having no pupils, all white.

Upon this mockery of a skull it possessed horns not unlike antlers. It had cloven feet and its entire body was like that of a skeleton. Very thin pale skin covered bones, but it appeared to have no blood in its veins.

But he knew however that he would have to raise the beast again, for one of the pages of the book was missing. The creature must have taken it out to cover against any trick. Yet the mage did not consider this a problem. However, unknown to Soren, deep inside the Netherworlds the demon planned its revenge.

*   *   *   *   *

"By my honour, by my life." Sasha saw engraved on the blade. On the hilt was the seal of the first house of the town Knight on Race Island.

The owner of the magnificent weapon, the soldier, was standing at the far corner of the room, gazing out of the only window.

"Time to go," Ace abruptly said upon opening the door. "Hey, who owns the sword?"

"This knight," she replied as the guard turned to face the swordsman, "who saved my life."

"Your life?" Ace said in surprise and approached the bed upon which she was sitting. "What has happened?"

"It appears either my father, or Soren knows what we are up to and is trying to stop us."

"How could either find out?" Ace stuttered.

"They have ways." She replied simply.

"We had better leave immediately."

"Will you come with us?" Sasha turned to the knight.

"I have nowhere else to go." He sighed.

*   *   *   *   *

It was well past sunrise when the company left the town and Ace was arguing with Procel, much to Sasha's frustration. She was relieved however that all had accepted the knight without question, though Ace had been annoyed that he had not been there to rescue her instead of the soldier.

"Are you certain the guide will be there?" Asked Ace. "How can you be so sure?"

"As I have told you before," Procel snarled. "The world's guides assemble in Valerian in four days time. They all have to be there."

Their arguing was silenced by the sight of the Grieve Mountains ahead. The three most dominant hills of Grieve stood out from their younger and much smaller sisters by stretching into the sky, the tips hidden by cloud. All three were said to be unclimbable and so the company was forced to detour around them.

"Which way now?" Asked Sasha.

"Left leads to Masterwort and from there to Trefoile on Dina Island, and then onto Valerian. While the right leads to mountains and Marjerome, and then onto Dina Island by boat," Procel replied. "Left is obviously shorter."

"If it is so obvious, then why aren't we taking the left route, instead of talking about it?" Ace enquired.

"We are just about to. But maybe first we should drop you off here so you can climb these mountains?" Procel answered back sharply.

"Huh, I've climbed these hills many a time," Ace replied. "I could scale them blindfolded."

"Is that so? I have a piece of cloth right here!" Procel declared, and began rummaging through one of his many jerkin-pockets for the small rag.

"That's enough!" Sasha roared, drowning their arguing and creating an echo.

Myru almost fell off her horse in sudden fright, but the knight grabbed hold of the reins and calmed the beast.

"You're both acting like children. Procel is the guide, so Ace, you be quiet!" Sasha shouted to the swordsman who could say nothing, but stare at her in astonishment.

Ace said nothing more, but would have started up again if he had seen the smirk on Procel's face.

Before long they had entered an endless sea of grass, while off in the distance they could see a group of hills with the town of Marjerome lying some length away at the coast slightly southwest of the mountains. The journey to these hills would take another day, but on the good side, Procel pointed out that there should be no dangers from here to Masterwort. From the mountains to the town meant crossing a desert that would take another two days to cross.

"An experience not to be missed." Remarked Ace softly lest anybody hear.

CHAPTER FOUR

As the company began the third day of their journey, Segal Goodwin finally realised that his only child was missing. It did not come as any great surprise to acknowledge this oversight since he recently had locked himself away in his study absorbing knowledge of the art. He knew Sasha believed that was an excuse for not spending time with the only real product of his marriage. He considered this ironic as he broke his study of magick to seek her advice on preparations concerning the anniversary of her mother's death. However Sasha would find great mirth in this since he had been late for the actual burial. But that had been unavoidable.

None of the guards could inform him of her whereabouts, so leaving the task completely up to him. It was both annoying and dangerous to attempt, since it might cause a serious drain of energy in the process, and could therefore lose him the war at this crucial stage, and for what? She had most probably gone on a short journey with that friend of hers. He had tried on numerous occasions to convince her that Ace was completely untrustworthy in every possible sense, but in vain. He and Sasha could not see eye to eye on any matter whatsoever.

At one time he believed he could convince her that his efforts were genuine, and not those of an unfeeling callous brute. But instead she would argue viciously about his absence of compassion and his self-righteous attitude. But after all, he remembered bitterly that was her mother's greatest talent; arguing. Her mother had performed and practised it to an art-form. Yet time and energy were things he did not have in abundance at the moment. It would have to keep until later, after the war; after Soren was gone. Yes, he promised, then there would be time for family and no more talk of war and magick, then he would show her.

*   *   *   *   *

Tiny granules of sand suddenly blew up into Ace's face and he spat violently to quickly remove the foreign substance from his mouth. He cursed loudly and readjusted the cloth over his mouth and nose, since the previous occasion had obviously proved unsuccessful. Sasha laughed at his frustration, a hand to her own facecloth. They had only crossed a couple of miles into the small desert and much to their dismay, Procel informed them that there was still a considerable distance to travel before they would reach Masterwort. If that was not bad enough, he also mentioned that the light sandstorm they were experiencing would continue for some time yet.

They rode for what seemed a lifetime until Procel finally decided they should stop for the night. Under protest to the point of annoyance, Ace reluctantly agreed to go on first watch. He drew his sword and placed the weapon across his lap as he sat and relaxed against a small palm tree, gazing out at the sea of endless sand. The dying embers of the fire barely revealed the sleeping forms cuddled around it. A sudden noise made Ace snatch up his blade and stand to his feet. But it was only one of the many desert-hunters; a rat looking for insects. Ace sighed with boredom and relaxed again. Ace was just sinking into the oblivion of sleep when he felt cold steel against his throat and his eyes flicked wide open.

"If I was a thief," the unknown voice said, "you would be dead now."

Ace grabbed the hand which held the blade, pulled it forward, and threw the mysterious attacker over his shoulder as he rose. The man fell on the ground in front of Ace with a thud.

Procel laughed as he got to his feet. "My turn to watch. Get some sleep, you look as if you need it." Ace did not reply, but instead simply threw a blanket over himself and slept dreamlessly for the remainder of the night until the guide's shouts awoke him in the cold of the dawn. "Everybody up. We move in fifteen minutes."

Ace's body gave out in anguish at the sudden movement and he fell back with a moan. Yet he was quick to remind himself of the blistering heat that would soon follow in only a few hours. He rose to his feet and noticed with embarrassment that the others were already dressed and preparing themselves breakfast. But they did not notice his minor predicament, and satisfied none had been gazing upon him, he too settled down for breakfast.

The eating of the small cold meal was a cheerless affair, for everybody's mind was on the journey ahead and did not wish to waste precious time.

*   *   *   *   *

It was still daylight when they sighted the town Masterwort. The settlement was completely isolated with desert to the north and endless ocean to the south. Its nearest neighbour was the port-town

Marjerome to the west, itself likewise cut off by sea and mountains. Procel however was quick to remind them that danger was now all around them. The town was teeming to capacity with every kind of criminal who resided in a perpetual state of anarchy and poverty. The last Alderman of the community had tried in vain to cure the town of its grave disease, but failed and mysteriously disappeared. No attempt was made after him. The thought of entering the harbour-settlement filled them with apprehension, but to detour to Marjerome would waste precious time. They had to enter the town.

They approached the gates of the town less than an hour later. All were relieved, but not very surprised to find no guards at the entrance to the settlement. Their entry was not noted by the majority of the populace since many strangers passed through the town to the port to avail of the service of the boats. It was only when a few noticed the two females of the party that the company began to worry. Female strangers in the community were also nothing new, but respectable looking and pretty females were something of a rarity, and it became obvious they were tired of what they referred to as the 'old-ones' of the town. They wanted something new, something that would brighten their dreary and monotonous lives, not to mention the slave-market that would pay well for such fine merchandise.

The general crowd began to disperse as small groups of men advanced towards the company, brandishing knives before them. All five travellers drew swords, but two heavily-armed dwarves appeared which caused them to hesitate. The dwarves appeared just as roughly attired as the general populace, but upon their breastplates was the emblem of the local house of guards. The gathering of knife-bearing men moved back a step, but did not leave the scene. It was the knight Jual who first suspected something was wrong, especially when he remembered that guards in this particular town had ceased to exist some time ago. Looting of the nearby derelict barracks had probably taken place some time ago, rusty armour and various bladed weapons continuing to be passed around.

The dwarfs began to laugh and advanced on the travellers, the crowd close behind. Ace glanced in every direction for a sign or means of escape, but he now saw elves, dwarfs, and even humans everywhere he looked. The swordsman cursed and held his sword in front of himself, preparing to make a futile stand when he suddenly heard Sasha cry out from behind him.

"Meshlea, meshlet!"

The sound of the foreign words echoed around the area, making the rest of the company stare at Sasha in puzzlement. Suddenly there was a blinding flash and then followed a deafening explosion of fire and smoke from seemingly out of nowhere. The group remained unharmed, but at least half of the crowd by Ace's reckoning were blown high into the air to come crashing back to the ground with a dreadful thud. Ace turned back to Sasha in shock and gasped. Her long, flowing jet-black hair was blowing about her face and her raised right hand was aglow with a blue and red flame. Her eyes then turned up to the sky, and she fell off the horse to land on the road, unconscious.

Ace seized the opportunity and jumped off his stallion. He picked up the motionless female and put her over his own steed. He then remounted, slapped the reins violently across the horse's neck and rode down the open street towards the harbour, leaving Sasha's own beast behind. This sudden action spurted Procel into motion, and he followed Ace down the road, the others close behind. The population of Masterwort was left in a state of confusion. Ace did not hesitate, but rode directly onto the deck of the nearest boat. The ferryman appeared and began cursing aloud as the hooves of the horses crashed onto his deck.

"Take us immediately to the harbour-town Trefoile on Dina Island." Ace ordered as the man turned angrily to him.

"I can't do that," the ferryman replied. "We sail with the morning tide. It will cost one gold coin each."

"I'll treble that if we sail now!" Ace shouted in a growing state of agitation as he saw the crowd begin to regain their wits and run down the street towards them.

"Yes, sir!" The ferryman answered and cast off the ropes.

The men of the town arrived at the waterside and began to hurl abuse at the ferryman as the small boat drifted away from the harbour. The Captain seemed to take no notice, money was the only thing on his mind.

Procel tied the reins of the horses to the mast while Ace laid Sasha gently on the deck and wrapped a blanket around her still form.

"How did she do that?" Myru asked Ace, pointing back to the town which was still smoking.

"I wish I knew," Ace responded, and gazed down at Sasha in concern. "I wish I knew."

CHAPTER FIVE

The new dawn revealed to the travellers a liquid wilderness that was so barren in its infiniteness it hurt the eyes attempting to find land.

Ace came onto the deck to see Jual staring out at the ocean. The soldier turned and the young swordsman noticed his face disclosed signs of worry, its origin obvious and Ace was surprised to feel a tinge of jealousy.

"Is she all right?" The knight asked.

Ace subdued a sly grin as he suddenly felt an overpowering desire to say 'No, she's dead,' just to see his reaction, but he forced this morbid statement out of his mind. "I don't know. She appears to be in a deep sleep."

Ace turned to leave, but the soldier called out and he turned back to the knight.

"I have a feeling you find my presence uncomfortable." Jual declared.

"Whatever gave you that idea?" Ace replied, this time not bothering to hide the sneer.

"You must understand that I am not standing in your way concerning Sasha. I have no intention of winning her."

"Then why are you here?" Ace snapped back.

"Because she is the key;" he replied flatly, "she is probably the only one who might stop this never-ending war between her father and Soren. Because they have equal power, their fight is similar to a chess-game where the only pieces are the kings; the result is always stalemate. There are no winners. Do you know anything about magick, Ace?"

"No, I can't say I do." Ace responded, feeling embarrassed by his ignorance and annoyed to be in the company of this man whom he believed was not playing with a full chess-set himself.

"Energy needs to be taken from a source. That source is the world itself. The more power they use, the more they drain the land of its vitality and strength. Do you understand, Ace?"

"Yes, I think I do. But what part do you play in all of this?"

"I intend to be part of her fight."

"How noble," Ace replied, his smile returning, and with it, his confidence. "And just how is she going to stop the war?"

"She can arrange a truce between her father and Soren." Explained the knight.

"Splendid idea! Except you have overlooked two things; one, she hates her father and would have nothing to do with him, and second, Soren would never agree to any truce. He will not stop until Segal Goodwin is brought to his knees."

"But I thought if the war ended, Soren would then devote his energy to his own magick, pursuing higher levels of consciousness instead of continuing a meaningless fight and draining the land of its strength." The soldier replied.

"Any normal mage would. But Soren is a lunatic! When he sees that he no longer has any visible opponents, he will take over the country and become a tyrant. Like the chessboard with the two kings, Goodwin and Soren will keep fighting perpetually. But someday, the two kings will meet, and then it will be checkmate for us and our world. That is what will happen if either one gets the dragons in the Cavern."

"Then we are finished." The knight despaired.

"Maybe, and then, perhaps not. A wizard at the School of Mages might have an option we cannot see."

*　　　*　　　*　　　*　　　*

The whole of that day passed quickly as the travellers lay asleep on the deck or stared trance-like out to sea which was still devoid of land. By this time, Ace was now seriously concerned for Sasha for she still lay in her unbroken deathlike slumber. However relief came as they sighted Holl Island, and soon after passed under the colossal wooden-bridge that separated the island from its neighbour; Dina Island. By sundown the following day they had sighted the harbour town Trefoile.

Ace was the first to smile at the end of this particular part of their journey. The large settlement before him was overshadowed by mountains; hills he had never climbed. "Another time, maybe," he sighed. Ace gazed upwards and gasped at the massive tower of stone at the end of the pier. Two armoured men stood at the top, staring out to sea. "I did not think they would require a lighthouse here." Ace said to Procel.

"Unfortunately they do. There are reefs to the west of here which cause many a shipwreck. We will have to pass through them on the return voyage."

Ace stared fixedly out and frowned, but could not see any sign of the reefs.

The guide stretched out a hand and pointed far out to sea. "There," he shouted. "See where that rock juts out of the foam?"

Ace nodded. "Can we go around it?"

"We would lose too much valuable time."

"Have you mentioned this to the Captain?"

"No," Procel replied sharply. "And I do not intend to do either. We will need a more skilful sailor than he."

"It will cost a fortune for a man of that experience."

"I know. We can only hope that the mage we find is powerful enough to persuade the sailor to settle for a reasonable price."

"That will not be easy, especially here!" Ace laughed.

"We are approaching the pier-wall," Procel stated. "Go below deck and tell the others. We will probably have to carry Sasha."

Ace went below deck and passed the Captain's quarters on his left. Their cabin was dead ahead, at the bow. He hesitated as he noticed that the door was slightly ajar, and he glanced through the gap into the room. Myru was placing a fresh damp cloth on Sasha's forehead. She did not even blink at the touch of the rag. Ace sighed in disappointment and entered, closing the door behind him. The room before him was small, but sufficiently large enough to contain beds for all five of them. The only compensation on this sea-voyage was that the food on board was not full of weevils. He sat down by the side of the bed. Beside him, Sasha lay quite pale, but her pulse was strong and regular.

"No change?" He asked.

"None." Myru sighed and rose to her feet. She resisted the temptation to lean against the wall for it was not vertical. She gazed down at her patient without saying a word.

"Is there anything around here which we can make a stretcher out of?" Enquired Ace, as he glanced around the bare room.

Yet from the female came no response. Either she had chosen to ignore him, or her full attention was on the still form of Sasha. He did not repeat the question. After a brief search of the room, he came to the conclusion that there was indeed nothing he could use. In fact, besides the beds, there was very little else present at all in the cabin.

The swordsman went back up onto deck to see the boat dock and the Captain throw a rope over to a waiting sailor on the wall. His chain of thought was broken by a shout from Procel informing him that it was time to leave. Ace hesitated at first, but then returned below deck to pass on the message which he had not done so previously. He halted for an instant and turned his eyes upwards while he rubbed his face in fear and confusion. "I'm losing it," he whispered to himself. "I really am losing it." Movement from up on deck shook him out of his contemplation and he approached their cabin to pass on the message. It was midday however before they had left the boat and were well on their way towards the town Purse.

Ace had become the only rider, his eyes wary for any rocks on the path ahead that might crack one of the four wheels of the wagon trailing slowly behind him. This delay caused further frustration to Ace, but they had purchased the wagon back in Trefoile specifically so they could transport Sasha. Myru sat at the back with the unconscious female while the knight and Procel sat out front, his hands firmly on the reins, guiding the two horses pulling the wagon. Procel smiled at the swordsman's actions, knowing this was Ace's only way of concealing his fear and worry for Sasha, and even he could not but frequently glance back at the inside of the wagon for any sign or message that might ease his mind. But no such indication came.

*　　*　　*　　*　　*

The remainder of the journey to Purse was uneventful, but Myru was now fearful for Sasha as her condition slowly deteriorated. It was dusk when they approached the town and the lights of the settlement acted as a beacon for any arriving night-traveller.

"Because of Sasha's condition we will stop here to find the mage instead of going to the guide in Valerian as we had planned to do first. Come daybreak, I will try and locate the School of Mages and find probably the only hope for Sasha." Procel stated and jumped down from the wagon.

As they approached, the gates of the innermost part of the town appeared dark and uninviting. Yet the company had no choice but to stop here, for now Sasha had become deathly pale and her breathing laborious. Myru could now not even risk attempting to force water down her throat in case she might choke. She leaned out of the wagon and whispered to Procel, her voice stern and cold. "She is getting much worse. I do not expect her to live much longer than a few days at this rate."

A sudden cry rang out into the night, making them all turn to the source. "Halt! State your purpose!"

"We seek the residence of the School or Guild of Mages, or the otherwise location of any of its members."

"I do not know where they might be found, and frankly, I do not care. Here, in this hell of a town, you are likely to find them everywhere. If you want my opinion, try the local sewer!" The guard snarled.

The soldier departed and the group entered the settlement. At first inspection, Ace began to believe the wastelands they had just left might be better than what was before them. The sight of the majority of the populace living in abject squalor was both surprising and shocking. The town was by far the poorest settlement they had come upon since the beginning of their journey.

"Like every other community," Procel said. "This town has its own laws and views towards strangers and its own population. But all jump and bow before the name of Segal Goodwin. They are acutely aware of who their master is."

The only close and seemingly habitable inn with rooms for hire appeared near to the same condition as its surroundings. It was situated on a corner overlooking the entrance to the town. Several windows were cracked and the walls appeared to be crumbling from rain-erosion. Ace began to wonder that if the coma did not kill Sasha, this house just might. He turned to argue with Procel, but the guide's expression of exhaustion made him reconsider, and he kept his silence. Ace now knew why the mages always had their assembly in this settlement, simply because no other community would put up with them. He suddenly felt very sick. He remembered upon travelling to other towns, and especially the huge isolated city Colewort. He always believed that the bloodshed, poverty and cruelty he had witnessed there could never be copied anywhere else. Yet these towns were generally all the same. They stank of corruption and greed.

Upon entering the tavern Ace saw another fine example of humanity was threatening the serving-girl. Yet Ace could only laugh at the situation. 'Serving-girl' wasn't the word to describe her. The woman standing behind the bar was definitely the most grotesque female he had ever seen. Even the barmaid in Grieve could not match her in repulsion. The robe which she wore which at one time might have been blue was now a dark brown. It was torn in several places as if it could no longer contain her monstrous body. She was being threatened by a small, but muscular man who appeared to be half the size of her. However, he had the advantage. His sword was pointing one inch from her stomach, yet she seemed to take no notice of the weapon's presence.

"It's like I said before, fatty. You pay a tribute of ten gold coins a month, and we won't burn down this disgusting hovel of yours." The man stated.

But the woman just smiled, revealing black teeth. "You take your miserable carcass out of my house right now, and I won't shove that blade up..."

"Excuse me." Ace interjected, in a mood as ever for a fight.

"Who the hell are you?" The man shot back.

"Your carrier to the gods." Ace answered flatly.

The assailant in reply smiled and Ace thought with much disappointment that the man had ignored his challenge. However, the intruder began to approach Ace, his sword hanging limply from his hand, down by his side. He halted close to Ace and his eyes fell to the ground. Ace followed the man's strange gaze to the floor. The assailant then seized his chance and brought the blade back up in an arc, meaning to behead Ace. Yet Ace simply ducked, and punched his attacker in the stomach. He stumbled back a few steps, thus allowing Ace precious time to draw his sword. The small assailant's face was red with rage and embarrassment, and he began swinging his blade back and forth wildly in anger. Ace easily knocked the weapon from the man's hand, and with a counterstroke, drove his own blade through the attacker's arm just above the elbow. The man cried out in pain and staggered back, clutching his right arm which was now free of the metal. However, he still managed to stare at his attacker in defiance. Ace prepared to deliver the death-blow. Yet it was never carried out. A mysterious individual appeared in between Ace and the injured man, blocking his path.

"Enough!" The stranger roared.

Ace could only stare speechlessly at the complete opposite of the barwoman. The newcomer threw back a hood to reveal flowing blonde wavy hair which stretched to the small of her back. Her piercing green eyes shone like beacons beyond a deathly-pale face which was extraordinarily beautiful. Ace could only let his gaze uncontrollably then wander down further to admire a slender, yet voluptuous body. He was vaguely aware of hearing Procel gasp in surprise behind him. The injured man cringed behind her in fear and respect. She suddenly spoke and Ace could swear an angel could not have spoken more softly. It was like music.

"I am Elisa," she said and glanced down at the man kneeling before her in adoration, "and the leader of this idiot who is but one of the many members of my company."

But Ace said nothing in reply.

"Oh, come now. Let's be civilised about this," she pouted, pleading for the man's life. Yet a smile that was more of a sneer crossed her face.

Still Ace kept his silence.

"Two tankards." She turned and stated to the fat servant.

But the barmaid stood motionless and as defiant as she had done for the injured assailant.

"I won't tell you again," Elisa snapped. "The drinks, now!"

The servant-girl hesitated, but then reached down below the bar and revealed an opened bottle. She filled two small mugs and left them on the table. The female took both and handed one to Ace. Yet Ace did not lift a hand to accept the gift. Elisa suppressed a grin of approval and respect.

"I don't accept drink from the likes of you." He lied.

He tried to stare her down, but she just smiled. "You are the first man who has ever said no to me."

"Must not be your day then." Ace retorted.

The mysterious woman had no reply, though she betrayed a sly grin. The injured man waited in excitement for a fight to occur. But she instead approached a side-door leading to the outside world with the confused man following close behind. However, she turned before leaving, her hair sweeping across her face for a moment with the sudden movement, before returning to its perfect position.

"We will meet again, and next time, the encounter will be a lot less friendly, I can assure you." She declared and left the two mugs on the table.

Ace watched her leave and a smile lined his face for a second. Then she was gone.

"A room?" The grotesque barwoman asked, as if nothing had happened.

"Yes... yes, of course." He stuttered.

But Ace did not move. The rest of the company approached the table while he stood motionless, staring fixedly at the open door and drank from the tankard she had tried to give him.

CHAPTER SIX

Ace was the first to wake and he did so with a shudder of coldness. The room was both freezing and deathly-silent. He glanced across at Sasha who was now paler than ever, but to his relief, he could see her chest rise and fall with the action of breathing. He let his gaze move and fall on the occupied beds of the rest of the company. Suddenly he frowned, and then rose to his feet. Procel's bed was empty. Ace ran to the bed and ripped the blankets off. Yet his eyes had not deceived him. The guide was indeed not present. Procel had gone without him. Ace approached the open window and peered out into the filthy streets in hope of catching a glimpse of him. But in vain. Procel knew the town like the back of his hand. It would be pointless to try and follow him. He scratched his chin in puzzlement. 'Where was he?'

*   *   *   *   *

Every single street appeared the same. No path or alley seemed to have any originality. To Procel, they all seemed filthy and teeming to capacity with the most unspeakable kinds of criminal life he had ever seen. This to his shock and disbelief increased in strength as he progressed further on through the town towards the centre.

He thought it best he go to the Guild of Mages alone, since he was the only one who knew the town while the others could keep a wary eye on Sasha. Her life depended on how quickly he could find a wizard, and with this in mind, Procel walked faster towards the town-centre.

He however did not have to search for very long, for the entire centre surrounding the fountain was alive with mages. The first one Procel came across was using a small mug to collect water from the fountain. He was in the act of beginning to drink from the mug when Procel hailed him.

"Excuse me, could you tell me where your assembly is taking place?"

The mage was slow to respond. Yet when he turned to Procel, he did so with a sneer. "You are not magi." He said flatly.

"No," Procel sighed, "but it is important I find it."

"Very well. Follow me." He replied gruffly.

Their short journey led them through winding streets until they came to a huge rectangular-shaped building. Its sheer size made it clearly stand out from its bleak colourless neighbours. It was two-storey with a flat roof of straw and mud. The four fifty-metre high walls were also composed mainly of mud, but also betrayed the existence of brick and stone. The interior of this unusual structure as they entered through giant double-doors was completely bare but for a vast oak table with forty to fifty seats which encircled it. Strewn all over its surface were herbs and instruments beyond the knowledge of the guide. Their owners stood talking over them. To Procel, it was unusual to see a white-cloaked mage and a black-robed wizard talking openly like they were old friends.

"The assembly holds a truce here annually for mages of every cloak, whether they be black, white, or grey makes no difference. Grey as you probably know is neutral."

"I see." Procel answered.

"No, I don't believe you do, or ever will, Procel Sanicle."

"How do you know my name?" Procel snapped back, now beginning to wish he had brought Ace after all.

"I know many things. Wait here." He commanded, leaving Procel to the mercy of a mysterious large company of mages.

Everywhere he looked, Procel could see sorcerers. It was as if he were in a dream, or more likely, a nightmare. Just as it seemed he would go mad, the wizard returned. Beside the mage was a younger man clad from head to foot in a flowing thick black cloak. He threw back the hood to reveal all of his young face and short spiked brown hair. His voice was deep and strong like that of an orator.

"I am called Barrius Fetherfew, foremost among the Guild of Mages. What is it that you want exactly?"

"I need your help to cure a friend."

"Sorry, but I've heard more sob-stories than I can bear, and besides, I'm busy."

"How can you be so heartless?" Procel snapped.

"I do not wear the dark-cloak for nothing, and I certainly did not obtain this rank by helping every unfortunate that might cross my path."

Despair began to slip into Procel like a knife, and he knew he had to act fast if he was to save Sasha. It was time to play his ace. "The patient is someone of great importance."

"I could not care less if your friend was the town-Alderman himself. Whether he lives or dies is of no concern to me."

"This he is a she." Procel retorted angrily.

"Whatever. Sex of the patient does not matter. I still do not care."

Procel snarled and moved closer to the mage. "This she is Sasha Goodwin, daughter of the High-Lord Segal Goodwin." He whispered, expecting to see him react, but he only stared at the guide fixedly.

"I have no time to waste on jokes."

"I can assure you, this is no jest."

"I don't think you quite know who you are dealing with, peasant." Barrius snapped back.

"I am no peasant," Procel retorted, "I belong to the first order of the Guild of Guides in Valerian."

"If you are lying," he said sharply, "your death will be slow; very slow indeed."

Procel sneered in reply. "Follow me."

The black-robed wizard collected his herbs, and turned to his fellow mages before leaving. "This will not take long. Do not do anything important in my absence." He announced, leaving the confused sorcerers talking ceaselessly.

"This way." Procel said in a gruff tone.

The wizard did not bother to reply.

"If you are foremost among the Guild, then which of the two High-Mages do you consider to be your superior, since they both wear the black-cloak like you?" Procel asked, seeking an opportunity to insult the sorcerer.

"Firstly, I answer to no man. But true, they both wear the dark cloak like me, yet I do not trust

Soren. You will always find one follower of the dark-arts you cannot trust."

"What a coincidence." Procel laughed.

The mage reached for the short wand strapped to the inside of his cloak and considered striking him down. But then decided not; not yet, since it was obvious that the guide was lying and there would be time enough to make him pay for his insults. They turned and entered the tavern.

The fat owner suddenly appeared and hailed Procel as they began climbing the stairs to their room. "Hey! No visitors allowed after sundown or I will have to throw you out."

"You had better get his coffin ready then." The mage retorted.

Procel ignored the comment and continued up the stairs. He opened the door to their room with the sorcerer following closely behind.

"Where the hell have you been? I've been looking..." Ace began, but halted at the entrance of the dark-robed warlock. "Is he-?" He began again, but Procel put a finger to his lips to keep silent.

The wizard slowly approached the bed in which Sasha lay, while simultaneously preparing a death-spell for Procel in his mind. As he approached, he instantly recognised the occupant of the bed and gasped. He ran to the sleeping form and closely examined the face to see if he had been mistaken. Yet there could be no error, it was indeed her.

"She has lost a lot of her psychic energy." The mage said, as he began to untie the top button of her jerkin to allow greater freedom to breathe.

"She has lost what?" Ace asked.

"It is the energy every magick-user has." Replied Procel to Ace, who was now even more confused than before.

"I see you are not a complete fool, guide," the mage sneered. He turned to Ace. "It is the energy of our body derived from food which is then used for sorcery."

"But we have given her food. Why is she still unconscious?"

"The energy must be directed correctly. She does not know how to use her gift properly."

"Naturally," snapped Ace. "She is not a wizard."

"But her father is. It was ridiculous to believe she would not inherit her father's powers."

"You say this *gift*," interjected Procel. "Surely she would know somehow?"

"Not necessarily. Think if you will of the gift as a serpent lying dormant until its master knows how to awaken it."

"That could explain her hatred for magick," Ace said. "She might have believed she would be shunned because she is different and so hid it away within herself."

"Or her father could have exploited her, which might explain her knowledge of the spell." The mage stated, taking out his knife.

"But that doesn't explain Soren and his interest in Sasha. Surely she can't be a threat to him?" Asked Ace.

"One of the prime laws of sorcery states that when a power is inherited, it becomes doubled in strength." Barrius replied, causing all present to glance at him nervously.

"Why didn't Soren have children of his own then?" Procel asked the warlock who began to play with the magick-knife between his fingers.

"Simply because the magick has made him sterile, like Segal Goodwin is now. When you seriously begin to follow the arcane-path, you become infertile. It is the price you pay for the knowledge of sorcery."

"And you are also?" Ace asked, watching the mage playing with the short blade.

"Oh, yes. I became sterile long ago." He remarked, and to everybody's amazement, suddenly drove the knife deep into his left palm.

He removed the blade without a sound an instant later and approached Sasha. Ace made a move towards him, but Procel was quick to hold him back. The mage moved his injured hand over Sasha's open mouth and let the blood from the wound drip into her mouth. He began to mumble something in a tongue the others could not decipher under his breath. The company were all speechless at this foreign act while Ace was both shocked and disgusted.

The warlock chanted the spell twice more before turning to the travellers. "She will be all right in a few hours. Now I, myself, must rest."

So saying, he was quickly fast asleep on a nearby bed and did not wake for several hours, by which time Sasha had opened her eyes.

*   *   *   *   *

Dusk was fast approaching and Ace's impatience demanded the company move on since Sasha's health had been restored. He had also vowed that he would not stay another night in this vile town. Sasha thanked the mage and bid him farewell, but he did not accept the latter.

"I am going with you." He responded.

"Why?" Asked Ace, "What about your assembly?"

"The convention is over, and the Guild will survive without me. I am travelling with you because on your return to Goodwin City, Sasha can introduce me to her father. Besides, even though you did not wish to impose, you know you need my help for the Cavern."

"My father is a recluse. He won't see anybody, not even his own daughter." Sasha said in anger.

"Oh, he will see me, do not worry of that." He replied and gave a sly grin that uncomfortably reminded Ace of the mercenary leader Elisa.

*　　*　　*　　*　　*

Before long they reached the massive wooden-bridge linking the two islands. This bridge however was well worn and did not appear very sturdy. The company were therefore forced to cross the quarter of a mile long bridge one by one. Ace was the first to cross and there was an ominous loud creaking sound in his wake. He approached the half-way mark and the sound increased dramatically, the horse almost bolting in fear. Yet Ace drove the reluctant beast on. Too late he realised his mistake. In his haste, the boards gave way below him and the horse fell to the ocean waters below. He reached out in panic and grabbed onto a board. Myru screamed in fright far behind him, while Sasha gasped in shock. The gods he had just thanked for his life now began to desert him as his hands began to slip. But just as he began to believe he was about to meet his maker, a sudden hand from Procel grabbed onto his wrist and pulled him up. Both collapsed onto the surface of the bridge in exhaustion. He was about to offer his thanks to the guide, yet Procel acted as if nothing had happened as he rose to his feet. Ace began to get the impression that the guide no longer treated him as a friend, but now only as a fellow-traveller. He suddenly felt jealousy grip him. The relationship of Procel and Myru was no more than friends, and he began to ponder on what Procel's feelings for Sasha were. After all, he was the one who had risked his life obtaining the mage.

Ace shook the absurd idea from his mind as he too rose to his feet. Yet he could not completely dismiss the thought, and decided it was time to keep a wary eye on the charming guide. The remainder of the company crossed safely. The short journey to Valerian was gratefully uneventful. They arrived at the town gates just as the last light of the day left the land. Procel was concerned that the guides' convention might have ended in their absence. The guards were quick to allow him entry because of his reputation. With a prominent guide present, all members of the company were heartily welcomed without prejudice at the house of the Guild of Guides and Travellers.

Upon entering the building, Procel ran ahead to the main chamber in hope to witness the last few moments of the convention. A fellow guide who recognised Procel as he approached the door to the room grabbed his arm in excitement.

"The prize for best guide is about to be presented." Said the man and began to drag his captive towards the chamber.

Procel's heart was beating fast. This event was both the conclusion and highlight of the annual convention.

"Do you think you will win?" Asked Myru as she drew up alongside him.

But he sighed in pessimism. "There is pretty stiff competition here this year, especially from the favourite; the guide we came here for."

An oratorical voice could be heard as they entered. "And I now am proud to present the coveted prize for best guide and traveller to...Amon Rusheus." The man on a stand at the front of the crowd in the chamber announced.

A young individual rose from out of the crowd and quickly approached the stand. He shook the hand of the orator, collected the prize and just as rapidly left him and re-entered the crowd which greeted him like a lost son returning home. Procel watched the tall red-haired man receive the medal for best guide without envy. The man had mapped earlier that year the region at the coast surrounding the infamous town Tamerindes. Such an individual deserved respect, not petty hatred.

Procel's attention was momentarily drawn away from the prize-giving spectacle to Ace behind him who appeared to be staring intently at something. Then he realised in disgust what it was. He followed the swordsman's gaze to the black-robed mage Barrius Fetherfew who was talking to Sasha. He knew Ace's jealous mind was working overtime.

"He's sterile." Procel said quietly to his friend.

"What?" Ace asked, and turned to see the guide.

"I said he's sterile, so there is no need to fret concerning him and Sasha."

"Yes, but that does not mean he has no interest whatsoever in women." Ace sneered, and Procel sighed in annoyance.

"He is completely dedicated to his magick, he doesn't care for anything else."

"Perhaps. But you do, don't you?" Ace snapped back.

"What?"

"I mean you recently appear to be especially worried for Sasha."

"Just what are you trying to say?" Procel shouted in anger.

"I won't waste time here," Ace replied, his arms folded. "Just how much do you really like Sasha?"

Procel's face became twisted with rage as his self-control exploded. He struck out blindly at Ace. In his fury he discarded the knowledge that he was but a guide, while Ace was a highly-trained fighter and swordsman.

Ace easily blocked the blow with his left arm, and in reply, sent his own right fist smashing into Procel's face, breaking the man's nose. Procel was sent crashing onto his back. The crowd of guides turned silent at the sudden commotion, while Sasha instantly ran for the centre of the disturbance. Throughout his long career of combat, Ace had always sworn by one definite rule of combat: never, ever fight fair. He now prepared to kick the fallen guide, but Ace's code of combat also suited Procel. As Ace approached the guide, Procel suddenly kicked his attacker in the shin. Ace grabbed his leg in pain while Procel seized the opportunity to rise to his feet and draw his sword. At this action, the watching crowd moved back a step in fear of being struck by sharp metal.

Ace let out a laugh at this development. His blade was both of a finer and sharper quality than Procel's, and he had training in swordplay. Ace drew his sword very slowly, listening with pride as the metal scraped off the inside of the scabbard. Procel was not intimidated by this action. He was in fact the first to strike. He drove the blade in an arc towards Ace's unprotected head, but Ace easily blocked the blow, and as a counterstrike, considered lifting the guide's head from his shoulders. Yet decided not. He wanted to have some fun first before he delivered the death-blow. Ace very neatly and with devastating speed, swung his blade down and slashed the skin just above the left knee of his opponent. Procel cried out in pain and almost fell onto his one good remaining knee, but he managed to keep his balance.

"Next time, it will be your neck." Ace laughed.

Yet Ace's good fortune deserted him when he suddenly felt a sharp pain in his back and fell to his knees with a cry of pain. He knew his nameless attacker was very strong and had an expert knowledge of exactly where to hit. Ace turned his head towards his assailant and saw Jual standing above him, his face stern and emotionless. The injured swordsman had barely the time to contemplate his mistake, when the knight's mailed fist came crashing down onto his jaw. For Ace, the lights went out as he collapsed to the ground in a heap. Procel accepted the opportunity gratefully to sit down, out of breath and failing strength. He tore a strip of cloth from his jerkin and began to bind his injured leg. Sasha appeared from out of the midst of the watching dense crowd at that moment and approached the guide.

"Are you all right?" She asked.

"I'll live."

"Procel, what the hell is going on?"

"I think you had better ask Ace for explanations when he wakes." Procel replied as the knight helped him to his feet.

"Yes, I think I will." She said in a low voice.

"Thanks, big fella." Procel said to Jual.

"Perhaps you will get the chance to repay the favour sometime later." The soldier smiled.

Several hours passed before Ace finally awoke and he did so to the angry voice of Sasha Goodwin. "All right Ace, what is going on?"

"I can explain." He replied feebly.

"You had better, and fast!" Sasha roared.

Her shouting was doing nothing good for Ace's headache.

"I suppose I might have let my jealousy overtake me." Ace said, grinning.

But Sasha did not smile. "Ace, we've known each other since we were children; I've always known about your feelings for me, all you had to do was to say something. But now you've spoiled it," she stated coldly. "I want you to leave."

"I can explain further, truly I can." He repeated in a trembling voice.

"Get out!" She screamed. "I don't want to hear it!"

He stared at her in shock, speechless.

"Just go now, quickly, before I say something else I might regret." Sasha said sharply.

Ace could not say anything more, his voice had deserted him. He collected his belongings and left without any other member of the company noticing his departure and quickly disappeared into the night, while behind him, Sasha broke down, crying.

CHAPTER SEVEN

The night was several hours old when a small ketch could be seen leaving the harbour of the town Valerian. The ferryman seemed to require only a little persuasion from the mage to sail the company through the reefs. There was a new addition to the party. With Ace gone, the new guide and prize-winner; Amon Rusheus took the swordsman's place. He had refused point blank at first, but greed was an important part of his lifestyle. Procel was quick to point out the riches to be found in the Cavern. Amon would receive half the dragons' treasure in exchange for leading them using the explorer's map, which Sasha had memorised before it was stolen. He could not refuse such an offer. Sasha or the others had no interest in treasure, each had their own reasons to travel there.

A long five day journey stretched ahead of them to reach the port of Campion on the mainland. It would involve cutting through the treacherous straits to save precious time. Such a long voyage worried Sasha greatly, for her father would be preparing to leave for the Cavern in less than a fortnight. Soren was sure to be preparing also. Time had become the ruler of her fears.

*   *   *   *   *

The following two days passed without incident until they approached the reefs. They had passed the town Trefoile on their right and the straits lay only a few hundred metres ahead of them.

"All hands on deck!" The Captain shouted. He turned to Procel. "Pull down the sail. We have to slacken her speed, or else she'll..."

His feverish orders were abruptly halted. A huge body of seagulls seemed to rise out of the very sea itself, and began to approach the boat. He remembered with dread that the birds nested on the rocks that jutted out of the waves that made up the reefs. The creatures would die if necessary to protect their young from this intruder, and the Captain cursed himself for his stupidity.

"What is happening?" Procel shouted in confusion and fear as he felt great thuds against the hull and deck of the ketch as the birds crashed off the ship in an attempt to scare off the intruder.

The guide glanced around the boat to see the deck white and red with dead bodies, while more arrived from a sky filled with birds. The seagulls attacked all members of the company, their claws and beaks ripping cloth and drawing blood. There were too many to possibly fight. At the bow stood Jual striking down several incoming beasts with the massive blade he carried. One bird swooped down and struck Procel on the left temple, knocking him to the deck. He was momentarily stunned by the attack and began to wipe the blood away which threatened to blind him as it flowed freely down his cheek. He opened his eyes to see probably the largest bird he had ever seen swoop down on target for his eyes. But as he prepared himself for the blow, a huge sword suddenly filled his vision and cleaved the beast in half, sending the seagull to rest amongst the many of its followers that littered the entire deck.

"Get back inside, this is hopeless!" The knight screamed above the noise of the diving birds to the guide.

Procel noticed his face was marked with many bleeding scratches since this was the only part of his body which was not covered by protective armour. The travellers fled back into the deckhouse and began to board up all the windows except the centre window looking out onto the deck. Suddenly there was a massive thud that sent Sasha and Myru to the floor.

The Captain went below deck and returned moments later, his face pale. "There's a huge gash right across the starboard, and the water is pouring in like crazy!"

Nervous glances were thrown around the deck-house and all looked to the ferryman for guidance. But he just roared in rage and hit his fist off the steering-wheel. The water had now filled the entire bottom deck and was approaching their feet.

The Captain turned to Barrius Fetherfew. "You'll pay for my new boat, mage!" He shouted.

But the sorcerer only smiled and gave an order of his own. "Abandon ship!" He screamed to all present as the water rose to their ankles.

"Those damn birds led us right onto the reefs." The ferryman said as they ran back out onto the deck.

The majority of the attacking seagulls had left the scene, as if sensing their task was finished and left their victims to the mercy of the sea.

"Where's the lifeboat?" Procel shouted.

The Captain pointed across deck to a small rowing-boat tied to the end of the dying ketch.

"We'll be damn lucky to all fit in that!" Sasha shouted as the mage was the first to climb into the small craft.

"Hurry it up, this old tub of mine is going down!" The ferryman ordered as he let go of the rope that binded the small boat to its dying mother. "Start rowing. I would say we've got about three minutes before she goes down."

Jual and Procel took the oars and began to row until they believed they had reached a safe distance from the ketch. The deck of the boat was hidden under a fine layer of sea-water, and the deck-house was half obscured from view as it was steadily devoured by the dark waters. Barely two minutes later, even that had vanished and the ketch rapidly sank below the waves.

"Make for the harbour of Trefoile, and carefully, remember we're still in the reefs." The Captain said and glanced at the warlock for a sign of impending payment for the loss of his ketch.

But the black-robed mage did not lift the dark hood that hid his face and his drooped head. He ignored his surroundings as he calmly studied one of his many books, trying to commit the contents to memory.

*   *   *   *   *

The death of the ketch did not go unnoticed by the inhabitants of Trefoile and they rapidly gathered around the harbour to watch the arrival of the small boat with its irregular collection of survivors. Fishermen glanced up from their work to observe the craft and recognised the ferryman. They too then ran towards where the main crowd had gathered.

Upon their arrival at the port-wall, the travellers were helped out of the small craft. But the fishermen let the mage tend to himself, especially after the ferryman explained through a mouthful of curses how his boat had died and who was going to take responsibility for its replacement. The large crowd which had now assembled shoved the company into the nearest tavern to hear the full tale concerning the watery death of the ferryman's ketch. The mage was left to follow behind. The company and the majority of the crowd had disappeared from view into the inn when the wizard faintly heard a mysterious sound from behind him.

The warlock hesitated and glanced behind, but could see nothing out of the ordinary. Yet he could sense something was amiss. He had the sensation that he was being watched; observed by a creature of magick and malice. But whoever or whatever it was, he could only sense the familiar aura of sorcery, not see its source. He decided it would be safer inside with the rest of the company. He began to walk towards the door of the tavern, but he turned around a second time. The sensation of dark magick was stronger now, far stronger. The creature was close.

The wizard drew his magick knife and now frantically searched the sky and empty street for some sign, but in frustration, could see nothing. Then he suddenly heard the flapping of wings and saw a giant golden eagle swoop down towards him. Was this the creature he had sensed? He brought the knife up in front of his face to prepare for the coming blow. But he had acted too late. The massive bird struck him full force in the face with its claws. The small blade left the mage's hand to land at the far end of the street. He himself was knocked to the ground and blood flowed heavily into his eyes from the gash to his forehead, blinding him. In panic, he desperately tried to regain his concentration in a mind filled with fear and confusion. He began to mouth softly a spell when the beast swooped down a second time, and everything went black.

*   *   *   *   *

The commotion of the tavern was approaching its zenith as the ferryman was reaching the climax of his tale. But Sasha was bored with the telling of the story for the tenth time and wanted to leave. She glanced around the densely crowded room for the others. But something was wrong. The mage was missing.

"What's wrong?" Procel asked, noticing the distress on her face. "If you're worried about the boat, don't be. The next ferry to the mainland leaves in one hour and we should be able to lose our current ferryman quite easily. He's quite drunk and in no condition to argue about the loss of his boat."

"No, it's not that. Where's the mage?"

"Ah, don't worry about him. He can take care of himself." Procel retorted.

"I wonder if he can. I don't believe he is as powerful as he says he is."

"All right," Procel sighed. "I'll help you look for him."

The two left the crowded tavern, leaving the three remaining members of the company inside. However, what greeted the two was a scene that made Sasha's heart jump. Before them lay the still body of Barrius, his face awash with blood. Resting on his chest was the giant bird Sasha remembered with fear back in Grieve. The beast was about to tear out the throat of the seemingly dying wizard. The foul creature was so intent on killing its injured, frail victim, that it did not even notice the arrival of the two travellers. Neither did it see Sasha's blade which cleaved through its neck and end its brutal, violent life. The beast shrieked its death cry and attempted to take flight, even though it had been decapitated. But it stumbled, and fell back to earth and suddenly to Procel's amazement, burst into flames.

"Get some bandages quick." Sasha shouted which pulled the guide out of his trance as she saw with horror the damage to the wizard's face.

Procel ran back into the inn and soon returned with bandages and a cloth which she used to wipe away the dark red blood to closely examine his wounds. A small mark lined his forehead, and that would quickly heal. However, the second deep wound that lined his left cheek would not. Procel had to look away as Sasha stitched up his cheek. A large scar would run from the mage's eye to jaw, and he would have it till the day he died. He awoke as Sasha stitched and roared in pain. She flinched back as he ran a hand up his cheek and cried out a second time, this time not in pain, but in rage.

"Calm down." She said, afraid he would break the stitches, but he ignored her.

"The bird was Soren's, wasn't it?" he said and glanced out to sea as if he might see Soren there, gloating.

But Sasha said nothing.

"Wasn't it?" He screamed.

She nodded in reply. "Leave him be, he's not worth it. Leave him to my father."

"No," he roared. "It's personal now. I'm scarred for life, and he's going to pay." Barrius rose to his feet, collected his knife and walked down towards their ferry. He went on board and said not another word as the rest of the company arrived and they left for the open sea. The Great Sea stretched before them, beautiful in its bleakness; barren like the mage's soul, and the hatred that burned within him.

*   *   *   *   *

Dusk was rapidly approaching as the ketch sailed safely through the reefs and managed to avoid the nests of the violent seagulls. Sasha was careful to choose a more experienced sailor this time. They barely escaped the previous ferryman as he chased them down the harbour after they had set sail. He had screamed curses at the travellers, and in particular, at the mage until the ketch had disappeared from sight. Yet the warlock had said nothing in reply, he had fallen instead into a depressive state where silence ruled. The only actions he performed were to eat very little at occasions during the day. He otherwise remained motionless, staring fixedly out to sea. He persistently ignored any attempts by the others to break him out of the mood. His monotonous gazing out at the unbroken ocean was finally beginning to annoy Sasha, and she made a futile attempt to break his trance, but in vain. He had become a recluse. She began to wonder if he would be of any use at the Cavern. But she quickly reminded herself that she never really knew or understood magick-users, so she left him alone and ignored him for the remainder of the journey.

*　　*　　*　　*　　*

The voyage was without incident and they arrived days later at the harbour of the town Campion where they could continue the next stage of their travels. The River Sual and the River Stye flowed into the sea near to the settlement to their left. The scene appeared so peaceful that Sasha forgot for a few moments the death and strife that this land would face as she gazed upon its tranquil beauty. The town including its centre was also surprisingly quiet. The only sounds to be heard were the footsteps of an occasional passer-by.

"This place seems almost too quiet." Procel said.

Sasha nodded in reply. But she sighed at the guide's suspicions all the same. She knew Procel's mind was filled with anguish and anger at Ace's performance back in Valerian. Her mind also persistently reflected on that affair and her forceful banishment of the swordsman. If only he had kept his jealousy in check! It was preposterous for anyone but Ace to consider that there was something between herself and Procel. But she still missed him. They had not been apart since they were children. Yet even so, she could not bring herself to forgive his actions, however foolish or well-intentioned. The knight however was free of such thoughts and was just happy to have his two feet finally back on solid ground. He hated the sea; all that swaying and rocking. The five day journey from Trefoile was torture. The ground wasn't likely to betray him like the water might. At least he hoped it would not.

Sasha shook herself from the enchantment the town had put her under. They could not afford to spend long in the settlement, regardless of its tranquillity. A nearby horse-trader lay in the town-centre and Sasha quickly purchased six horses for the next stage of their long voyage. The others protested about the rush, for supplies were running low, but Sasha was quick to silence them. Mandrake was their next stop and whatever goods needed to be purchased, could be got there. Again the group groaned for they required rest, but she became obstinate on the subject. The mage ignored her command and watched instead the waves crashing off the rocks of the harbour.

"It is time to leave." Sasha stated quietly, but there was a taint of anger in her tone.

Barrius did not respond.

"I said..."

"I heard what you said, curse you!" The warlock snapped.

"Well, I beg your pardon." She replied sharply.

"And so you should." He answered, turning his back to her.

She snatched onto the hem of his cloak which resulted in a snarl from the mage, yet she did not let go of her captive. She calmly watched his gaze come up from where her hand held the robe to her face where their eyes met. Sasha expected to see his natural colour in those eyes, but with astonishment, she saw to her disbelief them darkening, and with shock and rage she realised quickly the reason why.

"You wouldn't dare!" She screamed and his mumbling of the spell ceased.

He instead stared intently into her eyes, expecting to see the familiar sign of fear. But no such indication could be found. Instead to his surprise, he saw the gift; the great serpent of magick growing within her as protection to the spell he had been preparing. Uncertainty turned to fear and he shrank away from her, the hem of his dark robe tearing.

"What's wrong?" She stuttered. "What did you see?"

She released her grip of the cloth and he ran to one of the waiting horses, and rode ahead of the others. He did not look behind him to see if she was pursuing him in her confusion. She decided to leave the mysterious subject well alone for the moment.

*   *   *   *   *

By dusk they had reached the River Orack with the town Mandrake nearby north-west of the waterway. Sasha had never heard of this settlement, and cursed her stupidity for not checking first before they decided to stop there. The town was the main market place and one of the largest centres for magick in the entire land. The guide Amon Rusheus finally spoke, breaking his seemingly religious silence.

"The name of the settlement comes from the most powerful and dangerous magickal herb in existence. It is difficult to obtain outside of the town so it is the most expensive, but also the most common herb to be sold in the community. The sale of this herb is so great, it forms a huge part of the settlement's economy, hence the origin of the name of the town."

They safely crossed the river and soon approached the settlement itself. The community received the strangers as it did so for so many others, with no open sign of welcome, but neither with any indication of hatred or scorn. The populace required their money, but it appeared that did not mean they had to like them. This cold reputation did not frighten Sasha or her companions for this settlement was just one of the many scheduled stops on their long journey, and so pass through it they would.

*   *   *   *   *

The company slowly entered the town of Mandrake, wary of every action made by passer-byes. But none made a movement towards the group and neither did any recognise the leader of this odd looking party. Inhabitants of other settlements might have questioned the reason for a high-ranking knight and a powerful black-robed mage being present in the same company. By tradition, they were natural and deadly enemies. As they travelled through the dirty streets, Sasha noticed with some amusement and relief that she was not the only one to bear disgust for this community before them. Jual sneered in repulsion at the scene before him. The squalor in Valerian might have been forgiven, but this town had no excuse. They lived only to sell the magickal herb, and would die in this poverty in an effort to clear their daily stall and feed their starving children for one more day. All other activities were discarded and ignored in the face of the selling of the all-important herb. Surely for these people there could be no worse a hell in the possible after-world than the life they now experienced.

"With this town ends my knowledge of the land. I know not the country beyond this point. The rest is up to him now." Procel said and nodded to the other guide they had obtained from Valerian.

Amon glanced over at Sasha before speaking. "I just hope you remember your promise." He said quietly.

Sasha stared back at him in reply. "My interest lies solely in the dragons," Sasha responded. "You can have it all if you so wish."

"No, you are very kind, but half of the gold will be sufficient," Amon answered and moved to the head of the group. "Now that we have got that business out of the way, I will take charge. Rule one in this town is not to converse with anyone. Leave all the talking to me."

"All the talking?" Asked the knight who had taken an immediate dislike to the guide.

"All," the man snapped. "Foolish talk costs lives, and in this place, it may cost you more than your life."

All members of the company bar the mage gazed at Amon in puzzlement at this remark. The sorcerer just smiled in amusement.

"Rule two is to act like a wizard, and nobody will harm you."

"How do we do that?" Procel stuttered.

"Act solemn, wise, non-talkative; in short, behave as if you were in a perpetual fit of depression."

"You mean, like him?" Jual laughed as he nodded to the mage who sneered back at him in reply.

Amon nodded nervously as he glanced at the warlock for a sign of anger, but to his great relief, there was none. The sorcerer appeared to be too deep in contemplation to notice or care. They had just dismounted from their beasts when Procel halted in the middle of the main street and frowned.

"What is that noise?" Procel asked and glanced up and down the road for an indication of the origin of the loud and steadily increasing sound.

Sasha also frowned in puzzlement. It was a noise which was vaguely familiar, yet she could not immediately place its meaning. Then it came to her and she froze in fear.

Amon realised the source of the mysterious sound also. "Market day," he said quietly. Then he shouted. "Quick, into the nearest house!"

Procel who had been gazing idly down the street, now stared fixedly in awe as a sudden wave of people rushed up the road towards him. It was spearheaded by children and followed close behind by people of every possible description. It quickly became clear to the guide that they had no intention of stopping, even though he was in their path. The travellers ran and attempted to reach for the nearest door at either side of the street, but in vain. It was too late to try and flee, the mass was upon them.

The crowd crashed into them and swept them away without even decreasing in its urgency. The travellers became separated, each becoming part of the massive flow of bodies. The mage however managed to grab onto a passing door-handle and with a huge effort, was able to open the escape-portal, and promptly jumped in. He slammed the door behind him and stopped to examine his new surroundings. The giant room was completely bare but for a lifeless hearth in a far corner of the chamber. The warlock realised that there was no way he could go back the path from which he had come. Across the room, set in the wall lay a small wooden door. He approached this alternative exit, opened the door and groaned in frustration at the sight of his new position. He had entered directly into the town-centre which was teeming with people and merchants. He had walked straight into the main market area of the town, and there was no turning back. He hesitantly entered the centre and began to rapidly walk past the stalls openly presenting their magickal merchandise. On public view were objects familiar to the mage, though he also noticed substances and instruments banned and strictly forbidden by the Guild. But of course the main article of sale was to be seen everywhere he turned, the herb Mandrake. In his haste to leave the market place, the mage had forgotten his cloak would reveal him as a strong potential customer.

Half a dozen men appeared seemingly out of nowhere and rushed towards him. The warlock was surrounded by arguing men in an instant.

"I have hemlock and mandrake here for you at a bargain combined price of only five gold pieces." Said a small man who practically shoved the two herbs into the mage's face.

"Liar, cheat!" Roared a second man and turned to the wizard. "I will sell you the same for just four pieces. You cannot do better than that!"

"You don't understand, I do not want..." Interjected the mage, but he himself was quickly interrupted.

"Three gold pieces." Announced the original trader.

"Two!"

"One!" Shouted another who stared at the sorcerer expectantly.

"I will sell it to you for cheaper than that." Said the first man again.

All looked at the trader trying to comprehend how he might manage this task, but one did not bother to wait.

"Oh, no you won't."

"Oh, yes, and why is that?" Laughed the first trader.

"Because you will be dead." Whispered the man and grabbed the merchant by the throat.

The mage suddenly heard the sound of a shrill whistle, though the fighting traders appeared not to hear the noise. Yet Barrius was quick to recognise the whistle as the arrival of the Military-Guards, who were quickly approaching this public disturbance. The warlock rapidly deduced that it was time to leave. One guard reached the crowd and the mage gasped in awe. The soldier before him must have stood at almost seven feet in full battle armour. The wizard turned to his left and took off down the street, as fast as his legs could carry him. The soldier hailed him, but the warlock did not stop.

"Hey, I told you to stop! Are you deaf?" The guard cried out. "Well, you are now." He said quietly, as he produced a large crossbow and attached a steel-tipped bolt.

He took careful aim, and fired. Barrius saw the corner of the street, and sighed in relief. This turn-off meant safety and escape. He was about to enter the side-alley when the bolt struck. He felt a sudden sharp pain in his back and fell to the ground with a heavy thud. He grimaced briefly in agony before the sight of the world left him in a blur of colours.

*　　*　　*　　*　　*

The door of the chamber suddenly swung open and light from the outside world scarred the rats, causing them to flee and revealing the still shape of the single occupant of the dark room.

"You are certainly one person that is hard to keep track of, mage!" Jual shouted into the cell and casually hoisted the unconscious warlock over his armoured shoulder.

Checking briefly that there was nothing else amiss in the filthy chamber, the soldier gladly departed from the foul stench of the dungeon, and was halted by the guard who had shot the mage.

"What I did was perfectly legal, and besides, he'll live," the man said quietly. "Next time, make sure he halts when I tell him to do so."

"I will keep him out of trouble in future." Jual said in a way of apology and the guard smiled. But the knight did not let him see the sneer of disgust and anger that was present on his face directly afterwards.

The other travellers were waiting patiently across from the prison. Sasha thought it best that the knight went in for the wizard since the Military-

Guards were unlikely to argue with him, considering his rank and occupation.

"Is he all right?" Asked Sasha as they approached.

"He'll live, no thanks to them," he sneered. "But he has lost a great deal of blood."

"Then it appears we are going to have to stay here overnight." Sasha retorted bitterly.

"He won't recover overnight!" Procel interjected.

"You forget that this is a town of magick." Sasha replied. "We will find another sorcerer who will cure him."

"It won't be that easy," the guide declared. "Have you forgotten who you are? How will you find another mage who has the same views as he does?"

"I will find one." She retorted flatly.

"Why don't we simply leave him here to recover in his own good time, and collect him on the way back?"

"Because we need him to destroy the dragons at the Cavern and..."

"Destroy the dragons?" Procel interrupted. "Have you gone completely crazy?" Then he paused and frowned. "Now I see. Ace did not tell me the entire story, perhaps on your orders."

This outburst made the other guide Amon glance over at Sasha oddly. It was obvious he also did not know this.

But the knight did know. He turned to Procel. "That is enough."

Both guides now stared at each other in confusion and rage while the others headed for the nearest tavern and shelter for the night. It had begun to rain, a soft drizzle to cool Procel's anger and he began to wonder just where this journey might take them, perhaps into the very jaws of death itself.

CHAPTER EIGHT

The lone man stared in seemingly catatonic fascination as the day finally gave over its dominance to the night, and retreated once more over the distant hills. He watched from his single window and smiled briefly as the day was driven into temporary slumber by the oncoming relentless darkness; that great symbol of death and desolation. Yet even death, that irrepressible unforgiving force, it seemed could not threaten or send fear into this particular human, for the man had lived with it all of his life. It was as if death itself was a living creature that hung perpetually over him like a shadow, but would not dare face him.

He knew however what a risk he would be taking. To waste much more of his energy might prove fatal in the coming battle, while Goodwin was preserving all of his.

"Never mind the loss," he argued with himself. "The battle is already lost if I do not do this. I must possess the rest of the spell."

Throwing several herbs and powders of various description into the water-filled cauldron, he began to chant in a low voice that rapidly rose to a piercing crescendo of sound. He continued for several minutes until with satisfaction the clear liquid began to bubble and froth until the entire surface of the water was covered in thick white foam. Suddenly, the surface of the cauldron seemed to cave in on itself, and then the water rose five feet into the air and turned from colourless to red, blood red. Slowly the wall of water began to change appearance until a form took shape, and a distinct head and torso could be seen. The creature of water before the mage was neither human nor animal, but rather something in between. Its claw-like hands were folded across its naked hairless chest and the inhuman head was an insult to nature. The skull it possessed was that of a large ram, with two horns twisting and curling until they nearly touched the shoulders, the tips sharp and jagged. The eyes the monster bore were similar to that of a cat sunk deep into a deathly pale skull. A long white pointed beard hung down from its chin and all of the many rows of teeth in the inhuman mouth were sharp and stained with blood.

The voice of the demon was rough and coarse. "Soren." It said in a low tone.

"Are you the demon Choronzon?"

"I am a creature of many names and shapes. But you already know who I am. I am also known as the soul-sucker, is yours now for the taking?" It hissed.

"No, but my arch-enemy's is."

"There will be a price, mage. You owe me."

"I am no simple mage," the wizard barked. "I have reached far beyond that low status. I am a master of the dark-arts, I am a Grand Warlock, the third highest attainable rank. With my rival out of the way, I will be able to reach the second highest, that of Magus, and then finally, the ultimate spiritual status, that of a god!"

"There are already enough deities. What makes you think I will allow another?" The demon snarled.

"You cannot stop me," Soren retorted. "And I will destroy every other god in my path, until only I remain."

The demon laughed in reply.

"Will you help me?" The mage said in a low voice.

"That depends. Return to me what you stole."

"Very well." Soren replied, but hesitated in handing over the black volume.

"Give me the book." It snarled.

"There is a page missing. Give it to me."

"The book!" The monster roared and began frothing at the mouth like a mad dog.

"The page." The warlock repeated calmly.

Finally the beast of magick gave in. "Take your cursed spell, mage." It growled, and threw a parchment to the floor.

Soren carefully studied the small manuscript before handing over the book. The demon snatched the dark volume out of his hands. The red waterfall returned to colourless before subsiding back into the cauldron, by which time, the demon had left. The warlock exhaled a great sigh of relief, but turned back to the cauldron in sudden fear upon hearing a cackle of laughter.

"I will return, mage. And when I do, I'll see you in hell for this!" The demon snarled, and then it was finally gone.

Soren put a hand up to his left cheek upon feeling a gust of cold wind pass quickly over his face, and then suddenly, it was gone. He glanced at the parchment and sighed. "That might just happen."

* * * * *

Although Procel objected at first, he eventually agreed to go with the knight and search for another sorcerer, or at least obtain the specific herbs to cure the badly injured mage. The rest would remain and watch over the sick warlock. Amon protested for his knowledge of the town was greater than Procel's, yet Sasha was quick to point out that he was too valuable to risk on such a small task.

They left the tavern and Procel turned to Jual in frustration. "Where to first?" From where they stood, the crowded town appeared huge and insurmountable.

"Not the market anyway." The knight quickly replied, and the guide agreed, for too much trouble had occurred there already.

"We should try a small herb shop instead. They would tell us how to use it, unlike the traders at the market-place." Procel declared.

They walked down an alley off the main street, and proceeded to enter down several more side-roads until they halted in front of a small house with no windows, and only one cracked filthy door set in the black stone of the shop. Above the door in faded letters were the words 'Herbs and Powders'. The knight was extremely reluctant to enter such a dubious establishment for he loathed anything magickal as much as Sasha. But Procel quickly reminded him that there were little other alternatives, but to enter. The soldier eventually agreed with a sigh, and so, keeping a firm hand on the hilt of his broadsword, they opened the door and entered, whereupon a great shock greeted both travellers. A large petrified ram's head dangled from a thick rope from the ceiling and hung bare inches away from Jual's astonished face. The beast had not the eyes according to its nature, but rather those of a human. It was those piercing brown eyes that held the soldier's attention. It was as if those eyes could see into the very soul of the knight. Both then heard a sound from the opposite end of the chamber whereupon a short old man suddenly appeared from beyond a dark curtain. His exact age was impossible to estimate from his strange appearance. Long white hair flowed down over his shoulders from the back of his head, but the remainder of his skull was hairless as was his wrinkled-covered face. Apart from that, he seemed to be in remarkably good health.

"Don't worry, it is dead." Laughed the man in a loud voice that seemed both young and strong.

The travellers nevertheless detoured carefully around the head and approached the small man.

"What will it be?" The owner asked and faced the two men before him with sincere, but cautious eyes.

"We require something special. We need a quick cure for a crossbolt injury." The knight interjected, careful not to reveal more than was absolutely necessary.

"I have what you require," he quickly retorted. "But you do not need anything outlandish. We sell a lot of curing items in a town like Mandrake," he laughed. "They are in high demand."

The owner of the shop then reached under a table and revealed a tiny green flask which appeared to all intents and purposes, to be empty. He also took out a second container, black of colour which hid the contents.

"Where's the written instructions for these things?" Procel asked, staring down at the man.

"Oh, come now. You do not really expect the spell for those on paper, now do you? They will work as they are."

Procel took the strange flasks and hesitantly paid the small man who snatched the few gold pieces from the guide's hand and began to rub the metal items between his fingertips as if they were not real. He glanced up at Procel and smiled briefly, revealing broken rotting teeth.

"Have to be very careful about money in this town. It can disappear when you least expect it." The man said slyly.

"Do I look like a mage?" Procel retorted, beginning to lose his temper at such greediness.

"Believe me, they come in all shapes and sizes," the owner replied. "Now, if you do not wish to purchase anything further, I will bid you good-day."

The travellers left quickly, the knight sneering in disgust as they departed from the house.

"Did you hear what he said to me? That was absolute rubbish! You would notice a magick-user straight away. You certainly could not miss our mage in a crowd!" Procel shouted in anger.

"I would not be so sure." The soldier retorted.

"What do you mean?"

"For one thing, the shop has disappeared."

"What?"

Procel turned back to the shop to see to his complete astonishment, bare wall. The house had disappeared. The knight in reply laughed at the guide's open jaw and began to walk back to the tavern. Procel eventually broke himself out of his trance and ran after the soldier. They were both soon back on the main street, leaving behind the shops and houses which mysteriously changed their appearance at random far behind them.

* * * * *

A second shade of colours filled the sleeper's vision as he left the desolation of unconsciousness. He left behind the peace and oblivion of slumber and greeted instead the world of pain and despair. He felt something being shoved into his face and this action brought him back to reality with a shot of agony.

"Drink this." A mysterious voice said whose face was still a blur.

Yet he took the object in the hope of regaining his sight and other senses. His strength rapidly returned and almost immediately with it, his vision. He suddenly saw before him the knight who despised him, and yet still helped him for what reasons the mage could not yet decipher. But it was honour to Sasha which drew the armoured human to this task, though honour was not a word known or respected by dark mages. The warlock slowly rose up from the bed and instantly felt nausea which forced him to quickly lie back down on the bed.

"Are you all right?" Asked Sasha.

"Why did you save my life?" Retorted the wizard, and attempted to raise himself up the bed a second time, this occasion succeeding.

Sasha stared at the warlock, speechless at his reply.

"I mean you do not bear any love for me or my kind."

"You are still a member of this company," Sasha replied angrily. "Besides, I am simply repaying the favour. You saved mine."

"So, does that entitle me to privileges?" Barrius laughed. "And about saving your life, I did that only because I want to see your father. So, don't flatter yourself!"

"What makes you believe he will see you?" Sasha snapped. "He never had time for me."

"From what I've seen, I am not surprised," the mage responded. "You're just a spoilt child who had too much of a good thing and threw it away in arrogance."

"Spoilt?" Sasha screamed and grabbed the bars of the bedpost so she could be face-to-face with the wizard. "He even missed my mother's funeral because of one of his spells that just could not wait!"

Yet the sorcerer only laughed in reply. Jual approached the bed and began to slowly draw his huge blade, but the mage only laughed the harder as he faced the soldier.

"If you try and use that sword against me, I will blow a hole in your chest so large, the moon will be able to shine through it."

Sasha turned to the knight. "If you start any fights, you can leave."

"Like Ace?" The warlock interrupted and Sasha swung sharply around to face him in rage. "But he was no longer any use to you, was he? But I am. You need me for the Cavern, so don't give me any of your pompous rubbish!"

Sasha was silent. All the anger had suddenly left her, and she ran from the room.

"Brilliant, perfectly executed!" Procel remarked and ran after Sasha.

"That's not all that's going to be executed." Jual said angrily as he once again began to unsheathe his sword.

Yet the mage appeared to betray no fear at this threat. "Can your pride and honour protect you from me, soldier?"

The knight in reply fully drew his blade, but the warlock only sighed and calmly walked out of the room, leaving the rest of the company to stare at the soldier in confusion.

But Amon finally broke the silence. "We must leave now that he is all right. I will go and inform the others."

Jual watched him leave and growled in anger and frustration before packing his belongings.

* * * * *

The travellers were beyond the sight of the vile town by daybreak and quickly entered the range of mountains which obscured the settlement far behind them. They rode slowly through the narrow valley in fear of sudden avalanche of rock and stone which was common with the region. The mage took no notice of this activity. His full attention was focused on his shoulder which still persisted to annoy him with random flashes of pain. If this was not bad enough, there was a foul taste in his mouth. One of the flasks the knight brought back for the injured mage was to be poured directly onto the wound, but the other had to be swallowed, and it tasted awful.

This made the warlock grumble and complain all the more. The journey to Coltrop, their next planned cessation, would take two days. Beyond it was one more stop and two rivers to be crossed before the Cavern. Jual was at the rear of the company and allowed himself to grin as he noticed the wizard's agitation concerning his wound. Although for Sasha's sake he would not harm the warlock, any discomfort the mage might have brought a smile to his face. The travellers continued to be wary for any signs of oncoming avalanches, but forgot that a valley such as the one before them was ideal for a possible ambush. Both the guides and the knight cursed their stupidity as from beyond hidden cavities in the nearby rocks appeared several armed bandits. Jual was the first to see the intruders and quickly counted two dozen before shouting a warning to the others.

"Look out!" He screamed as their attackers rapidly surrounded them.

The armed bandits fell on the travellers like wolves. But one however decided to choose the knight as his first victim and instead fell foul of the soldier as his mailed fist broke the attacker's jaw. He collapsed at the feet of his conqueror, giving Jual enough time to draw his massive blade as more bandits quickly surrounded him. One large man jumped alongside the knight's horse brandishing a giant double-headed axe which he used with deadly efficiency as he swung and sliced the horse's stomach wide open, narrowly missing the soldier's leg. The beast instantly collapsed into a warm pool of its own entrails, bringing its rider down with it. The horse fell on the soldier's right leg, breaking it and leaving its master helplessly pinned as he cried out in pain. He glanced quickly around the battle-scene to see the condition of the others, fearful they might be in the same predicament as he. He saw one man attack the mage, believing he was weak and frail. But the warlock removed his wand from beneath his cloak and in one quick movement, struck his attacker across the face. The man clutched his cheek in agony and fell back, only to be instantly replaced by another fighter, ready to do battle. It appeared the company was heavily outnumbered and it was only a matter of time before they all fell. Even the knight himself now felt his moment had come as the axe man stood over him, a broad evil smile on his face as he lifted the weapon over his head to strike the soldier down. Jual held his breath and waited for the final blow.

Yet it never came. A sudden gasp of surprise and pain appeared on the axe-man's face and the confident smile vanished. Jual tried to move out of the way as the man began to collapse towards him. But the bandit crashed onto him, forcing the air from his lungs. The knight looked over the shoulder of his fallen attacker to see a narrow shaft sticking out of the man's back. Jual was just recollecting that nobody in the company possessed a bow when a shadow passed before his amazed eyes. A large man in a flowing black cloak abruptly moved in front of his vision. The stranger then drew two swords of equal length from scabbards on his back as he turned to face the raiders. Two men immediately came towards him, swords waving through the air before them. The stranger simply kept the blades horizontal by each of his waists and moving between the two attackers, cut both their stomachs open simultaneously. Another bandit charged directly at the stranger with a spear aimed towards his victim. Yet the swordsman simply, to the knight's complete amazement, leaped over the raider and upon landing behind him, swung one sword which neatly severed the man's spine.

Jual could only stare on speechless, as the stranger struck down every bandit that was foolish enough to attack him until the odds against the company changed, and the raiders fled in fear of the stranger's skill and ferocity. Procel and the other guide approached the fallen knight and began to pull him out of his predicament while Sasha made her way to their mysterious saviour.

"Do not bother yourself with thanking me. I do not usually help others, but I had my reasons," he said and as if in explanation, began to search the dead bodies for money.

Sasha turned away in disgust at their saviour and ghoul and heard him curse as he discovered little gold for his troubles. But she turned back to the man. She felt he deserved a reward no matter his reasons. "Do not trouble yourself with them. I will compensate you for your help."

"Oh yes, how?" The stranger retorted as he looked up from his foul task, betraying a sneer.

Sasha felt regrets already, but it was too late now. If she angered him, he might very well turn on them. "You may have a share of the giant treasure at the famous Dragons' Cavern."

This outburst provoked a sudden look from the guide Amon Rusheus who had half of the treasure coming to him.

"The Cavern?" The man laughed. "Nobody knows the way."

"I do. That is where we are headed for and we could use the talents of a swordsman on this dangerous journey."

"Yes, that is true," the stranger replied. "This might very well not be the first and last attack of bandits you will have."

"So, you will accept?"

He hesitated before answering. "Yes, very well."

"What is your name?" Sasha asked.

"Kali Darnel, mercenary of The Tribar from the great city Colewort."

The knight glanced at the man in disgust. The infamous Guild of Mercenaries, The Tribar, were nothing more than a bunch of brutal cutthroats. Jual suddenly regretted being saved by such a person. The man was scum.

"And one more thing," the mercenary said. "Keep him away from me." His finger pointed directly not at the knight, but at the wizard.

Barrius Fetherfew frowned in surprise and puzzlement for mercenaries were often hired by mages, so why should this individual be any different? The warlock decided he would keep a wary eye on this saviour of theirs. Something was not quite right about him.

After setting the knight's leg with two sticks, and constructing makeshift crutches so he could support himself on his one remaining good leg, the company with their new addition moved quickly on towards Coltrop, the next stage of their journey.

*   *   *   *   *

Besides the attack and the sudden intervention of their new companion, the remainder of the day passed uneventfully and the company made camp on a small hill a dozen miles from the dangerous valley. The knight and Procel were preparing the main meal while Sasha watched the mercenary make his own separate camp beyond the other travellers.

She rose and approached their saviour. "Sure you won't eat some?" She asked, offering some of the hot cooked wild pig meat from the spit.

"Thank you for offering, but no thanks. I carry my own food." He responded as he revealed a small package of salted meat from his pack.

"Don't trust us much do you?" Myru asked.

"I do not trust anyone." The mercenary retorted as he began to eat his solitary meal.

Sasha sighed and returned to the other travellers. Jual was the first on watch after eating and glanced at the mercenary. His earlier comment had escaped him the watch. Nobody wanted such a man guarding over their sleeping form, even though he had previously saved their lives. The soldier was relieved by Procel some hours later and the guide prepared to settle down by a tree and relax. It was going to be a long night. But no sooner had he begun to relax when he felt the strange sensation that he was being watched. He then heard a sudden eerie inhuman cry far off in the darkness. But the creature a few moments later sounded nearer, much nearer. Whatever it was, it was approaching the camp. Procel began to ponder on whether he should wake the others when his mind was made up for him. The howls were now barely a short distance away and he instantly rose to his feet and approached the knight who was already awake and rising to his feet.

"Did you hear that?" Asked Procel fearfully.

"What do you think?" He retorted as he unsheathed his huge broadsword.

But Procel did not reply. The howls were those of wolves, and many by the sound of their screaming. They were well known in the region for their ferocity and the guide now began to visibly shake with fear. Procel rapidly awoke the others, but the mercenary was on his feet so quickly that it startled him.

"Quick, grab a stick from the fire." Jual ordered and got them to form a circle.

"Don't go disappearing on us now, will you, Kali?" The mage said to the mercenary.

"I thought that was your usual trick, fortune-teller. And please be good enough to call me Darnel. My friends call me Kali."

The warlock went bright red with rage at being called a fortune-teller which were widely cursed as false magick users. "You betray any of us, or insult me again," Barrius retorted angrily, "and I will kill you."

The wolves abruptly halted their arguing as the light of the dying fire suddenly revealed the beasts. Myru cried out in fear and Amon actually smiled, and Procel remembered that the guide actually enjoyed the danger and the prospect of being killed at any moment. No wonder he had won the prize for best guide, thought Procel. From beyond the trees came the sleek dark shapes and approached steadily from all angles to the waiting company. The travellers each stood back to back facing the oncoming merciless creatures with one flaming stick each in one hand and brandishing a sword in the other. The shapes appeared to the travellers, but hesitated before the fire which they hated more than the cold steel the humans promised. But the blood-lust was upon them and they suddenly leapt at the travellers. There was immediate confusion amongst the company as the beasts attacked. The knight cursed in anger. He forgot the guides and the women were not fighters and would naturally break first. He in vain attempted to retain the circle, but it was soon every man, or woman for themselves. There were soon sudden cries of pain mixed with the harsh sound of cold steel as metal or fire met flesh as the company fought off the relentless attacks. One of the foul beasts was about to seize Procel by the leg, but he stopped its fangs with his sword.

"Do something, sorcerer!" Jual shouted to Barrius Fetherfew.

"I thought you did not trust me enough to allow me to do anything." The mage retorted.

"I don't," Jual responded. "But death as another option could be worse. Yet, then again..."

But the soldier was halted in mid-sentence by a sudden flash that both blinded him and the rest of the company. The wolves fled in terror from the piercing bright light which hurt their sensitive eyes. Jual turned to see the tip of the wizard's wand which he held high above his head was alight with a bright golden flame.

"A simple trick, but effective." The warlock stated, smiling for the mercenary had not saved the company a second time, much as he might have liked to.

However Kali only sneered in reply before settling back down to sleep as if nothing had happened.

"Better put two on watch this time," Sasha said to the knight. "I don't believe the wolves will be back, but all the same."

The soldier sighed in agreement as he sheathed his blade after cleaning and went on watch with Procel. Both Myru and Sasha had offered, but Jual would hear nothing of it. The two settled down and talked unceasingly through the starless cold night to keep themselves awake until dawn.

The wounds from the incident with the wolves were not of the visible physical kind, but rather scars of utter hatred between the mage and the mercenary. Both of their trades or ways of life involved the occasional blood-letting of some poor individual and in this way, their code of practice sometimes intersected either by choice or by accidental means. So the warlock pondered, why should this person be any different? There is definitely something not quite right about our friend the mercenary, and I mean to find out what.

The mage clenched and unclenched his teeth in frustration and anger as he gripped the reins of his horse so tightly that his nails digged deep into his skin, drawing blood. But he did not feel the pain. He only felt anger and distrust. Anger for the others who ignored him on this matter, except perhaps the knight. But I can't trust him. He would kill me at the first opportunity if her back was turned. No. This is something I will have to do myself. Jual on this occasion did not notice the mage's agitation as the warlock stared fixedly at the mercenary, as if attempting to inflict upon him a vile disease with his evil-eye. But the wizard did not possess such a power and he knew from experience of such men as the mercenary before him, that his death would not be an easy one. He would not be able to murder the man in his sleep. But what did it all matter? We are all probably going to die at the Cavern anyway. They all appeared to follow Sasha like willing lambs to the slaughter in search of something. The mage wondered if they would ever find it. And what do they expect to find? A mass of treasure perhaps? For some maybe, but were the others actually looking to this woman as some almighty great saviour who would stop the endless battle between the two High-Mages, and the damage it was causing to the land? The warlock began to laugh at this notion. He felt he had to laugh at such blatant stupidity and he laughed so loud and with such ferocity, he thought he might fall off his horse. The others glanced back at him in puzzlement before returning their gaze to the road ahead. But one did not look away.

"Why laugh when you already have one foot in the grave." The mercenary sneered, but the mage continued to snigger.

"And what do you expect to find at the Cavern, Kali Darnel?" Barrius retorted.

"What is due to me." He replied flatly.

"And you'll find gold coins and jewels, right?"

"You said it."

"All those precious dragons' teeth that you will pluck from their willing mouths, right?"

The mercenary nodded in reply.

"Oh, you will have your dragons' teeth, but only if you can pluck them out of your chest." The warlock laughed.

"I am after something much more precious than any object to be found in the Cavern, and I won't have to fight any dragon to get that prize." The mercenary stated which halted the mage's laughter.

What does he mean by that? The warlock pondered anxiously. What does it mean? And as the mage tried to solve this puzzle for he was sure the mercenary had let something slip, he felt Darnel had told him something dangerous; danger maybe for his own life, he did not see the sly grin on the mercenary's face.

*   *   *   *   *

The company sighted the town of Coltrop just before dusk of that same day, but they were considered unwelcome. Strangers were frowned upon at this time of year for they were only allowed free passage through the town in spring, when the traders came to the settlement. This trade which originated from the north was the only real acceptable contact with the outside world for the community. No other contact was permitted. Like most of the other towns situated along the south coast, Coltrop was a recluse. The large distance from its neighbouring settlements played a major part in its seclusion. Such a town as this would arrange and enforce boundaries such as a given number of fields around the settlement and farmers were prohibited from utilising land outside their given perimeters. This system of segregation kept the populace safely within the town's jurisdiction and therefore was able to provide adequate protection from invading bandits from the outside world. Strangers outside the designated season of trade were considered bandits, and the town refused to see any difference between the two. It was the law of the land and the town never made exceptions. Every member of the company noticed the passing farmers' agitation and curiosity as they travelled past the crop-filled fields on the rough worn road to the town gates. Dusk was fast approaching and Sasha did not wish to spend another night in such a dangerous area as this. Before them lay the town, barred by two massive iron gates and a thirty foot wall enclosing the entire settlement. Even as they observed this wall, several dozen archers appeared along the walls' battlements and took aim at the travellers. Sasha's eyes drifted down to the gates to see two heavily armoured guards standing apart and brandishing eight foot length lances which they used to form a cross against the gates, therefore barring entry. Friendly bunch, thought Sasha.

"No strangers allowed at any time, except market-season." Boomed one of the guards who appeared to wear armour much too large for him.

Outlandish multi-coloured feathers sprouted from the helmet he wore which danced in the air as he moved. The company had not come to this place to bring about a rebellion to overthrow whatever tyrant held rule, but simply to obtain supplies and move on. But it seemed the guards were not going to allow even such a minor intrusion lest they might inform the populace of events of the outside world the guards would prefer they did not know.

"We have travelled far and wish only to enter to obtain provisions for the journey ahead," Sasha said, but the soldier did not flinch as she pleaded. "It is a two day journey in each direction and so we badly require those supplies. It won't take long."

"Out of the question," he retorted. "I have strict orders to prevent any strangers to enter and will enforce that law by violence if necessary."

"But you can clearly see we are few and desire no such trouble."

"No trouble? You are a strange party of travellers to look upon - a mage and a knight? You have two such people in your party of opposite occupation, and you say no trouble?" Laughed the soldier. "You are either very stupid, or you are trying to make me look stupid. Be off, before I have you all hanged."

"Yes, there is a wizard in this company," barked Barrius, "and he is a very bad-tempered and dangerous one at that!"

"Don't try to intimidate me, scum. You do not frighten me." The guard replied angrily, now moving his spear to a striking position.

"No? But I should," the mage sneered. "My name is Barrius Fetherfew of the Guild in Valerian and my reputation is known and feared all over the land."

"Yeah? Well, I ain't never 'eard of you!" The guard sniggered and caused the other soldier to burst into laughter in further mockery.

The warlock replied by releasing his wand from the inside of his cloak and leaning over his horse, struck the top of the short-staff off the rocky-ground below. In reply, a deep split appeared in the ground and the fissure continued to widen until the noise and sight of the crevasse abruptly halted the soldiers' laughter.

"The black-cloaked bastard has caused an earthquake!" One of the guards screamed in panic, and pulling on a nearby hanging rope, a loud bell in response began to ring out from the town beyond the gates.

The bell continued to ring out until the gates swung slowly open and a company of fully armoured guards approximately thirty strong appeared from out of the town. They were followed closely behind by a large crowd. This mass of people gave way to more soldiers on horseback until there were shortly nigh on four hundred heavily armoured guards with hundreds of ordinary civilians crowded around them for protection. Sasha waited anxiously with the others as a giant man on a huge armoured horse made his way through to the vanguard of this small, but formidable army. Upon approaching Sasha, he turned to glare angrily at the gate-guard who had prevented the company's entry to the town.

"You brought out The Guard for this?" He shouted to the soldier who now cringed in terror.

"I beg your pardon, sire. This mage here caused an earthquake that might have very well damaged the town's foundations." He retorted feebly.

The soldier turned to the warlock and smiled. "Well, well! There's a face that is easily recognisable; Barrius Fetherfew of Valerian and wanted by many a bounty-hunter!" The soldier roared in such a strong overpowering voice that it scattered Sasha's thoughts.

Kali looked up at this remark with apparent interest and the knight, noticing this, thought it strange that he did so, for every mercenary in the land knew the wizard was high on the wanted-list.

"And none have succeeded, as you can see." The sorcerer laughed in reply.

"Give them their supplies." The Captain said, giving a false smile of friendliness to the sentry at the gates.

"What?" The soldier retorted in surprise. "But it is against the law."

"We made the law, and we can bend it. Besides, it does not pay to mess with this man, you don't know how powerful he is," the Captain whispered so only the guard could hear the conversation. "And how crazy." He added.

The sentry sighed in frustration and left his post to perform the task. The group were silent and remained motionless until the guard returned with bags of bread, salted meat and their refilled water-sacks. The warlock smiled at the soldier's embarrassment, causing further anger to the sentry, but he could do nothing. After handing over the provisions, he returned to his post and waited anxiously for the company's departure. The travellers quickly released him of his mental burden and had left the town's boundaries less than one hour later.

The mercenary glanced back at the mage and smiled to himself as he thought of the sorcerer on the wanted-list. An unexpected bonus. He almost laughed aloud as they left the town Coltrop far behind and began to slowly approach the River Swallow and another long step in their journey.

CHAPTER NINE

The lone man at the bar was busy getting drunk, creating oblivion for himself until he was interrupted by a shout more painful to the ears than any possible pain a blade could enforce.

"Well, well. Fancy meeting you here. Love life in a mess?" The person laughed and lightly pushed the victim of her torments, but could provoke no response.

Ace glanced up in anger and as his blurred vision began to clear, those feelings turned to utter amazement. But he managed to smile weakly at his attacker and turned to the barman to order drink for this newcomer.

"Ace, isn't it, if I remember correctly?" The stranger asked with a sneer.

"That name is dead." Ace replied flatly.

She smiled in amusement. "I said we'd meet again. Remember me, Elisa of the mercenaries from the town Purse? I also mentioned that when we met again, the encounter would not be so pleasant."

Ace gave a light laugh.

"I could easily kill you, you drunken slob." She barked.

"Then why don't you?" He retorted and turned to smile at her.

She did not answer and he laughed. He ordered another drink, but the servant glanced at the already large quantity of small tankards before him and refused. The alcohol had taken hold of Ace and the swordsman began to spout curses and abuse concerning the man's dubious parentage. The barman began to go red with rage and reached over across the table towards Ace as Elisa shoved something into Ace's limp hand. He glanced down to see a transparent flask and the barman relaxed. Ace clumsily removed the cork and without hesitation, swallowed half of the contents immediately.

"Hey, this is good." He remarked, but then suddenly felt an excruciating burning sensation in his throat and stomach and realised that he had just taken raw alcohol. He fell back towards the ground and was unconscious before his body hit the wooden floor.

*   *   *   *   *

Ace awoke suddenly and sat up. He put a hand up to his right temple and felt sweat all over his face. But this was forgotten as fear entered his aching body as awareness to his surroundings came clear. He briefly glanced around at the strange and unfamiliar room in which he inexplicably found himself. The room was tiny, perhaps even smaller than the one room he occupied back in Goodwin City. There appeared to be no sign of any ornaments of any kind. The only furniture to be seen was a single chair. His clothes lay strewn all over the floor and he noticed with sudden shock that his sword was missing.

But that apprehension was not foremost on his mind. His eyes fell on the bed on which he lay. Slowly he let his gaze move to his left and those eyes opened wide in astonishment. A fair-haired woman lay sleeping on her side, lying away from him so he could not see her face. But he was fully aware of her nakedness. Ace slowly threw over the covers on his side of the bed and placed one foot on the ground. He however became aware of his own nakedness. He pulled back the covers over his body in surprise and in doing so, awoke the woman. She turned over on her side and made no attempt to cover her body.

"Where am I?"

"In my room." She answered and rose from the bed and began to retrieve her clothing, which was also strewn across the chamber, while Ace stared on in amazement, speechless.

Elisa turned and smiled at him and his apprehension vanished. He could not remove his eyes from the sight before him. Her long flowing blond hair stood out distinctly over her white unblemished slender body. Her body was surely idolised by every man, but she was so thin Ace thought she was almost deathlike. Yet she moved with graceful movements towards the only door of the room and anxiety returned to the swordsman. He felt he must ask one question lest she disappear and not return, leaving him in the agony of ignorance.

"Did, did anything...happen last night?" He asked hesitantly as he tried to deny the overwhelming evidence before him.

She turned, and upon approaching the bed, placed a hand onto his cheek. He felt that he would never forget that touch because of its warmth and softness. She gently lifted up his head and bent down to kiss him lightly on the lips.

"You were wonderful." She smiled before fleeing the room, leaving Ace in a confusion of thoughts.

However, he rapidly regained his senses, yet stopped momentarily to put his fingers to his lips as if to bring back the fading memory of hers. He jumped out of the bed and quickly dressed. The door to his surprise was not locked and he stepped out into a narrow hall with several doors at either side. A small staircase lay to his left and this was the most obvious means of escape from the building. But as he was considering this path, a large man of at least six-foot four stepped out of one of the doors, saw Ace and stared. Ace was unarmed and suddenly was full of fear for his life, but instead of attacking, the man abruptly burst out laughing and rapidly walked past Ace and went down the stairs. Ace quickly gathered his thoughts and slowly made his way down the stairs and around a corner to arrive in a room. He hesitantly approached the chamber and awaited the arrival of more men, but to his relief, none came.

He noticed a door across the room which led into what appeared to be a kitchen where several men and two women were seated around a giant table. His host, Elisa was discussing something he could not hear and as he attempted to listen, the leader of the assembled company saw him and briefly said something before leaving the room. They all immediately in her absence burst into conversation. Upon approaching him, she grabbed hold of his hand, motioning for him to move with her out of the room. They entered the hallway leading to the stairs as she closed the door behind them.

"Why did you bring me here?" Ace shouted in anger.

She hesitated before speaking. "To join my company, of course."

"Why should I?" He retorted with a sneer. "You're nothing but a band of cut-throats!"

"And what are you? You love to fight as much as us and expect a reward for it."

"Why should I join?" He repeated angrily.

"Because I am here and Sasha is not. What can you get from her that you cannot from me?"

He could not find the words to reply. His mind was full of a mixture of thoughts; memories of Sasha's anger when she bid him to leave, and most of all, the thoughts of last night, although he could not remember them. But he looked forward with an almost feverish desire to the next night when he would not be drunk. She smiled and revealing his missing sword, placed the blade into his hand. He accepted the weapon back without a word. She left the hallway, and he followed her. It was all he could do.

*   *   *   *   *

She presented him to people whose names he almost immediately forgot. They only nodded and glanced in his direction in recognition of his existence. But Ace noticed that they appeared to be in some haste and in a state of excitement as they donned their light armour in preparation for the task ahead of them. He noted that only one of the group, a woman, carried a bow for it was a bulky weapon, for this company relied more on speed rather than on the art of fighting. However Ace reckoned this party could handle themselves adequately if it did come to that.

"What is going on?" He asked Elisa, but suspecting what they planned and that he was to be in on it.

"He's not going to be of any use." One of the group sneered and Ace noted with great distaste that it was the same bandit he had easily defeated back in Purse.

"He will be all right if there's any trouble." Their leader snapped and smiled briefly at him just before they all quickly left, leaving him alone in the room.

Ace sighed and rapidly followed. They carefully avoided the main street of the town Ruas, but travelled instead down dark dirty back-streets and alleys. It was now the fourteenth day in the long journey of Sasha's company as they approached the River Swallow. But this knowledge or concern for Sasha was presently absent from Ace's mind. His thoughts were for the safety of Elisa and her dangerous company.

"We are making for a rich fat merchant's house, if you could call it that. The dwelling is more like a palace and littered with hired soldiers and dogs." Elisa declared.

"How are we going to get through them?" Ace enquired.

She gave a sly smile. "Not through, but from above. There is a skylight on the roof. It is his cutlery we're after. He gives extravagant meals to the important people of the town to gain influence. The silver gleam of his cutlery blinds them to the real state of his wealth for he quickly gambles it all away, and needs to steal more from their gullible pockets."

"I see now you don't do this just for the money, but a sort of politics is involved also." Ace stated.

"There are more pleasures to be got in life than from just mere money. His despair at discovering the cutlery missing will be fine indeed. He will find them difficult to replace." She added and smiled broadly.

*   *   *   *   *

The journey to their planned destination was short and thankfully without event. They arrived just before nightfall and Ace gazed upon the building for the first time while the company made a final check on their equipment. The house was indeed more similar to a mansion. It stretched far above the street with dozens of windows looking out at the town below it. The sight was remarkable. It could contest against the castle of the High-Mage Goodwin back in the capital. The man who resided here was very rich or at least, kept up an incredible pretence. Ace could not see their entrance on the roof of this magnificent structure and hoped his mysterious lover could. As if in answer, she approached him, and pointed towards the massive roof of the house.

He followed her hand until his gaze caught the gleam of the skylight as the moon reflected off it. The mercenaries waited until it was fully dark before approaching their target. One member of the group threw up the grapnel and it caught onto the roof almost instantly. Then one by one, the mercenaries hauled themselves up the wall to the roof. Ace was almost the last and as he climbed onto the surface of the roof, he noticed this was not the merchant's house, but a smaller neighbouring dwelling he had seen earlier. He noticed a second rope which was hooked from this roof to the chimney of the merchant's mansion some fifty feet above them and across a large gap of nothing but hard street below them. Ace glanced over the roof to the street below and gasped. To fall would be fatal. Their leader went first, her legs wound around the thick rope as she climbed rapidly up towards the merchant's house. She betrayed no sign of fear or lack of strength in defiance of her sex and apparently weak body and Ace now realised why she was the leader of this company of cut-throats. This time he was not allowed the privilege of being one of the last, but was quickly forced to follow her up the rope. She had reached the mansion and was waiting impatiently for him. He slowly positioned himself on the rope and began to carefully climb. It seemed all his mountain-climbing skills had deserted him. He dare not look down. More than once his muscles ached and cried out for release, but fear of death kept him glued to the rope.

Eventually with much relief his hands touched stone and she lowered a hand towards him. Ace accepted it gratefully and once on the safety of the roof, almost fell into her arms with relief. He glanced back and noticed one of the group following up the rope after him, but much quicker than he. The swordsman realised they had performed this task many a time. One mercenary stood over where the rope was bound to the smaller house to make sure it did not break. Fifteen minutes passed before all were across and they quickly, but silently made their way across the giant roof to the skylight; their objective. Elisa was the first to reach it with Ace close behind. She unsheathed her blade and used the tip to lift the ledge up and a moment later, she had disappeared inside.

The others gathered around Ace and peered into the darkness where their leader had gone. None appeared to be concerned that she might not return. The minutes that followed seemed like hours before she finally returned and gave the all-clear. Ace jumped in and the others quickly followed. He leaped into complete darkness, but immediately felt the reassurance of her presence close by him which dismissed the bulk of his fear. She led the way until they were suddenly in the kitchen. Even in the darkness, Ace marvelled at the enormous size of the chamber. He could just make out shapes and the walls of the giant room as his eyes became accustomed to the darkness. He remained motionless while he heard the faint sounds of the mercenaries ransacking the shelves for the all-precious cutlery. In a matter of moments they were finished in their task and prepared to leave.

The robber who had attacked Ace in the town Purse led the way back towards the skylight. He approached the exit out of the kitchen, but abruptly halted. Faces cloaked in darkness glanced at each other in puzzlement and the man turned to stare at his leader in terror. Elisa frowned, then her eyes opened wide in surprise as she saw the reason for the man's motionless state. Wrapped tightly around the mercenary's right foot was a thin length of wire.

"Don't move." She whispered which was not only directed at the robber in question, but to the whole company.

But it was too late. Fear caused a reflex in the man's legs and his foot moved back a few inches. It was enough to trigger the trap. Ace faintly heard a click from the opposite end of the room and a low whistle which he instantly recognised. A crossbolt suddenly struck the bandit in the chest and the momentum carried him back onto the kitchen-table with a loud crash where he remained, motionless. The plates and glasses on the table were sent flying. The wire attached to the bandit's foot came away from the wall, though the man did not notice. Elisa checked the mercenary, but he was obviously dead. No man could have survived such a blow.

"Move!" She screamed, but the others were already running for the door.

Ace would only remember briefly-seen shapes afterwards as he fled upwards with the others towards where the skylight and escape lay. But as they approached their precious exit, the group halted so suddenly that they almost fell over each other. Before the open skylight were a dozen fully armoured guards who had just discovered their intruders' entrance. There was no time for tact or planning, the mercenaries fell on the soldiers like wolves. The guards were taken completely by surprise and three fell before they could even draw their swords. Still, a furious and short battle followed.

The soldiers put up a brave resistance, but they quickly fell before the highly trained robbers. A loud bell rang out from somewhere within the house and Ace could hear the approach of several more guards. But the mercenaries were already at the skylight and climbing onto the roof and out into the safety of the night. He ran across to the skylight where he saw his lover standing, motionless. She turned at his approach and her hand reached out, clasped onto his tunic and ripped it, before falling to the ground. He fell also with her weight and then noticed with despair the thick blood on her left side. Ace got to his knees and attempted to raise her off the floor, while all the time hearing the approach of the soldiers. She cried out in pain and he found out that it was quite useless to try and move her.

"Go, quickly." She whispered, but he ignored her.

Again he tried, but in vain. This time she refused to move.

"You must go, save yourself."

"No," he sobbed in grief, as he glanced down and saw that the floor was awash with her blood. "I am never going to leave you. Not now, not ever."

But she gave no reply, only smiled. Ace glanced down and saw that her eyes were devoid of all expression. She was gone. He had just closed her eyelids as he heard a noise behind him. A dozen more heavily armed soldiers had arrived and saw the kneeling swordsman immediately. Ace glanced at the dead men littered all around him. But for them, he was all alone. The robbers had all fled, bar three. Their bodies lay motionless next to their slain enemies.

"You, halt!" One of the guards shouted as Ace carefully put his dead lover's head down on the floor, before leaping for the open skylight.

His fingers clasped onto the ledge first time and he realised that he would not have got a second chance. He heard the whistle of a crossbolt and knew that he was completely vulnerable where he was. But the bolt struck the ledge instead of flesh, barely missing him by inches. Ace hauled himself up and just avoided having his legs severed by a sword as it was swung below him. He ran quickly across the roof, forgetting all cause for caution in his fear and slid rapidly down the rope to the neighbouring house from which they had come. The rope singed his hands, but he ignored the pain in his haste. The second rope to the street was also fortunately present and he was soon back on the dirty streets of Ruas. He glanced all around him, but did not look back at the house of the merchant where they had sought for silver and found only death, before fleeing into the darkness of night, never to return.

CHAPTER TEN

The River Swallow became distinct as the company approached this broad watercourse barring their path to the town Mullein. The shallow sweeping waterway wound before them similar to a long winding snake; a serpent which possessed its own brand of poison, much more subtle, but just as deadly. The reputation of this dangerous river was well known, and the display of the convulsive spasms of the water as it dashed off the rocks of the banks caused the travellers to have second thoughts on the real depth of the river.

"I tell you, it is really only a few feet deep," Amon sighed, but also knowing caution was necessary this close to the Cavern. "What do you see, mage?" He stuttered.

The warlock acted at first as if he had not heard, but then leaned over his horse and peered deeply into the dark waters below. The horse moved back a step from the water's edge in nervousness. "It is truly only about four feet deep," he replied and Sasha smiled, however her relief was short-lived. "But I sense a hidden malice, something of great power and evil."

Sasha sighed in frustration, though could not ignore his warning. The mage had been accurate on previous occasions. Procel and Jual however began to argue about precious time and how much would be wasted if they sought a detour around this obstacle. While they continued to argue, the wizard began to chant unnoticed in a soft rhythmic tone. The company's chatter was halted by the sudden approach of a lone wild wolf. Swords were instantly drawn, but the mage motioned for the blades to be put down. The beast did not hesitate in approaching the warlock until it stood alongside his horse.

"Get in." He said flatly, without even glancing at the animal.

The company could only stare on in amazement as the wild creature dived into the water and began swimming for the opposite bank. The beast had almost reached the bank when the water surrounding the animal began to froth and even the mage gasped with the others as a huge inhuman creature reared suddenly out of the water and seized the wolf between two giant claw-like hands. It glanced back at the company on the safety of the bank with a look of utter hatred, and hunger. The monster before them was beyond even the warlock's knowledge and comprehension. It was humanoid in shape, possessing two arms bulging with muscles and a massive torso making up its twelve foot stature. Of its lower-body parts, nothing could be seen. They were obscured by the depths of the water. Its head however was more snakelike than anything resembling human bearing an enormous mouth professing lines of inch-long fangs. The creature tore the unfortunate wolf apart with its claws before devouring the animal to the disgust of the travellers.

"What hell-world spawned this?" Jual declared as he drew his enormous broadsword.

As if in answer, the creature abruptly reached down into the depths of the water and suddenly drew forth two large broadswords, each twice the size of the knight's and uttered an inhuman laugh. "What hell-world spawned me, is quite right, soldier!" It shouted in a rough raspy voice.

"Who, what are you?" Procel stuttered, amazed the beast could actually speak.

"Of what I am, even I am not quite sure. But I was once a servant, or rather a spawn from one of the sorcerer Soren's more disastrous experiments," it retorted and saw the look of hate on Sasha's face. "I see you are no friend of that scum."

"But how did you get here?" Procel stated. "The town Tamerindes is far from here."

Amon glanced up at this remark for he himself had explored that very settlement, and was lucky to escape with his life.

"Quite easily, human. I simply followed the eastern coast until I found this river where I might find peace from Soren. But unfortunately this waterway is barren of food."

"Will you let us pass?" Sasha asked, getting back to their present predicament.

"Sadly, I cannot. You are no enemy and actually hate the one person that I despise, but my stomach does not like the taste of fish, you understand?" It sighed.

"Perfectly," retorted the mage. "But I'm afraid we can't oblige, much as we would like to, we have urgent things to do. But we would be happy to call on you when we return back to this place..."

The creature retorted by snarling at Barrius before diving beneath the water.

"Clever, real clever." Sneered the mercenary.

"You can't bargain with a monster," the mage replied. "But if you want to try, go right ahead. Perhaps you'll even find in it a relative."

The assassin was off his horse in a second and had drawn his blade before he had even landed on the ground. He was almost on top of the warlock before anybody could act. But the wizard was not afraid; he was even smiling, as he raised his right hand, thumb, index-finger and smallest finger extended. The mercenary leaped up to strike, his sword stretched behind his left shoulder in a striking motion. Yet the sorcerer did not even flinch. Something appeared to fly out of Barrius' hand and hit his attacker in the chest, sending him crashing to the ground. Kali was immediately back on his feet, expecting to see blood on his chest, but only felt instead a dull aching pain.

"How, how did you do that?" He asked in amazement.

The mage relaxed and sighed. But he had not finished mocking the mercenary. "A simple trick, changing energy into a physical force. Even a moron could do it. But then, maybe you could not."

The mercenary snarled in rage, but restrained himself. It was both useless and dangerous to attempt and harm a powerful mage in such circumstances.

"Have you two finished?" Sasha said. "There's still the problem of crossing this river."

In answer, the mage sighed and began to chant. Suddenly streaks of lightning shot from the tips of his fingers and struck the surface of the river. The water began to froth once more and the beast appeared, rising out of the waterway and roaring in anger and pain. It glared at the wizard and revealed the two swords. The creature began to move through the water towards the company, swinging the double-blades back and forth across the surface of the river.

The mage turned calmly to the mercenary. "Shoot it."

The assassin removed the bow from his back, but did not notch an arrow. The monster was now almost upon them, for both sorcerer and mercenary were nearest to the bank.

"Shoot it!" The warlock shouted.

But Darnel only smiled as he observed the wizard's growing agitation. Barrius snarled in rage. But was there also a hint of fear, thought the mercenary.

"I don't know if that thing can get out of the water," barked the mage. "But we're about to find out all too quickly."

The others stared at the assassin in nervousness for they would be next in line after them. The horses would normally have bolted at the sight of such an approaching creature, but they refused to move. It was as if the monster had some power over them. Darnel notched the arrow, but did not shoot. He was smiling again. But the grin abruptly vanished upon seeing the face of the mage. Barrius was chanting a death-spell for the mercenary. It appeared the time for jokes had ended. The water-beast had now reached the edge of the bank and had ceased its swinging of the blades. Instead it now drew them back as it prepared to strike down the wizard. But the warlock was taking no notice of the impending danger. His full attention was on the mercenary. Darnel momentarily gazed across to see the mage raise both his hands towards him. Those hands were now aglow with a blackish colour. He rapidly turned back to the oncoming monster and instinctively fired the arrow in time to save both his own life and the wizard's. The strength behind the arrow was weak, but the accuracy was true. The wooden-weapon struck the creature through the right eye and the beast dropped the swords with a great roar of pain to clutch the thorn protruding from its skull. The mercenary instantly notched a second arrow and drew this one all the way back on the bow, all his strength behind it. This arrow was steel-tipped, specifically made and designed to pierce armour. The arrow flew from the bow faster than the eye could follow and entered the beast's chest at point blank range. It went straight through the creature's heart and the steel-tip passed out through its back. The monster cried out in pain once again, before crashing heavily into the water and sank quickly into its dark depths, creating a giant wave of water in its wake.

The travellers seized this opportunity to immediately cross the shallow river lest the beast rise again. But it did not. It was gone.

The company made their camp not far from the river with one day's journey ahead of them to the town Mullein; the last stop before the Cavern and the refuge of the dying explorer, Patrius Turbith. His discovery was the reason for this long journey and the potential apocalypse it could create. Sasha felt that he had a lot to answer for. The travellers settled down to sleep, seemingly unaware of the evil thoughts of one amongst them; thoughts of murder, and dark events to be carried out this very night whilst they slept.

*   *   *   *   *

The oncoming night slowly began to drain the remaining segment of light from the dying day, forcing the company to set a fire immediately, for there was no moon to give them light to see by. Myru volunteered to take first watch as the others settled their tired bodies on the soft grass with an audible groan. She herself rested against an old tree-trunk and proceeded to shift her shoulders back and forth in an effort to relieve some of the day's tension. She did not however notice the shadow that slowly crept towards the mage's sleeping area. Nor did she hear the mysterious figure curse violently upon finding the blanket empty, its owner amiss. It was when the shadow began its retreat that she noticed the sudden movement. The mystery figure heard the familiar unsheathing of a blade and hesitated in its movement. Myru approached the stranger with her sword at the ready, but relaxed upon discovering its identity.

"I'm on watch. What are you doing awake?"

"Where's the warlock?" He retorted, ignoring her question.

"He's out somewhere collecting some herbs that he says he can only get at night."

"I'll bet." He snarled.

"What do you mean?" Myru replied nervously.

"What I mean is this." He whispered as he placed his left hand over her mouth while knocking her sword away.

She tried to push his hand away, but he was too strong for her. He moved so he could be behind her which meant she could not reach to get at him. She attempted to cry out in absolute terror as she heard the sound of metal being drawn from her right side. The sound was confirmed as he placed the short blade before her eyes to show her the instrument of her death. Myru could only stare transfixed at the small knife in seemingly morbid fascination and hoped someone, anyone would come and stop him. But that hope was taken from her with her life as the mercenary skilfully slit her throat, before letting her lifeless body fall silently to the ground. Darnel smiled at the bloody weapon and almost laughed aloud, but restrained himself lest someone hear and wake to discover his foul crime. But he glanced at each blanket and saw with satisfaction that nobody stirred.

"First to claim my prize, and then that bastard mage." He snarled as he made his way carefully amongst the figures until he came to the desired blanket.

He grinned at finally getting the chance to kill this victim, but momentarily hesitated in performing the foul act as he observed the calm steady breathing of his target. The assassin kneeled before Sasha Goodwin as if in prayer, hesitated again, and then raised the short bloody weapon in his right hand above his head. Darnel brought the knife down with all his strength behind it, but then suddenly felt an almighty jolt as his right arm was halted in mid-flight. Neither fear nor curiosity had time to enter his deranged mind before his hand which still clutched the blade was brought back behind his head and pain forced him to drop the weapon. He now began to feel an overwhelming curiosity to see the identity of this assailant. However he quickly realised who it had to be. The mage wasn't strong enough to perform such a task. Only one member of the company could - the knight. He began to wonder if in these delicate moments whether he could possibly bend or twist Jual's honour and code enough to let him escape. But all such thoughts were stripped from his mind as that powerful hand of the soldier suddenly brought the mercenary's arm up further and broke the frail bone of his elbow with an audible crack that made the assassin cry out.

The shout awoke the remainder of the company and they rapidly gathered around the strange scene. Sasha awoke and looked up to see the mercenary kneeling before her, and above him, the stern face of the knight. She rose and heard the mage approach. He was grinning in satisfaction.

"What is going on?" Sasha asked in puzzlement.

"He was going to kill you." Barrius retorted as he stepped forward into the centre of the scene.

"To have saved our lives and now try and take mine? It does not make sense." She stuttered and backed away from the mercenary.

"Who are you, Kali Darnel? You are certainly no mercenary. I always had my suspicions about you, but I always believed you would attempt to take my life, not Sasha's." The mage sneered as he gazed down at the injured mystery assassin.

"So what if I'm no mercenary," he snarled. "You were not powerful enough to see through my shield." He grinned, but the smile was a bitter one.

"Shield, what shield?" The wizard retorted in puzzlement and then gasped. "You're a magick-user, or at least an unregistered mage. You're a servant of Soren!"

"And now finally you know." He replied flatly and bowed his head with the constant pain of his arm.

"But why didn't you let the bandits kill us all that time back in the valley?" Sasha pouted. "They would have saved you the trouble."

"Simply because my master wanted an undamaged souvenir to prove that you were truly dead, and to show that I had killed you myself. He wanted your head!"

"Over here!" Procel abruptly shouted and all but the knight came running to where the guide knelt, his face buried in his hands to hide his grief.

They stopped short upon seeing before them the lifeless body of one of their own, her neck slit from ear to ear. They all bar Procel returned slowly back to Jual. The guide remained motionless over his fallen childhood friend.

"You bastard!" Sasha screamed and kicked the kneeling mercenary in the stomach, causing him to double over.

They all broke out into an argument about what fate should be enforced on the assassin. All but the mage continued to bicker. Nobody seemed to want his opinion. But none had stopped to consider that the warlock hated the mercenary more than anybody else, and especially now, since the assassin had seemingly so easily deceived him. The sorcerer glared at his fallen rival and his eyes narrowed with hatred for this man.

The assassin seemed to sense the wizard's dark thoughts and shrugged in apathy. "So be it," he said flatly. "Do what you will. My life is already forfeit for failing in my task. If you do not kill me, Soren certainly will."

Barrius Fetherfew nodded silently in agreement and decided that he was not going to be denied his prize. Jual noticed the mage's intentions as he approached and gave a sudden shout. The others turned and began to react, but the warlock was too fast. The knight began to shove his prisoner down to save him, but the short blade that flew from the wizard's hand caught his victim in the throat.

The rest of the company could only stare on, helpless as the assassin coughed and was dead in moments. The knight let his dead prisoner fall to the ground. The mage smiled in triumph, but it was a bitter win. Kali's betrayal of the company's friendship and his treachery showed clearly the extent of Soren's hatred and power. It was planned well. But it had not counted on Barrius. His constant arguments with Darnel had weakened his resolve and made him make mistakes. The mage decided again that there would have to be a confrontation between himself and Soren.

"We were going to talk about his fate!" Sasha shouted in anger.

"And what then? You would have killed him anyway." Barrius retorted, and then smiled. "Besides, my way is quicker."

Sasha could only stare on, speechless, as the mage calmly settled down to sleep once more, as if nothing had ever taken place. It seemed to her that she was leading them all to their deaths.

The wizard did not stop to ponder that she could be leading him to his early grave also. He had come too far and had too much hate within him to die so easily. "Later for that," he remarked to himself. "Much later."

*   *   *   *   *

The following morning was bright and free of rain or mist, revealing to the company, now less in number, the path ahead to Mullein. The strong presence of guilt on Sasha's face over the death of Myru at the hands of Darnel the previous night had now decreased in appearance, but the mage could still feel the emotion in her downcast gaze. Procel also noticed it in her silence and placed a gentle hand on her shoulder.

"You mustn't blame yourself. We never could have guessed as to his true identity."

But she only sighed in reply. "First Ace, then Myru. How many others will be lost before this is all over?"

"Ace chose his own path, Myru also knew as we all do, the risks she was taking in coming along on this journey. We are doing this because we believe you may be the only one who can stop the endless war."

"Am I?" She groaned. "I really don't know anymore."

The guide turned to see the mage smiling at her distress and he cursed the sorcerer, but Barrius only laughed in reply.

"This is no lover's trip." The warlock retorted sharply.

Procel turned away from him in anger to Sasha. But she was gone. He glanced around the small camp until he saw her preparing with the others to leave. He sighed before joining them in their task.

The wizard sniffed the air around him, and coughed, cursing in mid-rasp. "Must you burn that awful weed?" He growled at Amon Rusheus as his horse passed by the mage.

"You should try some, it's good." He laughed and blew the fumes straight into the sorcerer's astonished face from a small straight pipe protruding from the guide's mouth.

The mage threw several curses at the guide who only laughed back again in answer. He cursed with distaste for Amon's attitude to plants and herbs. To a magick-user, they were vitally important and not to be abused. The warlock glared at Amon one last time before leaving the camp area, forcing the others to quicken their pace and catch up with him.

*   *   *   *   *

The day's journey to the town Mullein was without event. The settlement symbolised the last scheduled cessation before the Cavern. They arrived just before nightfall after traversing yet another stretch of barren uninhabitable land.

"Procel and I will go and locate the explorer Patrius Turbith," Sasha announced. "The rest of you, find an inn for us for the night."

The knight nodded in reply and left the duo to their task. Sasha watched them leave, but Amon Rusheus did not depart with the second company.

"This does not concern you." Sasha declared.

"I think it does. Half of all treasure to be found at the Cavern is mine, and that explorer is the key to a safe path to the mountain. Therefore, it does concern me."

The two travellers saw that it was quite useless to argue and so Sasha finally sighed in acceptance. The three travellers rapidly passed through a town now cloaked in darkness, towards a large house situated near to the town-centre and adjacent to the Alderman's house. But as they approached this building, something far off in the distance caught their attention; their destination. A bright orange fire blazed brilliantly into the night sky from one of the many volcanoes located in the huge region surrounding the mountain of the Cavern. It was the first time Sasha had ever witnessed such a spectacle, and even seen from afar, it filled her with dread because of the many of those dangerous fire-towers they would have to pass through to get to the Cavern. She cast her eyes away from the scene and concentrated on the giant structure directly ahead of them; the Healing-House. The massive building before them contained four levels each possessing up to a hundred beds for the sick and the dying. During periods of war, the enormous house of the Alderman was also used. It appeared many inhabitants of this town had suffered at the hands of the fury of the volcanoes. Sasha considered that not even both buildings would be enough to contain the dead and dying in the war to come if they failed in their mission.

They arrived at the house and entered without first fully examining its gigantic size. Finding the location of the explorer would be a daunting task. Even finding a healer would be difficult. But they sighed with relief upon seeing one who was tending to a child. Sasha's mind drifted again, this time bitterly back to the occupation she had placed upon herself in the capital, that of caring and protecting orphans. Times and events that would never come again. But she once again cast her eyes away and forcefully banished the thoughts. She turned to the healer who was dressed in the familiar white robes of his profession. Procel had earlier recommended that the mage not be included in this task, and Sasha now realised why. Healers and mages were of opposite sides which might have caused a confrontation.

Sasha approached the man. "Can you tell me where we can find a man called Patrius Turbith?" She asked and the healer sighed.

"In the dying section," he replied bitterly. "You can't miss it."

He then turned away from the travellers and again began to tend to the living. The dying did not receive much attention, but to help and ease their path to the other side. True to word, it indeed only took mere minutes to locate the section on the third floor of the building, and they discovered it with great shock. There were approximately fifty beds of both men and women alike of which men were in a majority. Some of the blankets of beds were red with blood of those with incurable open wounds and the healers could do nothing to stop the person from dying from loss of blood. As they passed, they observed others who appeared to be suffering from a fever or disease until they finally reached the remainder, the victims of burning. This was surely the worst part of the section, a glimpse into hell itself. Amongst these were simple farmers who had foolishly strayed from the boundaries of their fields in search of new possible pastures and found instead a fate of death by a shower of ash and burning-rock. Lying unconscious between two such farmers was a thin middle-aged man possessing little hair and many burns, one of which had taken his left-arm at the shoulder. His hairless face was devoid of mutilation, but was red from the intense heat it had endured. There was no mistaking him. He had to be the explorer Patrius Turbith. The famous explorer who had made the greatest discovery of his career only to pay for it with his life. Sasha wondered if her father would really save this man, or simply leave him to rot. His wounds were beyond the power of their mage. Only Segal Goodwin would have that kind of energy and magick at his disposal. Their approach did not disturb his deep slumber and they considered waiting patiently for him to awake, until Sasha gently called out his name. His eyes opened slowly and focused on the daughter of his promised saviour.

"Do you know who I am?" Sasha asked the man.

The explorer attempted to raise himself up onto his one remaining elbow, but only succeeded in moving himself further out of the comforting blanket and collapsed back onto the pillow with a sigh. "I do not know you by name, but your face is oddly familiar. Of whom I cannot exactly say," the man replied in frustration and then smiled in triumph as he realised. "You have your father's eyes."

Sasha smiled back in reply, but did not think of it as a compliment, only as a curse.

"But you do not have your father's ideals. Am I right?" The explorer added. "So what do you seek of me?"

"The safe route to the Cavern." Procel answered and the man laughed.

"There is no such thing."

"But you know which path is the least dangerous, which route has no lava-pools to cross." The guide added.

"If I had such knowledge, I would not be here."

Procel and Sasha glanced at each other and the explorer saw that they had never considered this.

"The path I travelled on to the Cavern, and the route on which I came back on were quite different," he said which relaxed them. "You have to understand that I'm not a fighting man, us explorers only confront danger when it's absolutely necessary. After leaving the Cavern, I suddenly got the feeling that something was watching me. I couldn't see it, but I could feel eyes upon me, you understand?" He said and Procel nodded. "But I believed my hunch to be right and so took another path, and this is my punishment for cowardice." He sighed heavily as he gazed over his blackened body marked with sores and wounds.

The travellers listened attentively as the dying man related to them his precious hard-won knowledge. The guide Amon nodded in reply as he tried to remember his own knowledge of the paths while memorising these new ones. Later he would have to decide on which one they would take to the mountain of the Cavern. He was fully aware of the consequences of his actions. If he chose poorly, it would most probably be fatal.

"Your father will heal me?" He stuttered, his eyes betraying the fear at the thought of death.

"I...I don't know." Sasha stuttered and moved away from the bed so quickly that his hand reached out and ripped her tunic as she rose.

Without looking back, she fled out of the building, her mind full of despair and confusion.

"Half of the treasure is mine!" The explorer cried out after her and Amon's face lit up at the mention of his pay.

Procel ran after her, but the second guide did not follow. He stood momentarily by the bed, pondering on whether he should venture to ask the explorer as to the exact amount of treasure to be found in the Cavern. But he dismissed the thought and walked quickly out instead, knowing Sasha might revoke their contract in disgust at his greed if she discovered this act. She might still be close by. But Sasha Goodwin had already reached the meeting-place where Jual, standing on a makeshift crutch he had forged, comforted her and helped her on towards to the tavern for the night.

The company left the town early the following morning and left behind their last real sanctuary. From here on in to the mountain, everybody was fully aware that the path would become gradually more dangerous and potentially lethal. This last stage of their long journey would have to be crossed with extra caution in mind, but with also great haste. Sasha's father planned to leave the capital in six days hence, and arrive at the Cavern one day later, travelling on the back of his fastest dragon. Amon had given great consideration to the route outlined by the explorer. He had no choice but to accept it. His old paths might be blocked or even destroyed altogether by the molten lava.

The travellers gazed momentarily at the road ahead and let out an audible groan of relief, for it marked the final stage of their journey. But the sighs were also tainted by some trepidation for it could also symbolise the final stage of their very lives.

CHAPTER ELEVEN

This night the darkness ruled absolute, with no moon or any stars to challenge the blackness. No creature of the night witnessed the swift passing of one of its own briefly across their path. What meagre light there was, created by passing travellers and buzzing fireflies, could not hope to betray the presence of beast and rider, seemingly fused into one by their darkness of nature and soul. But although they could not see the intruder, they could sense its evil nature and in their terror, fled back to their underground home where they hoped the presence could not venture. But whether it saw or cared, it ignored their presence, and as suddenly as it had appeared, it vanished, swallowed up by the night, leaving no traces of it ever being there. It passed by countless towns of insignificance on its great journey southwards, but did not stop to mock the hated living. But its living rider did, and silently vowed to himself that he would correct that on his return. These towns would shortly know and bow before his name. He would pay back all those who had once scorned him. He remembered with hatred how they had branded him a renegade; a wizard who had gone rogue. But they would all pay, he sneered. Especially the one above them all; the one who had him exiled to the Dark-Regions, the so called High-Mage Segal Goodwin, who himself left the Society of Mages not long after. But Goodwin had resigned in honour, not banished in disgrace like me.

Soren cursed aloud and drove the magickally created horse below him to move even faster to reach its destination. Yes, he vowed, Goodwin will not leave the Cavern alive. It was time to settle the old debt.

*   *   *   *   *

All thoughts of every member of the company were on the dangerous voyage ahead and in particular, what lay at the journey's end. Soren might already be at the mountain, waiting for them. Sasha's mind in particular was on the Cavern. She knew with a bitter heavy heart that some, perhaps all, of the company might die there. Even if they wished to now leave, which she knew they would not, she was not brave enough to even ask them to, and face Soren alone. All were prepared to see it through to the end, whatever fate awaited them there. Every member of the company faced death almost every other day, even if this appeared more dangerous than usual and perhaps more certain of occurring.

"We're approaching the River Mamba." Amon cried aloud.

They followed his gaze to see one of the most unusual waterways they had ever seen. Steam billowed from the turbulent water and the surface of this large river was broken frequently by violent bubbling. They could clearly feel the great heat being given out by the waterway as they approached.

"Why is the water boiling?" Sasha asked in amazement at such a sight.

"Lava must be flowing into the river at some point and boiling the water. This is a common sight around this region," the guide replied. "The question is how are we going to get across? I can't see where the explorer might have found a way across."

"Leave that little problem to me." The mage interjected.

All stared at him both in nervousness and wondrous expectation. Jual waited to see the very river suddenly disappear, but instead of something disappearing; something was in fact appearing. Before the amazed group, the rising steam began to thicken and form seemingly into a dense mist. It then began to take shape. Within mere moments a bridge of thick ice took shape two feet above the boiling water. Even though the ice was several feet thick, it was already melting heavily, producing a very dense mist, much thicker than the one which had given it birth.

"Ride!" The dark mage cried aloud and was the first to dash across the path of ice.

Besides the slight rise at the front of the bridge of ice, it was otherwise very level and surprisingly not slippery. The others hesitated before rapidly beginning to ride across in single-file. Large chunks of ice were now falling into the river and disappearing into its depths almost instantly. The wizard's spell was supposed to produce non-slippery ice, but the heat from the river was disintegrating the artificial bridge so quickly, that it was reversing the intended effect. Sasha's horse suddenly slipped and fell heavily down onto the surface of the bridge, breaking away a giant section. She was the last to cross and fortunately so, for the magickally created overpass now began to disintegrate completely from the blow. In panic, Procel reached out and grabbed hold of her hand, pulled her onto his lap and rode off the bridge just as the overpass completely collapsed and vanished into the river, taking her horse with it. Sasha almost passed out both from the heat and the shock of almost meeting death and fell to her knees, breathless on the ground before the river.

Everybody was fully aware that it was most unwise to remain in such an area as this for long, and so Procel helped Sasha to her feet and placed her on his horse with him. He took the lead for Sasha was still disorientated. The mage then glanced to the sky and frowned.

"There's a storm coming." He stated as he observed the dark clouds rolling in from the coast towards them.

Already the weather was dramatically changing. The strength of the wind began to increase and it suddenly blew dust up from the barren ground and into their unprotected faces in its fury. Wrapping clothes or pieces of cloth urgently around their mouth and nose, they urged the beasts on. The reluctant creatures cried out in frustration at the dust, but obeyed. The storm increased in ferocity and crashed all about them, blowing their cloaks violently about, robbing them of protection. The wind began to approach a crescendo of lethal energy and attempted to force the company back. The horses began to cry out again as their hooves slipped over the hard glass-like basalt rock.

"Head for the coast!" Amon screamed.

"But what about the waves; the sea." Procel retorted in panic. "We'll drown."

"Possibly," he retorted, "but the cliff will shelter us from this blasted wind."

"Possibly." The mage remarked to himself with a sneer.

The travellers left the explorer's path and urged their horses down a break in the cliff leading to the sea. This collapsed eroded section in the cliff-line managed to support both horse and rider as they rode rapidly down the large mound of stone and sand. The steep cliff did indeed shelter them from most of the storm and the horses rode more easily on sand rather than on the hard basalt created from the raging nearby volcanoes. Unfortunately the tide was in, leaving them with only a few feet width of beach to ride on, but it was enough. No lava flowed into this part of the coast and Amon quickly led the way to a small cave eroded into the very rock-face of the cliff when the sea used to come in this far centuries ago.

"We can shelter here." Amon declared and was already off his horse and walking into the giant dark cave.

The rest hesitated until they saw the sudden light of a lantern and they too then entered. They slowly ventured deeper into this natural cavern until the powerful outside wind could no longer be felt. The guide was kneeling on the cold clammy rock and gathering nearby branches for a fire.

"What are you doing?" The knight shouted in alarm. "You'll suffocate us with smoke in here!"

"Don't worry," Amon replied. "There's a hole in the roof to let out the smoke."

"Have you been here before?"

"What do you think?" He laughed, pointing to the lantern.

The wind continued to batter against the cliff-face and showed no sign of wilting.

"Better get some sleep," Amon stated. "Looks like we're going to be here for some time."

But even Amon could not have reckoned on the amount of time they would have to remain in the cave before the wind calmed enough to enable them to leave. It was now the second day since they had left Mullein and it was already dusk, forcing them to remain until morning.

Both Procel and Sasha paced the corridor of the cave in silent anger and the guide frequently thumped his fist against the cavern-wall, causing the stalactites to tremble. "More wasted time!" Procel growled.

The night passed without event, but the following dawn did not break without interruption. They awoke to the first faint rays of the rising sun outside the entrance of the cave. But it was not dawn that broke their slumber, but rather a slight tremble in the rock surrounding them.

"What the..." Jual stuttered.

But Amon quickly relaxed him and the waking others. "It's probably only a nearby volcano cracking open a new fissure." The company began to pack their provisions as Amon related the grim news of the path ahead. "We'll have to head back to the explorer's path because the coast from here is impassable. I now have to remind you that the journey ahead is on a passage unfamiliar to me and the same route the explorer said he was being watched on."

The group were just beginning to leave as the slight tremor returned, but with a new and greater intensity. The very rock walls of the cave began to shudder.

"Get out," Amon blurted in panic. "Move!"

They fled their natural shelter mere moments before the cave disappeared under an avalanche of rock and sand. They looked up over the cliff-edge to see a volcano one mile away explode in a fury unlike anything they had ever seen. The normal blue sky above the mountain disappeared from vision as a huge cloud of ash and grey smoke rose high into the air. All turned to the guide for an answer to which path they should take in order to avoid the river of lava which even now, was winding its way rapidly down towards the coast and the sea. This confusion turned to absolute terror as without warning, an enormous crack in the sand suddenly appeared and opened up to reveal a crevice of incalculable depth. The jolt sent all flying to the ground and the horses bolted. Jual reached out and grabbed onto the reins of one of the frightened beasts, but was carried away along the beach. Loose sand flowed into the crevice like a river of water until the crack closed with an almighty crunching sound. All slowly rose to their feet. Procel ran after the knight who had managed to get to his feet, despite the injury to his leg. He was tugging on the reins of the horse, bringing the beast to a halt.

"We must get off the beach immediately! This whole area is shortly going to be covered with lava and this won't be the last earthquake." Amon shouted and the others obeyed the order without question in their confusion.

They were off the beach in minutes, having managed to recover the horses and some of their wits. They mounted and immediately urged the beasts into a gallop as a river of fast-flowing lava approached the beach. The company would only have a matter of mere minutes to cross this particular patch of land before the lava created an impassable path before them. The horses cried out at the harsh basalt rock below them and began to choke on the ash which was becoming increasingly denser in the air around them.

"Ride." Amon roared as the river of liquid fire came closer with every passing moment.

It flowed down towards the coast, a meandering snake of fire, bringing sudden and lethal destruction to everything that lay in its indivertible path. It travelled at an incredible pace with no hill or mountain to bar its path. The mage attempted to slow its pace by placing huge boulders of rock before it, but the lava destroyed the obstacles almost instantly upon contact, and continued unchallenged and undefeatable towards its inevitable destination. The riders urged their horses to collapsing point until it seemed the entire company would meet the river of lava head-on. But the group passed by the flowing lava, missing death by bare inches, almost sending the horses into a frenzy of fear in the process.

"By the gods, that was close." Amon declared when they were a safe distance from the river of lava.

They all breathed deeply in relief and coughed with the ash and sulphur which was still all around them in a heavy mist.

"Almost too close." Procel stuttered as he glanced back to see the lava block his sight of the route they had just crossed.

"But we can't stay here," Amon retorted, denying them of rest. "The lava might change course, and besides, we've already lost too much time." He glanced at Sasha. "And your father will arrive at the Cavern in a matter of a few days."

"You don't need to tell me that." Sasha snarled.

There was now a constant air of caution about the company as they travelled the rest of the day, wary for more volcanic eruptions and the resulting earthquakes. But the day was without event, bar the occasional argument due to the high degree of tension amongst the travellers as they drew ever closer to the Cavern. They made their camp that night far away from any nearby volcano, but were awoken by the distant light of those same fire-mountains and not the light of the dawn, which made them aware of the long day ahead and the many dangers which awaited them.

*   *   *   *   *

Wary attentive eyes observed the mountain-ranges for any early sign of disturbance that whole morning from dawn to noon, and it was this that saved their lives. Before the mage's amazed eyes, the mountain he was observing seemed to inexplicably change or alter its shape and begin to metamorphosize into something incomprehensible. It appeared to have grown wings, and was now moving towards them, revealing to the wizard its true and frightening familiar shape and identity.

"Dragon!" He roared and urged his horse into full gallop.

The sudden scream drew the eyes of the group first to the giant predator, and then to see the destination of the mage to which he was approaching. The sorcerer almost fell off the beast in his terror as he brought the horse to a sudden halt before the back of a steep hill, hopefully obscuring him from the sight of the dragon. He turned to see the remainder of the company come charging to join him. They had just reached the hill when the sun disappeared and its great heat was no longer felt on the travellers. A massive golden-coloured shadow passed quickly over their frightened bodies and continued flying at an incredible speed north. They hoped they had reached the cover of the hill in time and waited anxiously for the creature's return. But it did not and the company decided it was safe enough to move on. The dragon had not the intention of taking their lives, but it might as well have done. The quick motion of the beast had alerted the interest of the native creatures of the region, and within moments, had surrounded the entire area. All felt the watchful presence and fear petrified them to the spot. They dared not move. The company began to seriously consider the explorer's feeling of being observed by unknown eyes. The creatures did not keep them in suspense, but slowly began to move in towards them. As they appeared steadily from beyond small hills, the travellers could only gasp in fright and awe at their number and physical description.

"Fire-wolves." Amon breathed, announcing what the company already knew.

The vile beasts before them were the native creatures of the Volcanic Mountains; animals well known and feared for their ferocity and cunning. They desired the great heat given out by the raging volcanoes above all, but faced starvation in such barren lands in return for the warmth. But every once in awhile, they were rewarded for their devotion to the fire-mountains by the arrival of human-prey. Their size was similar to that of a donkey, possessing teeth sharp enough to easily pierce flesh and jaws strong enough to break bones in one single bite, their coats a bright red with thick wiry fur, even on their paws. The company counted at least twenty in number. Each knew that this would be a fight to the death. These creatures would continue until either the company or they themselves were dead. Such animals had no leader to follow and would not stop to consider their losses in the hunt for food. It was the universal law of all beasts; only the strongest and fittest would survive, or perhaps the most hungry.

The demons of this desert attacked swiftly, not giving the company time to prepare themselves or the mage to perform any spell. One struck the knight in the chest with such a ferocious blow with its paw, it would have killed the soldier but for his thick breastplate. But even so, the strike still knocked him to the ground and his gigantic sword fell from his grip. The other wolves seeing him fall, immediately gathered to finish off the largest of the prey in sight. Sasha ran one through the chest with a quick stroke of her blade as Procel stabbed another as it passed by him. But the third ran on unhindered, diving through the air to crash heavily onto the knight's chest, knocking the breath from his lungs and preventing him from rising to his feet. None could reach the soldier in time, since they were all totally occupied with their own opponents, and the wolf now dived for its victim's unprotected throat. Jual in panic, placed his armoured arm in front of his face and neck and the wolf in response, sank its giant fangs into the soldier's arm. Jual cried out with the pain, but this move gave him precious time. He fumbled for the small blade at his hip, but in agony, he almost dropped it. He then brought the knife swiftly up to his attacker's throat, and in one quick motion, thrust the dagger into the beast's neck and up into the brain, sinking the blade to the hilt into the creature's neck. The beast did not even get the chance to cry out before the life left it and it collapsed onto the knight, pinning him with the weight. The other wolves fortunately now ignored the fallen soldier, believing one of their number was now gorging itself on its prey. Jual eventually managed to push the dead animal off himself in disgust and gasped at the pain in his left arm as he remembered its huge teeth which had penetrated deep into his flesh. He however sighed with relief that it was not his sword arm. He began to consider what had brought on all this bad luck. First his leg, and now his arm. He consoled himself though that it surely could not get any worse.

The wolves though great in number, had not reckoned on the company's own ferocity. The travellers had confronted many a danger in order to reach this far, and the thought of dying or even losing the precious time necessary to reach their destination increased their anger and heightened their skill in swordplay. Even the fire-wolves' small brains quickly began to realise that they were losing too many of their number and not inflicting any serious injuries. So for the first time in known recorded history, the infamous species known as fire wolves, began to retreat and soon disappeared by fleeing into the barren land, never to be seen again by any member of the company. Once they were certain of their departure, the travellers fell to their knees with relief and sheer exhaustion. The weapons fell from their tired limbs. The knight tore the armour off his injured arm and examined the wounds. He realised grimly with a sigh, that they were indeed deep.

"Let me help." A voice uttered and Jual turned in amazement to who had offered.

The mage was standing over him, holding in his hand several unfamiliar herbs which he had taken from the large bag strapped to his waist next to his knife. Jual held his own dagger in front of himself protectively, but then lowered it. The warlock knelt down by the soldier's side and began to place the herbs which were anointed with some foul-smelling liquid the identity of which the knight could not decipher, though he certainly felt the presence of. He grimaced silently in agony at the placing and sting of the cold herbs and held his breath patiently while the warlock wrapped bandages around it and the wound to keep them both in place. All eyes turned once again to Amon as the guide rose to his feet.

"I'm afraid we have to ride again immediately. The fire-wolves could return and we have to cover several more miles before we can allow ourselves rest."

All groaned in annoyance and exhaustion, but mounted their horses once more and rode swiftly, leaving the battle-scene in the distance. The mage now remained with the knight on his horse to keep a wary eye on him, for the teeth of the wolf had carried poison. Not enough to kill, but enough to sicken. Sasha now rode on the wizard's horse, and they rode all that day, travelling long through the wasteland until all around them were active volcanoes.

*   *   *   *   *

The dawn arrived, and with it, new dangers. The company awoke to the shakes and shudders of further approaching earthquakes and threats of eruptions from the nearby volcanoes. But they had left the camp long before these threats could be carried out. It was now the twentieth day of their long dangerous voyage and each member of the group knew that they were finally almost at journey's end. But only two days remained for them to reach the Cavern before the arrival of Sasha's father. He would leave the capital for the mountain tomorrow and arrive one day later. They had also lost much time as they travelled and could find themselves arriving just that little bit late. But the thought of having traversed almost the entire length of the nation just to arrive by even a few minutes late appalled them. They travelled once again on the beach for it was now passable from here right almost to the very Cavern itself. They would be able to now avoid the main body of the Volcanic Mountains and most of the lava rivers which would have barred their path had they travelled normally on the land beyond the beach. The explorer Patrius Turbith had considered the options very carefully. But lava could still flow into the sea and thus block their path, costing them precious time. However, it was a chance they had to take. They would not make it in time otherwise. But the gamble paid off.

The sun was beginning to surrender its power to the night once more, when all yelled out in triumph. They halted and looked up over the steep cliff to the land above, and all gasped in speechless amazement. Situated approximately half a mile away from where they stood and towering several thousand feet high into the sky, the tip obscured by a mass of cloud, was their destination. They had finally reached it. Before them stood the largest, the highest, and the most volcanic mountain in the land, the mountain of the Cavern; Dragons' Mountain. It was aptly named for the enormous number of dragons reputed by legend to exist there. But only when the explorer Patrius Turbith returned did that myth become reality. Segal Goodwin could have travelled by one of his own fire-beasts here at any time, but without knowing the exact time of their mating cycle, the voyage would have been pointless, especially as he required confirmation of the legend. That is why he had commissioned the explorer to travel to the Cavern and determine exactly when and if the dragons actually rested at the huge mountain.

Here stood one of the last remaining magickal wonders of the land, and they had come here to destroy it. Men had killed and died in the vain pursuit of claiming this prize and their grim task was to make sure nobody would acquire it. They agreed to make their camp for the night at the base of the cliff before finding a path up to the Cavern come dawn for little light now remained for such a task. A full day remained before Segal Goodwin would arrive. They had plenty of time to consider their options once they arrived at the Cavern itself.

They awoke early, refreshed and ready to finish the last leg of their long journey. But as they prepared to march, the two guides returned from their long search and brought bad news.

"It's all sheer cliff. There's no broken path for horses to climb," Procel announced. "We'll have to leave them, and climb ourselves."

Amon nodded in agreement, but he wasn't pleased. He was eager to finish this journey and obtain his half-share of the dragons' treasure and so too, urged them all to climb. They decided to leave most of their belongings and the provisions in a small cave located at the base of the cliff away from the sea-line for they would now have to travel light, and with the utmost of haste. But as they finally prepared to climb in single file, the knight suddenly turned upon hearing a sharp noise to his right. He glanced over his shoulder to the nearby rocks, but could see no movement. He shrugged in apathy and began once again to unload his heavy backpack when he heard the noise again, only now sharper and closer. Jual reached for his broadsword, but a sudden whisper behind him warned otherwise. He slowly and hesitantly turned about to face a short filthy bearded man of un-guessable age, naked but for the small piece of animal-skin wound around his hips. This remarkable stranger was sitting upon a large rock adjacent to an outcrop of smaller ones. In his hands he displayed a crude, but nonetheless effective wooden crossbow which was currently pointed directly at the knight's unprotected face.

The man put a grubby finger to his lips, motioning for the soldier to maintain his silence. However, the remainder of the company had other ideas. Behind him, Jual heard the mage cry out in a language unknown to him, and smiled upon hearing a shrill scream of pain a few moments later. But then he felt despair as Sasha told the travellers to drop their weapons for they were completely surrounded. The others reluctantly complied and about forty of the mysterious silent strangers rapidly collected baggage and weapons, while others began tying up the company. As they were about to be led away, Sasha turned to glance up at the mountain of the Cavern looming far above her, as if in silent mockery and she cried out in frustration and anger. To have come so far, and now this. It was so close, I could almost touch it, she sighed. Even the guide Amon could not relate the path they travelled across until they finally arrived at a crowded clearing which was obviously their camp. They were made to kneel before the largest of their number who prostrated himself upon a makeshift throne of dried mud and straw. He stood at five feet displaying an enormous stomach and asked questions of the company that neither the guide nor the mage could decipher nor understand. But it soon became clear what their intentions were. They were all cannibals. The travellers were shoved into a cage made of bamboo for bars, but the prison did not leave much space to move. It was large in the sense of its height, that of at least ten feet, but its width was only five feet by three. There must have been at some time or other an enormous man in the cage for whom it was specifically built, but it was not constructed to house several confined individuals. All but the mage sank down to the barred ground in silent despair. He laughed aloud at the irony of it. To have come so far and to be so near to their target, only to end their lives here by being eaten by a bunch of savages. He laughed long and hard, but it was a bitter snigger for he had his own special desire to reach the Cavern. Day slowly trailed on until night eventually approached, and with it, came a new air of excitement amongst the savages. A massive metal cauldron was hastily erected over a blazing fire in front of the cage. Even the mage began to sweat in nervousness and decided in his panic that something had to be done. The tribe of savages now began to dance frantically around the prison and the giant pot, working themselves up into a frenzy of diabolical ravenous hunger. But one such native danced too close to the cage and the knight suddenly reached out and pulled him by the arm towards the prison, slamming his head off the bamboo. The cannibal was momentarily stunned, but not unconscious. He quickly awoke from his daze only to find the two intense eyes of the warlock gazing intently into his own, piercing his very soul. The sorcerer smiled when he saw the senses leave the native and fall into a trance. The other savages in their excitement had not noticed the predicament of one of their number. He was at the mercy of the wizard, and Barrius Fetherfew did not know the meaning of the word.

The mage then whispered orders to the native that none but he could hear. The dazed man then walked off, leaving both the warlock and the others pondering on whether he had performed the spell right. They might not get a second chance. But he smiled and the others sighed with relief as the cannibal grabbed a nearby knife and handed it to a second savage and gave him an order. This second native stared at the dazed brother cannibal in confusion, but then nodded. The second savage walked calmly to their captives and began cutting off the large ropes that binded the entrance bars of the cage. The sorcerer now began to sweat profusely, wondering if this native would free them before the hypnotised savage carried out his second instructed task. The dazed cannibal was now standing behind his Chief's throne with a short blade in hand. The man on the seat began to smile at the joke he was being told by the controlled savage over his shoulder. The knife came around and the cannibal chieftain was still smiling when the blade skilfully and quickly cut his throat wide open, killing him almost immediately. His tasks completed, the trance over the native abruptly vanished, and he was left staring fixedly down at his dead Chief in speechless fear and confusion. Just at that moment, the last of the bonds on the cage fell away and the company charged out. The dead Chieftain also fell to the ground at that moment and chaos in the camp reigned. The confused natives were easy victims to the travellers who had swiftly retrieved their weapons. They then left the remaining cannibals to their mourning as they ran into the wastelands. They kept fleeing until they eventually collapsed with exhaustion, their escape particularly hard on the knight because of his injuries.

All looked up to see the sun rising over the Volcanic Mountains, reminding them of their grim task. Far away in the distance, they could see the distant glow of the mountain of the Cavern; their destination. All slowly and painfully rose to their feet and kept running, only stopping to rest for a few brief moments. It was after noon when the company finally approached the entrance of their destination. Ahead was a wide long natural tunnel cloaked in darkness cut into the very rock of the largest mountain in the land. Before them was their long-awaited destiny, and perhaps, their death. All exhaled audibly in anxiety as they entered the dark cavern. As Jual lit two lanterns, Sasha glanced back at the outside world as they left it, wondering if she would ever see it again, and then suddenly, she saw it. A golden dragon reared on its hind legs just adjacent to the entrance. How could they have not seen it as they entered the cavern? Sasha almost cried out in surprise and fear, yet she frowned, for the beast seemed somehow familiar. But Procel grabbed hold of her arm before she could remember and the company ran on into the darkness, knowing fully that precious little time could be left. Already they might be too late.

CHAPTER TWELVE

An enormous golden shape passed swiftly over the largest city in the land. All who witnessed the spectacle in the sky recognised the massive beast, but none knew its grim purpose. It flew at an incredible speed, passing over the capital's crop-filled fields in a matter of seconds. Few could travel like this. It was a privilege only granted to sorcerers and, even then, only to a few of them. The dragon covered vast areas of land in mere minutes that might take travellers days on foot. Strapped to its back just beyond the neck was its rider, his dark cloak dancing in the air, the wind cutting into him like knives of ice.

This was the day prophesied by the mages in ages gone by. Here sat one of the key players in the coming event, and he was in the prime of his power. At no other time in his long life had he been this powerful. He was unmatchable; undefeatable at this moment. He had awaited this event the whole of his life, this was his time; his moment. The beast ferried its master over the vast area of land that took Sasha over three weeks to cross in a matter of a few hours and arrived at the town of Mullein in the early hours of the following morning. He had arrived at the settlement just as his daughter and the company had escaped from the natives and were already approaching the mountain of the Cavern.

The huge creature landed in the centre of the main street of the town. Many noticed its presence and cowered back in fear. Its rider dismounted and approached the massive Healing-House situated in the very centre of the town. The doors opened without touch before him, allowing him easy entry. A frightened male healer in between stutters gave him directions and he followed them from floor to floor and passed by bed upon bed of the sick and dying until he eventually approached the one he desired and sat on the edge of the bed. The dying man beneath the cloth slowly opened his weary eyes and gasped in both fear and joy.

But the man towering above him did not smile in welcome and that joy left the dying explorer. "I can't heal you." The man stated flatly.

To Patrius Turbith, the voice was seemingly without regret or remorse. "What...?" The sick man pouted faintly.

"I need all of my power. Even the little energy required to heal you might cost me dear."

"But you promised!" The explorer screamed, and almost burst into tears at the thought of death. "It was part of the deal."

"I'll cure you on my way back."

"But I might be dead by then! And what if you don't come back?" He retorted, now almost hysterical.

"I'm sorry," the mage answered bitterly. "It's all I can say, I'm truly sorry." He repeated and left the Healing House while the dying explorer cried out behind him in not only physical and mental pain, but most of all, in anger.

"Come back, Goodwin!" He screamed. "A curse on you and all your kin. Come back!"

The dragon left the town with its rider as quickly as it arrived and the settlement was soon left far in the distance. A large gold medallion banged against his chest and suddenly burned with an inner light, a faint heat as if in anticipation of the magickal battle to come. His mind was focused on the task ahead, as even now, not far away, loomed the mountain of the Cavern. He cried aloud in triumph just as the sun rose to its zenith in the sky, announcing mid-day. The dragon flew even faster now, its nostrils filling with the scent of its brethren and was becoming increasingly excited to land. But it was no way near as anxious as its master; the High-Lord and High-Mage Segal Goodwin.

"Yes!" The warlock cried. He was finally going to claim what was rightfully his.

*   *   *   *   *

The comforting rays of the mid-day sun quickly drew away from the company as they ventured deeper into the cavern and disappeared from view. It opened up into a wide area of rock with two more tunnels stretching off to the right and straight ahead. The passage straight ahead appeared to lead downwards, further into the ground. This particular tunnel was large and the darkness was occasionally broken by sudden flashes of red light. A strong smell of sulphur came from beyond the passage. The right was short and appeared to end in rock, but a dim piercing ray of light came through a small hole in the wall. However, as they began to fully examine their surroundings, they could only gasp in amazement as a lone figure began to stumble up from the tunnel straight ahead of them. The man was clad all in black and this stranger appeared not to notice that he had company, until he was almost face to face with them. He halted and gasped aloud in complete surprise and astonishment.

"Sasha!" He cried aloud, and started to move towards the company's speechless leader.

Barrius stepped forward upon recognising the stranger and smiled in silent triumph. He approached the man and held out his hand in welcome. "I'm Barrius Feth..." He began to pout, but his magickal superior ignored him and kept on walking past him until he stood two feet from Sasha.

"Father." She stated simply, without any sign of emotion.

"You've come to stop me," he said flatly, and she nodded. "You're too late."

All groaned in despair, but Sasha suddenly held up a hand, motioning for their silence. "Father, I want it to stop."

"It will, once Soren is dead."

"You'll destroy this land first in your fight. He won't die easily."

"He hasn't a chance now that I possess the dragons." Segal laughed.

"And what about all the people who will perish in the process?" She retorted. "What about me?"

"What about you?" He replied back sharply.

"You bastard!" She screamed. "All you care about is your precious magick!"

"How can you be so naive? My work is my life, it means everything to me."

"Everything is right!" She snarled. "Don't patronise me. My mother died trying to deter you away from your precious magick for just a few hours a day. But no, you wouldn't hear anything of it."

"That's a lie, I loved your mother. She understood me and my work."

"You had a strange way of showing your love. You even missed the funeral."

"I couldn't avoid that, something came up." Segal sighed.

"He's right about that, I'm afraid." A foreign voice from the cavern abruptly uttered and all gasped.

But two smiled in satisfaction: the mage Barrius Fetherfew, and Sasha's father. Before the group was one of the most powerful and surely one of the most evil of men in the land. Before them stood the object of Sasha's real hate and her father's.

"He's right," the sorcerer Soren repeated and smiled. "He had to evict me from the Society of Mages."

Barrius reached for his magick knife, ready to evoke the long-awaited and most powerful spell he knew. Already, he was beginning to mutter it under his breath, but Soren did not notice.

"Goodwin, I want you! Come to me, let us clash at last!" He cried out and flung back his heavy dark hood to reveal himself in the prime of his power.

"You are no match for me. You never were, and you certainly are not now. I command the dragons of the Cavern now." The High-Mage Segal Goodwin replied.

"Even they will not aid you now," Soren laughed. "I have a far greater force at my disposal."

Sasha's father burst into laughter himself, but he frowned in sudden uncertainty, though he quickly dismissed the foolish thought.

Even Barrius was now frowning in suspicion. However he then smiled. *If Soren has a foreign power, let him waste it on Goodwin. All the more chance for me to destroy him.*

Segal Goodwin began to slowly approach his arch-enemy and Sasha snatched onto the sleeve of his cloak in anxiety. But her father only smiled in reply, and her hand fell away. He continued walking until he came face to face with his rival but then hesitated in attacking. Soren suddenly grabbed his great enemy by the throat, attempting to strangle him. Goodwin did the same as Soren smiled.

"Now at last. Let the power...flow!" Soren shouted and to Goodwin's utter amazement, his arch rival began to glow with massive power, the like of which had never been seen.

Even Barrius gasped in awe and drew back from the spectacle. The High-Lord attempted a protection spell in panic, but in vain. He instead then called upon all of the power of his dragons at his command. However, it quickly became clear to all present that nothing could save him. The sorcerer Soren laughed aloud as his rival cried out in pain and before everybody's astonished eyes, the High-Lord suddenly and incredibly crumbled to dust under Soren's fingers. Goodwin's black robe fell to the ground, empty.

Sasha fainted and the knight caught her while the others stared fixedly at Soren, and what remained of Lord Goodwin. The now High-Mage Soren turned away from the remains of what was once his great enemy, as Barrius Fetherfew walked slowly and carefully over to the pile of ash that was Goodwin. He continued to stare fixedly in awe until something caught his eye. Something was shining from the pile of dust. As he bent down to pick it up, far away and unknown to the mage, the explorer Patrius Turbith suddenly cried out briefly in pain and despair, before falling back dead. The warlock rose to his feet and carefully studied the mysterious artefact. It appeared to be a gold medallion, and as he looked, he noticed writing. *We are two, but we are also one and the same.* What could it mean? He pondered on the possible meaning, and then gasped in realisation. He quickly pocketed it before turning to the Arch-Mage Soren.

"It is time to claim my revenge," he whispered and began to play with his magick knife between his fingers as he turned towards Soren. "That was quite a feat," the warlock uttered to everybody's amazement. "How did you do it?"

"Who the hell are you?" Soren snarled.

"I am a mage who desires revenge."

Soren laughed. "You? You dare to insult my intelligence? You don't deserve to wear the cloak of a mage, you're nothing but a petty fortune-teller!"

Barrius snarled back in rage, but Soren only laughed the harder. The warlock turned to the Arch-Mage who had turned his back to Barrius Fetherfew. Barrius outstretched both of his hands in preparation for the command that would unleash all of his energy. "Selah Samael!" He screamed and a huge blazing ball of fire flew from his hands to strike Soren on the back, sending him off his feet and crashing into the cavern wall.

Such a blow would have killed an ordinary man, even a sorcerer, but Soren had become too powerful. He was now the single and absolute master of all the dragons and the dark-arts.

However, he still felt pain. He slowly began to rise to his feet and Barrius gasped in amazement.

The warlock took out Goodwin's medallion and threw it to the knight. "Get out now! I'll try to stall him. Move!" He shouted which awoke Sasha from her daze.

"What's going on?" She muttered, but the four of them were already beginning to run for the tunnel to the right.

They halted and turned to see Soren finally stand to his feet and scream in rage. Yet Barrius Fetherfew did not flinch. He held his wand in one hand and his knife in the other. Soren instantly unleashed his massive power and visible electricity shot out from his outstretched hand and struck the mage. He cried out briefly in pain, before his body hit the ground. All stared fixedly in shock, before turning to run for the small opening of light. Jual reached it first and began to increase the small size of the hole by striking the rock with his large sword. They could see the sun above and all almost cried out in anxiety. The hole was soon big enough and Procel was the first and rapidly emerged out on the steep side of the mountain. But he could still stand upright and quickly turned to help the others escape. The knight handed out Sasha next and she managed to stand to her feet. Amon soon followed, but Soren had now turned his attention from the fallen warlock to the remaining company. He unleashed a fireball of his own just as Jual Dittany began to climb out and it struck him on the back. His armour was not sufficient to protect him from such a blow, and he stumbled as Sasha cried out in alarm. She reached back into the cavern to pull him up, but he waved her away. His face was wracked with pain, yet he managed to reach up and hand something to her. She glanced at the object and gasped upon recognising it. She quickly pocketed it and turned once again to save the knight. But Soren suddenly appeared above the soldier. The Arch-Mage sneered down at him while the knight spat back at him in return. The master of the dark arts picked up Jual's own sword and drove the blade into the knight's chest and the soldier died instantly. Sasha screamed in rage as Soren laughed. Procel jerked her back from the opening just as a second fireball exploded at the entrance to the Cavern from Soren's hand.

The three remaining members of the company fled blindly into the wastelands, leaving behind their hopes, dreams, and fallen friends. And even as they ran, they could still clearly hear the supreme Arch-Mage Soren cry out in triumph.

CHAPTER THIRTEEN

The three fleeing figures eventually stopped to rest at the River Storm, a small tributary of the much larger parent River Leif, and decided that they were a significantly safe enough distance from the now distant Cavern of the dragons.

The aching pain in Sasha's legs had now reached the point of being excruciating, and just after even a few more moments, she found she could not even move due to both exhaustion, and the numbness in her legs. "How...how far did we run?" Sasha asked with much effort, and obvious trepidation.

"I'm not exactly sure. Maybe as much as fifteen miles." Procel replied, and also collapsed next to her.

She shifted upon feeling something bulky in her hip-pocket and removed the gold medallion which had once belonged to her late father. The object symbolised the very last action of the knight before his untimely brutal demise. She stared at the inscription. She handed it to the guide. "What does it mean?"

"I don't know," Procel retorted as he examined it, "Barrius would have known. But I can tell you this: It must be something of great importance judging by the mage's reaction when he picked it up. I saw his face, it was full of amazement and it was his final act to give it to Jual before his death. It is the only thing that remains of your father."

The brutal killing of Segal Goodwin came flooding back to Sasha and she burst into tears.

Procel held her close as she cried out in frustration. "It's all my fault. I thought of only myself. I was the one who created the rift between us. It's all my fault!"

Procel placed a hand gently on each of her shoulders and stared into her eyes. "Don't say that," the guide declared. "It was a two-sided argument. He was as much to blame for that rift as you were."

Sasha nodded feebly in silent agreement before relaxing down to sleep. As Procel began to place a blanket over her, he heard her say faint words. "I wish Ace was here." She mouthed before sleep finally claimed her.

The following morning's coldness could not dampen their spirits any further for their will had reached its nadir. The dawn had only reawakened the hopelessness of their situation.

"What do we do now? Where do we go?" Amon cried out in despair, echoing the general feeling. "By all the gods, what am I doing here? My job is done, I led you to the Cavern!"

"Well, you've now become temporarily re-employed." Procel retorted flatly. "Besides, where are you going to go? Once Soren recovers from his spell-casting, he'll finish the job he started; to plunge this entire land into perpetual darkness."

"Well, what can I do about it?" Amon shouted back in frustration.

"You can stop that defeatist talk for a start!" Procel snarled. "The nearest settlement is the town Heale north east of here. Sasha and I are heading for there. You can come along, or you can rot here!"

"From Heale, we'll be able to find a way to return to the capital before Soren decides to raze it to the ground." Sasha added. "We can plan our attack from there."

"Attack?" Amon declared in disbelief. "That should be fun!" The guide stared at them fixedly in anger as they rose to their feet and began the long trek to the town Heale. "By all the gods, I hate this job!"

*　　*　　*　　*　　*

With every night comes darkness. But to the population of the town Samhai, the darkness this particular night seemed to have a greater edge than usual, an increase in the blackness from previous nights. Some rapidly put it down to superstition, but others looked towards the north-east into The Dark Regions, to the city Soren; a community where the most violent and foulest of people resided, a settlement dedicated to the God of Death and its greatest servant, the namesake of the city. The settlement itself was populated with nothing but the worst kind of cut-throats, bandits and mercenaries; men who would do anything for money. Ironic that numbered amongst them should be bounty-hunters living alongside their prey; men who, if paid enough, would willingly hunt their own kind to the very gates of hell itself. It was fitting that the people of this massive fortified city should serve death in its every guise and form, but the ruler of the city was surely the greatest bringer of sustenance to the God of Death and amongst his people, he stood out clearly as the most foul and blackest of them all. It was also a sense of karma that this man himself should be close to death because of the extent of his evil deeds. Progress comes only through pain and effort, and this the sorcerer Soren had found out, though with a cost. But although he was very ill, he knew he would recover and this pain was nothing when he contemplated on his rival's own agony at the moment of death, and the rank he now bore: Magus, the rank of a demi-god, master of all magick. It was purely a matter of time and a little effort, he mused, before he reached the supreme rank, that of a deity.

"But even then, I will not stop, not until I am the only remaining deity." Soren declared to himself. "I will overthrow the old God of Death and assume his status and claim his plane on which he reigns. But first, there is still much to do, and as soon as I recover, I will finish the job I started and pay back the people of the nation who cast me out and made me a pariah."

*   *   *   *   *

The town Fumitorie loomed before him, offering fresh hope, and possibly a new path leading away from his old troubles. The population looked upon strangers with no real concern of any kind, but danger nevertheless was prominent everywhere. Many of the residents would not hesitate to take life and suffer no shame at such an act. But such actions and attitudes were commonplace and were to be expected. Neither such thoughts nor the constant pangs of hunger seemed to be a worry for the stranger. His confusion and total exhaustion excluded all other considerations completely as he stumbled into the settlement. He passed through the enormous town-gates and on into the community. People passed by him, seemingly unaware of his very presence. He might as well have been invisible. These people had long forgotten the meaning of pity or compassion in a settlement perpetually overshadowed by violence.

"Where am I?" He repeated several times and abruptly sensed movement behind him.

"In hell, that's where. But you already knew that, didn't you?"

The man before Ace could not have been more than five feet tall and was grossly overweight for such a small height, but possessed fine expensive clothes and large rings on each of his chubby fingers. He was despite this quite handsome, being about fifty years old and must have been popular with the ladies in his younger years. He had to all intents an air of royalty about him though all nobles had been wiped out by the purge many decades ago; the vicious act carried out by Segal Goodwin's father when he assumed power and deposed the rightful king.

"Brother, you look out of place." The stranger declared.

"In this town, I wouldn't have believed so," Ace retorted. "They all appear to be in the same state as myself."

The fat man laughed. "But I sense you are different. You are out of place here."

"Who are you?" Ace asked, becoming annoyed at this nonsensical conversation.

"Demur Galingale," he announced. "And yourself?"

"Ace." he answered flatly.

"Just Ace?" The fat man inquired curiously.

The swordsman was now beginning to seriously lose his self-control at this ridiculous discussion in the middle of the main-street. "Look Demur, or whatever you call yourself, just what the hell do you want?" Ace shouted, and to his surprise, a smile appeared on the man's bulbous face.

"Very well then, I'll come straight to the point."

"I wish you would." Ace retorted angrily, with a forced audible sigh of relief.

"I want you to become my personal bodyguard."

"You what?"

"I want you as my personal soldier." He repeated, his idiotic smile seemingly transfixed permanently onto his round face.

"Why?" Ace retorted with a frown of puzzlement.

"I need a guardian because I'm a merchant, and I travel, and..."

"Don't patronise me!" Ace interjected angrily. "I said why meaning why me?" Ace glared at him. "There must be literally hundreds in this town who would kill for such a job."

"And probably kill me," he remarked. "But it is mostly because most of them wouldn't be as good as you."

"Oh, and how can you tell that?"

"Look around you," the fat-man replied. "Most of the men around you are mercenaries right enough, but they all have three or even four different weapons each."

This was true. Ace could see the general population around him displaying an assortment of swords, knives, and bows on just about every single man, and some women also. "So?" Ace retorted.

"The point is this; a very good fighter requires only one weapon, he needs not the additional burden or protection of other weapons. You for instance, have just your sword."

"How do you know that I just haven't lost my other weapons?" Ace asked with a sly grin.

"I know swords, it's part of my merchandise. That particular blade of yours is from the capital where they specialise in making bespoke swords for mercenaries and nobles. You are not a noble?"

"No, I am not. But neither am I exactly a mercenary. Besides, I could have stolen the blade."

"The type of metal in question on that particular sword hasn't been used for almost two centuries. Only fighters of a very special quality could have obtained such a blade. Otherwise, the blade would have been inherited, and then only passed on to a son with exceptionally good swordsmanship. The owner of the sword would surely have killed you before handing over such a weapon."

"Maybe I had help." Ace interjected.

"The help you needed would had to been of a very high quality indeed, and they surely would have killed you for the blade afterwards."

Ace smiled broadly. "You're very clever."

"I thank you for the compliment. But all the same, in time I will see how good you really are."

"I haven't accepted the job yet." Ace remarked.

"By the expression on your face, you just have." The fat merchant laughed.

Demur Galingale led Ace through the crowded streets to a large house situated on the outer frontiers of the town.

"You said I would be your personal bodyguard, how many others do you have?"

"Just two others." The merchant replied.

"And they are so bad that you chose me over them?"

The fat merchant laughed aloud. "No, they're good, very good! But I have a feeling you will be much better."

"How can you tell that?"

"Experience," he replied simply as they finally approached the enormous house.

"You do very well for yourself." Ace remarked and remembered the mercenary leader Elisa's words about merchants and how they attained their riches; by fair means or foul. They would as soon take the food from the mouths of hungry children as quickly as they would publicly give them.

"I do all right. My job has its advantages."

"So I see." Ace remarked quietly to himself.

"What was that?" The merchant asked.

"Oh, nothing," Ace retorted flatly. "Nothing at all."

Ace followed into the massive mansion directly behind the merchant and as the enormous door of the house began to slowly close behind him, it was as if he could feel the closing of another door, locking away the whole of his previous life before this moment, signifying another chapter that had ended. However, he wondered just what the next chapter in his life would bring. Would it bring further grief and pain, or an end to those things? But Ace felt these doors were closing to reveal solitude instead and decided with a sigh, then if that was to be the case, then he would make the most of it; even welcome it. The door closed.

*   *   *   *   *

The morning sun bestowed no pleasure of scenery or heat onto Sasha and her two remaining companions as they finally approached the gates of the town Heale, the furthest, most western point from home.

Sasha put a hand into her pocket and revealed just enough money for several days' worth of provisions and three fresh horses. As they entered the town, they noticed that the population appeared to be in some strange state of agitation and distress. People of every description hurried past them from every direction, seemingly heading for the town-centre. Some occasionally glanced skywards and with a great gasp of surprise and shock, the companions saw the reason for the distress. Heading towards them at a fantastic speed from the northeast was perhaps the largest dragon Sasha had ever seen. This creature far dwarfed any of her father's beasts and she quickly realised the fire-demon's original home and the name of its new master. She sighed in exhaustion at such a sight and briefly wondered if the beast was about to raze the town to the ground. But no, the creature's hooked claws reached out instead to land in the middle of the town adjacent to the Alderman's house. It swerved at the last moment, missing the fountain in the centre of the square by inches to land on the smooth stone. The huge beast glanced around through slit cat-like eyes at the defenceless people who slowly and hesitantly began to gather around it. They realised that if the massive beast had intended to kill them, it would have done so before landing. The creature sneered at the vulnerable mortals for several moments, before speaking in a gruff raspy voice that echoed over the entire town. It was not necessary to crowd around the beast to hear its foul message.

"Hear me! I bring a message from my master, your new and omnipotent ruler. For a tribute to show your love and unquestionable loyalty to his almighty, each and every one of you must give half of your annual crop and a quarter of your livestock. All praise be to the Magus Soren, High-Lord!"

The creature then hesitated as if expecting to hear their reply to praise their new ruler, but they were speechless instead in shock and amazement. The beast took the silence as gratitude for sparing their pitiful lives. Though it might as well have taken them for such a tribute would result in many a death, especially for the smaller farmers who would be forced to sell out, or starve. But this would not be a concern for the new tyrannical ruler. He certainly was not going to lose any sleep over it. Sasha sneered at the departing dragon in utter disgust and rage while the two guides could only stare in likewise astonishment at such a request. Complete revolution was surely imminent. But how could they battle against such a force as only Soren could muster? Their situation was hopeless, and yet leaderless, thousands would die, before they would even consider accepting such a tribute.

Sasha's eyes fell to the ground in self-pity, realising her failure and her complete helplessness. What can I do? These people need a commander to lead them into battle...but my father is dead...and then she lost her breath in sudden shock and realisation. Am I that leader? But she was too afraid of the huge responsibility and shrugged away the thought. I came out here to end a war, will I be the one to start another? She glanced over the rooftops eastwards towards her distant former home and remembered the memories of the old days. But her confusion made it difficult for her to focus on them and they were quickly replaced with the bitter reality and the realisation that the past was gone forever, and would never return. She momentarily thought it ironic that she should even attempt to remember those days, back when she perpetually hungered for release, for her desired freedom and independence, and now that she actually had it, she would gladly forsake it to return to the old life. She perhaps believed this because those old days of her father's patronising and emotional neglect of his daughter were somehow better; more bearable or even preferable than what lay before her now. For the future that lay before her now was less certain, and she feared it; feared it like nothing she had ever feared before in her entire life. She had not chosen this future, but she would see it through to the end, whatever end that might be. She also sighed in despair when she considered that unlike her childhood past, her best friend and constant companion was amiss, and perhaps even dead; a friend that with only a gentle persuasion, could very well have become her lover. Her gaze remained fallen in bitterness and regret, and the world moved forward, shifting the present into the future, but leaving her trapped in the past.

CHAPTER FOURTEEN

The scene outside the window of the small house portrayed the same familiar sight. If there wasn't a fight taking place in almost every part of the city the whole time, the familiar scene of utter depression and poverty was evident the remainder of the time. This day was no different. This abject stare was present on the occasional passer-by on the filthy street portraying a face that lacked any expression of emotion, in particular any certain sense of joy which was not to be found anywhere under any guise in this massive settlement; the great city of Soren. One might ponder on the reason why people would actually attempt to live in such a foul city, but the populace more festered like an infectious disease than lived, for dirt always had a habit of clinging to other dirt.

Yet all this did not bother the man behind the window. He actually enjoyed the view, managed to find some perverse pleasure in the scene of despair before him. The solitary man glanced at the sundial in the centre of the street. It was almost noon and the scheduled fight, if correctly on time, would begin directly before him. He reached down and opened a small flask and began to drink. He then relaxed and settled back on the high-stool and waited patiently for the show to begin. He did not have to wait long. The crowds gathered rapidly from every possible entrance and entered the centre of the street, just outside the window. They quickly formed into two main parties and approached each other from opposite ends of the broad passage.

There really was no definite explanation or original cause for these skirmishes, it simply just began.

A single man on the left of the assembly was the first to light the flame of the fight by attempting to strike down his opponent on the right party with his sword. The man on the right in reply promptly ducked the fatal blow, and swiftly followed this up with a strike to his opponent's head with the metre long axe-handle he carried. This particular issue ended with the first man having his head split open like a ripe melon from the savage blow. He then quickly fell from the fray; his part in this fight had ended. The battle then got into full swing with men falling at either side. The mystery man behind the window appeared to have become bored with the feud and opened the door of the small house to leave. One of the fighters saw the newcomer and left the battle with great haste in fear. His opponent just missed him by mere inches with his short-axe before also quickly fleeing the scene. The reason for their terror was clear and apparently obvious. The mysterious man of the window was none other than Ortolan. Nobody knew his first name and nobody dared to ask. His surname was enough to mark his reputation. He was the single finest swordsman in all the land. Some drunken soothsayers would even venture to say that he was born with a sword in his hand and could use it efficiently before he could even speak.

The fight was rapidly beginning to break-up at his approach, such was the fear of him, but one man left the main part of the fray upon seeing the swordsman, and advanced towards him. It was clear that the attacker thought Ortolan was involved in the fight and did not recognise him. If Ortolan saw the man, he had decided to ignore him.

The individual attacked Ortolan from behind and was almost upon the swordsman before Ortolan reacted. He side-stepped out of the way of the fighter's sword which crashed onto the ground instead of Ortolan's unprotected skull. The man did not even get enough time to register what happened next. Ortolan's blade slid out from its scabbard with devastating speed and cut the man's throat with a single stroke and had returned to the scabbard, all in one motion, and all in one instant. Ortolan had already stepped past the man before he dropped lifelessly to the ground.

People who knew the deeds of Ortolan, knew well of his long and infamous history. He was a mercenary like his father, and his father before him. But he was more assassin than mercenary. The fine blade strapped to his waist bore the emblem and signet of his ancient ancestors and was rumoured to be worth a fortune. Some would say that the weapon was so finely made, it could literally fell a tree with a single stroke.

The enormous city was similar to a labyrinth of sorts, with its many winding back-streets following no definite set logical pattern, many ending in dead-ends. But a mercenary like many others of the population of this foul city, learned quickly of the city's such secrets if the need to abruptly flee arose. The swordsman's knowledge did not fail him and he soon found himself at the centre of the settlement.

Many of the faint-hearted would have fled at the scene before the mercenary. The sight was like to that of a glimpse into hell itself, enough to drive the foolish insane. Massive gates of black iron barred entrance to an enormous structure known as the Castle of Soren. Adjoining the gates were twelve-foot high walls that surrounded the building. The foundations of the castle gave birth to almost unbelievable high towers that appeared to have no end as they stretched far into the clouds. Numbered amongst these was the tallest of all seven, the one in the centre. Its height could not be determined by the eye for this particular tower stretched so far into the sky, the human eye could not follow. The castle and the outer walls were of the same colour as the gates: pure black, dark and mysterious as the night and which actually seemed to reek of the aura of malevolence; of untainted evil in its purest form. One might think a man such as Ortolan would feel perfectly at home in the vicinity of such a building, but he was distrustful of sorcery and the aura of evil from the structure was so overpowering, that even he shrank away from it in momentary uneasiness. But he sneered and snarled at his own disgust and fear of the building and suddenly reached out to touch the cold metal of the gigantic gates.

However, to his surprise the gates opened without his touch. He instantly snatched back his hand and glanced in all directions, before with some trepidation, he entered into the courtyard beyond the gates. The large barriers clanged shut loudly behind him and he turned around, startled. He faced the castle again and to his further surprise, twenty metres across the courtyard, the double doors leading to the main building began to slowly open, their creaking clearly audible. But all apprehension had left his body, and without hesitation, he entered the massive structure. With no surprise, the double-doors banged loudly shut behind him. The corridor or hall he was in led far off into the distance ending in a small single door. Likewise, a dozen other such doors were beside him at either side stretching off down the hallway. Not one of these possible entrances opened at his approach, so Ortolan took it upon himself to open every door that took a fancy to him. All revealed darkness as the mercenary made his way down the corridor. The swordsman would normally have been annoyed at such inconvenience, but curiosity was on the forefront of his mind. However, one offered light at the other side. He unfalteringly chose this incandescent portal and instantly heard a response to this action.

"Come in, Ortolan. I've been expecting you."

"You know me?" The mercenary enquired.

The swordsman could not see the owner of the voice since the light was blinding in contrast to the darkness in the corridor behind him before he had entered this strange room. But Ortolan knew one thing; he knew he was hearing the great Magus Soren because of the soft, almost musical tone of the voice which was so characteristic of mages.

"I know of your reputation." The hidden voice retorted.

Ortolan received the compliment with no obvious sign of pleasure or gratitude, but replied quickly to the statement. "Then know you this: do not waste my time, speak to me of money and I possibly will reward you with my services."

Soren did not show any resentment or anger at such impertinence, for he knew well indeed of the mercenary's long history and that his assassinations included many mages, which was testament to his great skill and nerve. On the contrary, he approved of the answer with much relish for it displayed much of the swordsman's brazen courage, but also his great greed, and here the two men had common traits. "I speak of great money indeed."

"How much?" The assassin retorted sharply.

The warlock stared at the young man in admiration. The swordsman before him was nearly thirty years old, but gave the appearance of someone much younger. He was slender and relatively handsome having strawberry blonde hair and a short moustache. However, what was most appealing was his piercing blue eyes, which even now gazed intently at the black robed man across from him. "I offer employment on a steady basis."

"I'm not one to settle down." Ortolan snapped.

"I'm not asking you to. Besides, I believe it is employment you will develop a fetish for."

"A fetish? You speak to me as if I was a sort of pervert?" Ortolan snarled, his eyes finally beginning to adjust, and he began to intently observe the large shadow striding briskly from one end of the room to the other, back and forth without cessation.

"You are one who unscrupulously eradicates the object of one man's hatred with death to fulfil your own greed." Soren retorted.

The shadow halted and Ortolan suddenly flung himself across the room and grasped the Magus by the throat. "I could snap your neck like a dry twig and no magickal power in your possession could falter this event." Ortolan sneered as he finally glared face to face with the warlock.

"I do not doubt it," Soren replied calmly. "But then you would forfeit the greatest opportunity of your career."

"Speak, and quickly, for I now rapidly tire of your odious words from this morning when you sent notice requiring a mercenary." Ortolan breathed into the mage's face in reply.

"I offer you leadership; the ruler-ship over Tamerindes; this city's neighbouring town."

Ortolan gazed fixedly at the wizard in speechless astonishment, before bursting into laughter. He released the warlock from his hold. "Oh, I might be a dealer in death, but you offer me the kingship of the dead!"

"It is no joke." Soren stated flatly.

"You cannot be serious. No man can be a ruler of that settlement, that town is a refuge for the failures of your dark magick at attempting to create life. Any commander would be torn to pieces as would any man who dared to venture into that foul community."

"I will give you protection." Soren protested, realising his insult to the assassin had backfired.

"There is none from those minions of hell."

"But they are after all my minions." Soren stated simply which halted the laughter.

"Then maybe you should offer me protection from you." Ortolan replied sharply.

It was now the mage's turn to laugh at the mercenary's audacity. "I like you, I really do like you."

"Be careful, those people who get too close to me, usually wind up dead as a result."

"I will take that chance," the Magus retorted. "Then you will accept the post?"

The assassin appeared to hesitate, but then smiled. "So be it," he said and then added. "When do I start, boss?"

"Immediately," the warlock answered. He then proceeded to pull the large golden signet ring from his left middle finger and bestowed the supposed gift to the mercenary who gazed down at it in apparent mystery and confusion. "Your protection," Soren declared. "Wear it and no creature of my making will harm you. On the contrary, they will serve you."

Ortolan did not question the act further, but placed the ring onto his ring finger and not the middle finger of his left hand since Soren's hands were so thin and slender from spell-casting.

"I have a single tower at your complete disposal in the centre of the town from which you can see over the entire population, and in which you will be completely safe from any danger."

"How do you know I won't get lonely?" The mercenary laughed.

"I don't think you will or ever had that problem. I would offer my familiar as a companion, except I killed it for failing me." Soren replied with a sneer, referring to the eagle which had tried to kill the mage Barrius Fetherfew, but met death instead at the hands of Sasha Goodwin.

But it was obvious to Ortolan that the Magus meant something else. "Just how long do you intend for me to watch over them?"

"Oh, I have a feeling that you won't have to wait for too long. I have plans for those creatures of mine."

The new ruler of Tamerindes began to head for the door, but turned around to face the sorcerer once again. "I won't fail you." He added without any sign of impertinence or sarcasm.

Then he left, leaving the Magus to stare at the closed door after him. "You'd better not."

CHAPTER FIFTEEN

Once again, new faces revealed no secrets or indications of their true meaning, but Ace was just grateful for the fact that neither of the two mercenaries were female. One was surely the largest coloured man Ace had ever set eyes on. His muscles bulged, the sinews of his arms quite noticeable. He would be completely naked but for the tight trousers and sandals he wore, displaying an enormous torso. But it was the massive broadsword he brandished that especially caught his attention for the blade must measure at least a metre and a half in length and its sharpness at a single glance, could not be doubted. The huge man was not only clean-shaven, but also completely bald. He was more a heavily tanned colour than actually black of skin, unlike some coloured individuals Ace had seen long ago back in the great city of Colewort. The swordsman let his gaze now fall on the second mercenary who was quite small in contrast to his companion who towered over him. This man in question did not appear to even have one tenth of the strength of his companion, and bore no sword. What he possessed to compromise this loss was a magnificent set of throwing knives, a dozen Ace quickly counted. The individual was in his early thirties Ace guessed, similar to the larger man, but displayed a crop of auburn wavy hair with a beard to match. Ace noticed his hands which displayed extremely slender fingers; a trait of knife throwers. Fingers which were graceful, but also very fragile.

What they did not readily bestow however was their names, it was up to the plump merchant to supply them to Ace. "The knife thrower is Genot Kassler, he's deadly with those small blades of his," the merchant stated and the small man nodded to Ace. "Our giant dark friend here is Karl."

"Just Karl?"

"I've never dared to ask of his family," the trader laughed, and added, "like you."

Ace smiled lightly and shook hands with the massive swordsman who almost crushed Ace's fingers with his grip.

"This is Ace, your new colleague; a swordsman of great repute." The merchant declared.

Both mercenaries appeared not to show any indication of interest whatsoever, but again acknowledged his existence with a simple nod. Ace believed this was the closest he was going to get to friendship for the present time, and he would have to be satisfied with it. The merchant then left the room. The smaller of the two mercenaries also then left the chamber as if to express his boredom while Karl began to seemingly attempt to stare down Ace. Ace retaliated by following suit until the giant swordsman suddenly burst into laughter and from behind his back he removed an equally massive sheath into which he shoved the broadsword. He then reached over to Ace and clapped him heavily on the back, almost sending him flying across the room.

However, Ace managed to retain his balance and the dark warrior placed a friendly, though large hand on his shoulder. "Now then, enough of that foolishness. Let's get some drink!" He boomed as Ace glanced up to his face and smiled.

"That surely must be the best idea I've heard for a long time."

The two men then left the chamber, their friendship established. The smaller mercenary would be more cautious to advance his valued companionship to Ace, but Ace cared not on this matter for once again, he had a place of safety to turn to, and for a brief moment, he could not care whether he ever saw Sasha again.

*   *   *   *   *

All around the travellers were dying shrubs and withered trees as if somehow heralding the arrival of some disaster. This uncomfortable thought caused the companions to travel faster and so they quickly left the vicinity of The Great Forest. The travellers did not hesitate to admire the forest, for their final destination was distant, and the desire to reach that place insistent. Their next temporary cessation was the town Rue, which was situated on the outskirts of the River Nandu, a shallow brook. Nevertheless, it was an obstacle, if only a minor one. The journey to that destination was a span of approximately twenty miles and at their present velocity, they expected to arrive there within just a few hours. Sasha greeted this knowledge with much relief for the sooner she reached her native city the better. She felt an inexplicable apprehension that her old home was somehow approaching the end of its life for she remembered the threats of the foul reptilian servant of Soren. She knew he fully meant to carry them out. This was the prime reason for their urgency, but there was also something else; something that was pulling at her; urging her to return, and she did not know what it was. It was simply a feeling; a sensation in the pit of her stomach that pushed her mercilessly onto that destination. This frightened her a great deal, perhaps more than she herself really acknowledged, for she disguised that dread from the others and kept it deep down within herself. However, that anxiety would have to manifest itself eventually. But for the present moment, she kept it well hidden. Minutes slowly dragged on into hours and the company found themselves before the River Nandu. They slowed their pace considerably before entering the shallow, but warm waters. They rapidly arrived at the opposite bank, wasting little time.

A short stride over a small hill found the wayfarers at the gates of the town Rue. Halting here the company considered would be a pointless expenditure of time and so quickly bypassed the small settlement, and almost immediately crossed the River Mamba with no problems. They decided to completely avoid the River Swallow and its many tributaries and continued in a north-east direction.

The next town was as much as thirty miles away and would take the remainder of the day to traverse, though the ground was more adaptable for travel now, or the journey would take far longer. Nevertheless, the voyage would be long enough and full of tension, for all knew that reaching the capital in time was imperative, and that it might already be too late.

*   *   *   *   *

As was promised, Ortolan was at his new post within one day. It was an employment that was surprisingly to his liking, much more than even he himself had previously anticipated. The town appeared vacant by day and as busy and crowded as if it were the festival season come nightfall. All this he could witness from one of the four windows facing each of the gates of Tamerindes, giving him both an adequate and safe overview of the entire town from the single tower situated in the very centre of the settlement. The only accessible entrance into the structure was a single porthole in the turret of the tower and a retractable ladder scaling one entire side of the building. Security and protection was all important. Even Ortolan himself wondered at just how easily and comfortably he fitted into this new employment for it was quite stagnant of action compared to the usually active job of a mercenary, skipping from one task to another, each almost always ending in death. But the pay was always meagre, and he wanted more from life than the simple bloodletting of one person for the petty hatred of another. This new employment however offered leadership, something he had never experienced before and provoked in him a perverse excitement he had not felt in his earlier vocation.

Laughter of an equally perverse kind suddenly rose from his throat at the sight of the approaching ambling foul creatures which began to roam and wander the streets below as night fell. The ugliness of their horribly mutated bodies was so pitiful it was almost beautiful to the mercenary, and he sniggered harder. Most of the people in the land who knew of Ortolan's reputation ranked him as one of the most evil men alive; completely ruthless in his dealings and possessing no trace or taint of emotion in his vile personality. Some with superstitious beliefs would remark that his very blood must be black and icy cold because of the foul black heart that pumped it. Many was the time he had massacred whole families in order to hide his existence in such a brutal slaying of one individual in the family. This could be considered ironical, since his mark was well known in such a matter. Nevertheless, he did it all the same, having a strange fetish for over-extravagant use of his sword as if he required practice. Such was the life of an extremely brutal and ruthless individual.

This was probably the first and only place he could actually call home, though it had no family to furnish it, nor would any grace its chambers with their presence, ever. The murderer felt no bitterness or regret in this reality and did not dream of any such possible future. Women and especially children were a burden in his opinion; a pleasure at certain moments, an annoyance at most. He glanced once more out of one of the windows to the town below which was now descending into darkness and the vile minions of the night were coming into view, crawling out of the gutters and slums. The sun had now completely disappeared over the horizon, leaving a settlement dedicated to death and its ruler; a single man smiling in satisfaction at his new position and status, but most of all, at the pleasurable prospect of bringing further misery to the land with Soren and he at its head.

"I think I'm really going to like this job."

*   *   *   *   *

Not since the incident with the mercenary leader Elisa did Ace consume so much alcohol. However, he could still not match the huge dark-skinned mercenary Karl for the liquid. The large warrior drank as if he had been born with a whisky flask in his mouth.

"Nev...never have...I seen any man drink like you." Ace stammered, oblivious to the fact that he could now not even stand.

"I have a great tolerance for alcohol." His friend boomed in reply, quite sober.

"So...so I've noticed." Ace slurred.

"Come on, drink up. You've only had eight pints. I'm on my twelfth!" Karl laughed and clapped Ace on the back, almost violently jettisoning the drink he had already consumed, not to mention his last meal from his body.

However Ace coughed heavily instead and smiled, before suddenly falling to the floor, unconscious.

"Barman, a bottle to take!" Karl ordered as he grabbed Ace by his other hand, threw him over his shoulder and walked soberly out of the tavern.

The icy air pierced him and he realised just how much alcohol he had really consumed. But he just shrugged off the cold and slowly moved on towards the direction of the mansion of the merchant.

Upon arriving inside, he deposited Ace onto a bed before sitting down upon another adjacent to Ace's and broke the seal on the bottle. The sudden crack of the seal did not wake the smaller swordsman and the flask soon touched the lips of the dark mercenary.

But instead of stirring, Ace began to twist and turn in his drunken slumber and mumble something inaudible. Karl's eyebrows pricked up in interest as Ace's mutterings increased and began to take form.

"Sasha, why did I do it? Why?"

The mumblings then turned back into silent breath, leaving the large mercenary in not only puzzlement, but also in great curiosity. He began to consider this information as the drink took effect. Eventually his head began to slowly hit the pillow and he quickly fell asleep. But his final thought before he was drawn into a drunken dreamless slumber was the urge that he would have to find out the nature of that name in Ace's mumblings, and also why it seemed so strangely familiar.

*   *   *   *   *

The foreboding darkness of the night seemed to gain in strength as the small company approached the town Ruas. It marked the second last planned cessation before Sasha's home city. This settlement would present few dangers if any, but the three travellers were cautious all the same upon entering such a town situated in the very centre of the land. The horses had become weary and required rest, so halting here was unfortunately inescapable. The heavy gold medallion banged against Sasha's chest as if to perpetually remind her of what lay before her, but she needed no reminder. She could not forget what events had passed, and what was still to come. She felt like a caged creature being goaded mercilessly onto one inevitable future, with no available choices of other possible paths, but that which led to the human slaughterhouse of war.

Like so many other towns in the land, this one treated the company's arrival with no great concern or interest. They headed immediately for the nearest tavern which had adjoining stables and after catering for the beasts, headed inside the inn. The scene inside the tavern was all too familiar - dusty, generally ill-kept being unhygienic with noticeable traces of dirt and grime, and of course it was practically empty. There was however a thin unshaven filth-covered servant, and two other likewise lone men sitting in the far right-hand corner of the small room adjacent to the stairs leading to the guest-rooms located on the second floor. The sleazy servant showed little, if any interest in the arrival of the travellers. He instead appeared to be entirely fascinated with a giant cockroach present on the reception table and poked at it with every available opportunity to prevent its escape from the arena. However, their entrance did prove an interest for one of the two middle-aged men in the corner, or rather Sasha's entrance. Sasha was not aware of this interest and its possible meaning. The now vaguely concerned servant snatched up the few gold coins strewn on the desk by Sasha. The resulting meals held no comfort for the company other than to fill their aching empty stomachs. They quickly retired after their essential, but non-conversational meal.

The night's sleep was not easy to arrive for Sasha for a persistent train of thought. She concentrated on attempting to sleep once more, but in vain. Slumber was an impossibility. But she then heard the click of the door, though could not see anything in the absolute darkness of the room. Perhaps I was mistaken, she contemplated, and settled down to rest once again. But the all too familiar fear returned as her suspicions were confirmed as a dim shadow passed near her. It suggested someone of heavy bulk, and yet quite quick.

"Procel?"

The darkness' reply was the sudden approach of a bulky person, much more different than the guide. Sasha instinctively reached for her slender dagger. However as she brought the short blade into view, it was knocked from her hand to land on the wooden floor. She raised a fist then instead to the foreign attacker. But her hand was seized strongly at the wrist.

"Who are you? What do you want?"

But no reply was forthcoming. The mystery assailant's hand then reached down and grasped the small bag containing the few remaining coins that she possessed. Greed however had made the attacker careless. Sasha placed one foot between his legs and swept his left foot out from under him, causing him to stumble. Sasha rolled off the bed and onto the floor and reached for her dagger. A moment later, it was at his throat.

"Nice move, my beauty." He whispered.

"Who are you?"

"From downstairs," was the reply. "I guessed rightly when I believed you had all the money. I didn't reckon that you would be so difficult to steal from though."

Both suddenly turned to the door as light flooded the room. The two guides stood at the door, swords drawn before them.

"Leave him be." Sasha said as they approached.

"Then you'd better gather your things. We can't stay now."

The thief turned to her as she rose to her feet. "Be careful, my beauty. You might regret your decision of letting me live someday."

"I don't think so." She sneered before leaving the room.

Dawn revealed the bleak landscape before the weary travellers. But they rode quickly away from Ruas and headed for its nearest neighbour, Peon. Another fateful step had been taken in their long journey which was approaching its end. They had almost come full circle. The time to finally face Soren was fast approaching.

CHAPTER SIXTEEN

Ace let out a loud heavy sigh and smiled in remembrance of the preceding night as he gazed at his large dark companion in the neighbouring bed. Even asleep, the huge man's great bulk had not diminished in impressiveness. But he was not so quick to awaken with the sun's burning light. The massive coloured individual had obviously consumed far more of the liquor then himself. He was dead to the world as a result. Ace contemplated on whether the fat merchant would be awake even at this hour of the late morning. The obese trader was not a man who gave the impression that he rose early. Ace believed that he presumed rightly for the entire house was seemingly devoid of sound of any such kind to hint otherwise. The trader would surely create noise as he moved around his giant mansion.

Suddenly he remembered the other mercenary. He would make little noise and commotion. Ace pondered on this small, yet deadly individual. An odd character; a loner with no apparent sense of values, morals or need for friendship. He seemed to possess nothing other than the same clothes he constantly wore and the impressive set of knives strapped around his thin waist. But Ace sensed there was more to this person than met the eye. Someone to watch very carefully. As if sensitive to this train of thought, the man in question; Genot Kassler threw the door open. He poked his head with a sneer into the bedroom.

"Well, well, well. Ain't this a pretty picture!" He shouted. "The master requests that you shift your ass. We don't serve breakfast in bed here! And by all the gods, wake up sleeping beauty!"

Ace sighed and glanced over at the dark-skinned man who was still dwelling in a drunken slumber. "Maybe you'd better do that yourself."

"Sore head, eh?" The small mercenary laughed.

"I would say one of the worst." Ace interjected and began to force himself to rise. But in vain, as he collapsed back once again onto the bed.

"Well, that's just terrible!" Genot boomed.

The roar had the desired effect as a subtle groan arose from opposite Ace and a pair of bloodshot eyes painfully opened. "What ungodly hour is this that you wake me?"

"An hour which you should already be awake and up at!" The short mercenary still continued to shout, much to his larger companion's annoyance.

"It will be also the hour of your untimely death, if you don't lose yourself this minute!" He screamed in reply, but Genot only shrugged and left slowly as if to provoke further the anger of the man. The dark warrior turned to Ace. "One of these days. Just one of these days!"

Ace smiled in reply. He then began to dress himself as Karl slowly and painfully removed himself from between the all too comfortable bed covers. His coloured feet hesitantly touched the cold wooden floor beneath and he let out a further groan, much to Ace's amusement. But Ace left him to his dilemma and closed the door behind him. He then walked down the corridor and entered the great dining hall. The obese merchant and Genot were already present. A meal had been placed in front of two unoccupied chairs adjacent the small mercenary while the trader sat at the head of a massive long table. Ace sat to the merchant's right in between he and Genot. As Ace ate, he observed the enormous infrastructure of the chamber. The dining room could have comfortably held giants. It was grossly over-sized for such a small company that was present. The ceiling stood easily thirty feet away with the length of the room twice the height of floor to ceiling. Width was approximately the same as height. The huge rectangular-shaped dining-table itself could seat at least sixty people placed as it was in the very centre of the enormous chamber. It had been waxed and polished, seemingly with a passion until shining.

The trader began to speak as Karl appeared and sat down. Once seated, all of his company present, the merchant changed the topic of conversation from short pleasantries to more serious matters. "In just two hours we leave for the city Ketherin. Certain colleagues of mine tell me that there is talk of war following the rumour of the sudden death of Segal Goodwin and the rise to power of Soren. War is good for business. I have a delivery of arms for that city, so we must leave this very day."

With this, the trader rose to his feet and left the room. Genot soon followed after him, leaving Ace alone with his large companion and giving him time to ponder on these new developments. There is talk of war, the merchant had said. Now why did that make him think of Sasha? A war against Soren. That meant there was a good chance that Sasha was behind it, or soon would be. As the daughter of the late High-Lord Goodwin, she might be able to rally the people behind her. For Ace, the old fear had returned; fear for Sasha's safety. Ketherin was a near neighbour of the city Soren. Thus Sasha might very well end up in Ketherin before proceeding onto Soren City. By all the gods, Ace hoped she did. It would give him a chance to see her and even perhaps stop her. The woman was all too anxious to become a sacrifice. Ace just hoped he would reach her in time.

*   *   *   *   *

It was the horses nearing exhaustion and not a member of the small company that forced their sudden cessation. The town Ruas seemed so distant that Sasha felt that she could finally relax. But she knew as always that her mind must forget the minor incident and concentrate on what lay ahead; the town Peon. The River Voce and the River Myall ran near to the settlement and would have to be crossed soon afterwards. Not far from there stood the capital, her home city. It was as if she could almost sense the great agent of death and destruction; the Magus Soren close by. His foul presence seemed so strong and consistent that it seemed to pervade and poison the very air around them. Her home city she knew with dire certainty would be a prime target for obliteration by Soren. It was imperative she reach it before him.

Such haste she felt was necessary for she felt something, she did not know exactly what, was missing. A piece in the puzzle concerning her late father's medallion and its obscure inscription which she now wore. She could not explain how, but she somehow felt that it was the key to the Magus' power and his possible downfall. She felt that the secret to this wordless feeling was to be found in the capital, somewhere. It was their last hope, no matter how ridiculous it appeared. She knew no other path to take.

Afternoon passed into evening and as darkness approached, there was still no sign of the town. However, in the distance, across the plains, was the dark line marking the River Orack. Its snake-like presence gave relief to the weary travellers, for they could go no further. Exhaustion had gripped them like a fever and they were forced to rest.

A light breeze blew gently across these sparsely covered grass-plains. The land here was utterly flat and barren for miles in every direction. If an intruder happened to approach, he would be easily noticed. These extensive grasslands Procel however observed were not natural, but man-made. This land before them had been annually tillaged. There were however no labourers' houses to be seen. But the land was obviously owned by nearby farmers who most probably marketed their produce in the towns of either Ruas or Peon. This otherwise barren flora before them was the only indication of life in this region. To Procel, the land seemed to reflect their present situation. Amon Rusheus would almost certainly desert them soon. But he might just wait long enough until they reached the capital so he would finally get paid, however small the amount. Procel reckoned that he might settle for anything at this stage. The urgent desire to escape from Sasha's dangerous, perhaps lethal company, was extremely evident on the frightened nervous guide's face. Trouble was coming her way and the timid guide wanted no part of it. He considered himself extremely fortunate to have survived the incident at the Cavern. But he knew he would most probably not escape the next occasion a danger as great as that exposed itself. Procel had to sigh in silent agreement; he found that he could not blame Amon. It was now purely only friendship that forced such an obligation on Procel to remain with Sasha to the bitter end. That obligation was now rapidly turning into regret.

His train of thought was broken by a sigh from the exhausted Sasha as she virtually collapsed onto the light grass. He smiled briefly before he began searching for wood for the fire. The search however proved futile as there were no plants to be seen, never mind trees. Amon also quickly came to the same conclusion and sighed in mutual agreement. However, the climate was warm. They huddled together by a small mound of earth and settled down to sleep. But slumber did not come easy to Sasha Goodwin. Forgotten memories of times long past arose once more to haunt her. Ghostly apparitions of her dead father and his powerful killer Soren possessed her dreams; his brutal death, the knight Jual Dittany and the mage Barrius Fetherfew. But what came most clearly and disturbingly were images of Ace. Feverish recollections of her lost friend haunted her into the early hours. She awoke long before the guides, weeping bitterly and trembling with guilt and fear. She dressed and walked several yards away from the camp and stared out at the bleak foreboding landscape before her. She was a stranger in a strange land. Not belonging to this nation; a country which made her fight seemingly for every step towards her inevitable fate.

It seemed she stood there motionless for hours. The passage of time of her stagnation was marked by the slow ascent of the rising sun casting bright golden rays across the dark plains to where she stood. She decided to return to the guides, however she could not join them in their deep slumber. Instead she wistfully observed the sky slip from dark to a pale light blue, promising a fine day.

"Yes," she remarked quietly to herself. "A fine day for travel." And sighed heavily.

But her tired body cried out for relief and she gave in to the powerful sway of slumber as it destroyed her resistance in an instant. Only a short duration of time passed before Sasha again awoke, but on this occasion not to silence. The guides' ceaseless chatter of their journey ahead invoked her unwanted sudden consciousness. Once more she forced herself to the monotonous ritual of self-dressing, feeding and the beginning of another step in their long journey. The morning meal was brief; another informal obligation before the horses felt their weight.

Ahead, the snake-like River Orack beckoned and they were forced to obey its summons. No easier or quicker path lay open before them. The watercourse became more distinct as they approached, but appeared to pose no danger. Still the river beckoned and before long, they stood before it. It flowed into a small inlet to the south and continued to flow into the distance, reaching for the coast. This small waterway which willingly embraced the soil was too modest to bother the travellers' worried minds. They ventured quickly across to the opposite bank and up a small mound to finally gaze upon the town Peon. The settlement possessed only a meagre protectoral outer wall and a likewise inner military force at their disposal. Like its neighbours, the boundaries of the wall was circular in shape, surrounding the entire town. The company decided now not to halt here after all since their provisions were enough to sustain them until they reached the capital and to stop here would cost them precious time, a luxury they did not have. They instead travelled rapidly through the River Voce, the neighbouring River Myall and soon sighted the great River Lead, the longest river in the land.

Once they crossed that obstacle, the capital city; the largest and greatest of all the four cities, Goodwin would soon reveal itself. Three days journey at most was all that separated Sasha and the guides from the city and their fate in the war to come. Finally, she sighed, I am returning home, however minus old and relatively new friends, not to mention a late obscure father whom I never really knew. She wondered grimly how the general populace would greet her now her father, their ruler was dead. She wondered how she could possibly cope with the massive responsibilities that might be forced upon her. Will they spurn me like I did my father, and cast me aside like I perhaps deserve?

The bleak landscape before her offered no comfort or answers to Sasha Goodwin. She was virtually alone in a nation which might see her as a possible saviour, or the bringer of its destruction.

*   *   *   *   *

Night crept in gradually, hiding the dark actions of an evil violent man. No other human was present to correct or criticise the absent conscience and deranged mind of the most powerful and dangerous man alive. It is said that power and death are close cousins; ultimate power and complete madness even closer. This was truth when one considered the mind of the Magus Soren. Never was madness more clear and profoundly evident than in this man. Hatred and its fulfilment can take its toll on any normal individual. But the complete revulsion Soren had held for his great late rival Segal Goodwin could never have been considered normal, and the eventual death of that same man was the instrument to throw the Magus over the thin line of what had already been shaky sanity. Even the former High-Lord's death had not quenched the mage's utter resentment of the very name of Goodwin. He wanted to eradicate every possible remaining reminder of the man.

One last such reminder remained. There stood one last festering bane present on the land, the capital; Goodwin City. This gangrenous virus, he decided in an instant; this thorn in his flesh would have to be immediately destroyed. He flew into a demented rage and reached for the nearest paneless window to vomit forth his deranged threats and promises. In the distance, his order was heard and acknowledged. His voice their will and life. The sky blackened further until it had become completely cloaked in utter darkness as three huge shapes suddenly took flight into the night, obscuring the Moon Goddess for one frightful instant, revealing it once again in another. He screamed into the night, only the dragons; his servants, heard the call.

"Destroy Goodwin, raise the entire foul city to the ground! Kill every single man, woman, child and even beast present. Leave no survivors! I want the city's destruction to be an example of my ultimate power and authority...Kill them all!"

He collapsed back onto a nearby seat, the sudden burst of madness had exhausted him and the pleasure of knowledge that his city would now be the capital. His fire beasts would soon arrive at Goodwin and wipe the city completely off the face of the map. Only ruins and the bitter pungent smell of burnt flesh would mark the grave of the once great capital; the last testament to the only man who might have been powerful enough to destroy him.

CHAPTER SEVENTEEN

The night seemed more ominous than usual, as if it were predicting a terrible evening of bloodshed. The company was approaching a small range of undulating hills and a high feeling of anxiety could be felt amongst them. Goodwin City; the capital, was close, perhaps even just beyond this series of hills. They began to increase their speed, driving the beasts to their limit. The hills in question quickly greeted them and they rapidly rode up the small mounds. Sasha however began to halt as they made their ascent. Procel drew alongside her in puzzlement. Then he saw the reason for her sudden cessation. A dim golden incandescent glowing was to be seen from beyond the tip of the hill. Procel struck a worried glance to Sasha and the same was reflected in her face. They spurred the horses on as Amon did also in wonder and confusion. The beasts and their riders finally reached the peak and stared uncomprehendingly into the distance in horrified fascination. The greatest possible nightmare in Sasha's life unveiled itself before her. Barely a thousand metres away lay the capital city Goodwin; their destination. The whole city was cloaked in light; the worst kind. The capital was ablaze. From their vantage-point, it appeared no single building had escaped the fiery rage which continued to hungrily consume the entire city. Even the turrets of the outer walls of the city were ablaze. From this distance, the company could clearly see figures fleeing from the open city-gates. The ones not so fortunate were strewn seemingly lifeless around the entrance. The reason for such utter devastation was not clear at first, such was the overwhelming scene of fiery destruction of the entire settlement. But breaks of sky-light in the dense greyish-black smoke which was rising steadily from the burning city below revealed a darker and more terrible nightmare.

Sasha sighed audibly in despair as she gazed upon the all too familiar huge golden creatures circling the city high above. They would normally not have been noticed such was the absolute blackness of the smoke rising, but their foul presence was noted by the sudden fiery jets which seemed to appear seemingly from nowhere in the sky above and rain down without warning on the vulnerable defenceless populace in fine orange streams. The wing-spans of the beasts appeared never-ending, as Sasha bleakly observed, stretching over twenty metres each in length. She counted at least three in number of the creatures diving to and fro repeatedly into the city below, causing massive destruction with each dive. However she forced herself from her trance and spurred the horse on with all of her remaining strength. She briefly turned around to the still transfixed guides and roared over the sound of distant screams of absolute terror.

"Ride, you fools! Ride!"

They shook their heads into reality and immediately rode down the small hill after her. Dirt and dust arose from beneath the riders as the horses sped on towards the city boundaries. People of every possible description were fleeing blindly in utter terror from the gaping wound in the city-wall, carrying what little they could of their possessions. Mothers carried young children, older ones fled on their own, halting occasionally to search for lost fathers. The elderly in the panic were left inside to perish. The scene was one of absolute total chaos.

A bedraggled middle-aged man ran in front of the company's approaching horses and they were forced to a sudden halt. Procel's beast reared up on its hind legs in fright, barely avoiding striking down the man. Procel grabbed tightly onto the reins in panic, almost falling off the horse.

"Stop, don't go in there! There's nothing left, everybody's dead." The man screamed before fleeing in fear and despair.

The small company hesitated at the entrance of their destination. To the guide Amon Rusheus, it was completely infuriating to have come this far and now not to be able to enter. To him, it appeared his long awaited wages were going up into smoke along with the capital city. He attempted to move towards the broken gates, but his horse had other ideas and would not budge. The guide growled in both frustration and complete annoyance. Eventually after several moments of contemplation, both Sasha and Procel dismounted.

She turned to Amon. "Stay here with the horses."

He did not bother to argue. The flames from the burning city were clearly giving off their lethal heat as the guide was sweating profusely. He watched the two disappear into the smoke hidden city and glanced at the fleeing population. They ran for the same series of hills they themselves had just left to hide from their flying persecutors. Amon glanced towards the sky, searching for the nightmarish creatures, but could not see them. Perhaps they have tired of their sport and have left, he thought and sneered. Amon scratched his fine red beard in frustration, and in boredom began to fiddle and play with the golden medal attached to his jerkin just above his heart. The symbol for the prize for the single best guide from the Alderman in Valerian back on Holl Island. A load of rubbish, he sneered, and yet he laughed at the sight of Procel's utter disappointment when he had first met him. All in all, it wasn't a completely bad journey, it had its moments, he mused and continued to observe the fleeing population leaving their dying homes. But he then however felt a strange shiver run down his back as if someone had just walked over his grave. High above, the largest of the three rampaging dragons circling the city, prepared for another dive. But it hesitated in mid-flight, reared back up in mid-air, an act no other flying creature could possibly copy, its spiny tail dangling at an odd angle beneath its sleek under-body. It noticed with much amusement the fleeing figures from the city gates.

It altered its course, and headed for them. Amon Rusheus now felt considerably uneasy and pondered on whether he should follow the others into the city. He felt as if they might be in trouble. His thoughts however were abruptly broken as a dark shadow appeared all around him and the nearby fleeing citizens, casting all into a state of semi-darkness. He looked up to see a massive head and snake-like golden body above him. It possessed a huge wingspan, stretching almost as far as the eye could see. Both Sasha's and Procel's horses bolted. The guide did not notice. He let the reins fall from his hands without a thought.

"In the name of..." He breathed before feeling absolute terror as he realised what the dark beast had in mind.

The horse below him also realised and reared up in blind panic. Amon fell heavily to the ground, the breath jolted roughly from his lungs and scraping the skin off his back on the sharp stones. He glanced up more in silent wonder than in fear as the dragon made its steep dive and the whole area was abruptly smothered in bright yellow flame. The guide did not even get the opportunity to let out a scream before the flesh was virtually seared from his body and the nearby bodies of the populace presently fleeing from the shattered city-gates.

The beast passed over, leaving as a testament to its awesome power a fleshy-charred skeleton, head still staring up skywards, blank sockets and a small gold medal clung to the charred left-breast ribs. An indescribable scene seemingly out of hell itself greeted the two travellers upon entering their home city. No single house or even street was immediately recognisable to Sasha, such was the extent of the destruction. Everything before the observing eye was ablaze, several houses already crumbling and falling down all around them. Screaming figures ran past them and all that Sasha could do was stare at them as they fled past, seemingly oblivious to her presence in their fear.

The atmosphere of sheer terror was stifling.

Procel led Sasha by the hand, such was her complete shock, through the smoke-filled streets towards the centre of the city, towards Goodwin Castle. What they witnessed when they eventually approached the structure was by far the greatest testament to the God of Fire. The giant great towers still retained their impressive height, but they were completely engulfed in flames. Some of the walls of Sasha's former home could not be seen for dense smoke and fire which blazed fiercely from open windows. Even as they gazed in shock and despair, they heard a low moan like that of an old man in great pain, and saw the centre tower; the greatest and highest of all seven begin to seemingly crash in upon itself. It brought down a second smaller neighbouring tower with it as it fell, bringing the two down simultaneously in its death fall. The rest were soon to follow.

The dragons which still circled above had obviously directed most of their attention to this particular target. No child under Sasha's care would ever again gasp in awe and admire its decorated walls, no mage venture here in future peaceful times to study or to consult the great man whose home it once was. The towers and the castle were built upon magick. It was fitting Sasha reckoned, that they should be destroyed by another form of that same power. To Sasha, it appeared that everything her father had once worked all his life for and built, was destroyed in mere moments; a lifetime's work and dreams consumed by fire. She also reflected bleakly in surprising apathy, that all of her worldly possessions were also going up in flames. What she presently wore and possessed was all that testified to her existence. But most of all, and more importantly was the secret she had to find, that blank gap in her mind and past would now not be filled. Its solution would have probably lay in the great library or even in her father's private study.

All that was now gone. There was nowhere left to go.

She fell to her knees in utter despair and turned her face to the sky where the dragons still circled and wished she could actually summon them to come and finish their task, to kill her. She had nothing left and no path left open to her. Soren had won. The game was over. Procel watched her fall to the ground in resignation, but did not follow her. He instead continued to observe the fiery destruction of Goodwin Castle in morbid fascination. He frowned as he turned his eyes to the left of the burning structure to see two figures moving quickly away from the dying building. Even though they appeared to be fleeing like all those around him, they were unusually out of place. They actually seemed calm as if they were no strangers to such destruction. As they approached, for they would have to actually pass the guide to reach the gates of the city, he noticed that one was a huge knight, his once shining armour now tarnished by soot and the other was an old man who the large soldier half-carried under him, the old man shuffling weakly. The massive knight moved quite rapidly as if the weight he supported under his left-arm meant nothing to him. The grey-haired balding old man carried a small bag over his shoulder containing what appeared to be bulky goods. It suddenly occurred to Procel that they had just looted the castle, greed overcoming any possible fear of the flames. He moved and stood before them, blocking their path.

"Hold fast, old man! What do you have there?"

The elderly individual did not answer or even lift his head. The knight turned to face the guide, his piercing green eyes cutting deep into Procel's very soul. For a moment Procel regretted his rash decision, but it was too late to back down now.

"Out of our way," a booming command from the soldier came, "if you wish to live."

Procel was momentarily taken aback by this impressive figure of a man. The soldier stood at just over six-feet possessing dark wavy hair which stretched down to his shoulders with a fine dark beard to match. An eerie snake like scar ran down from right-eye to top-lip. But still the guide did not move. The old man looked up in curiosity and frowned in contemplation. The boy seems familiar, he reflected; where have I seen him before? It was then he noticed that the guide was not alone. Another knelt nearby, the face obscured by flowing dark wavy hair. Procel watched the old man turn and whisper something to the knight. Procel thought the old man had said the word 'valley' and frowned in puzzlement. Then suddenly his mouth fell open in realisation. He felt great overwhelming shame grip him. The old man had not said valley, but Vali. The massive knight before him was none other than Vali Balder; Chief of Guards of Goodwin City, not to mention being widely recognised as probably the greatest of all soldiers.

He was acknowledged as probably the finest student to come from the training school based on Race Island, an incredible swordsman and brilliant battle-strategist. Before Segal Goodwin's father had rose to power and had no use for him, he had been the one man who had kept the city together against outside enemies back when the city had once been called Andrealius, after the last monarch who had died decades ago. Although he did not particularly like the ruler-ship of Goodwin, he had always trusted their judgement and supported their reign.

Procel fell to his knees before the knight, head bowed in both respect and complete shame. "Sire, I did not know it was you. I beg your forgiveness."

"Get up." The soldier replied gruffly. He was about to curse the guide when the old man interjected.

"Sasha?" He asked hoarsely.

The kneeling figure did not appear to hear at first, such was the extent of despair to which she had sunk. She vaguely thought she had heard a name carried by a voice she had not heard since childhood. Perhaps she dreamed it. But the voice would not let go, it slowly dragged her mind back to unwanted reality. She finally raised her bowed head to see the face of a familiar old man. She frowned at first, but then smiled. She rose to her feet and embraced the individual, the knight letting go of the old figure to Sasha's care. The man was Primus Rief, Sasha's childhood tutor, one of the few people she could turn to when there was no-one else. Only a deceased mother and a father dead to everything but magick symbolised her childhood years.

The old teacher turned to Procel and the knight. "We must leave. This whole place is falling asunder."

The soldier again half-carried the old tutor with Sasha supporting him on the other side while the guide led them out of the dying city. They walked at first, then half-ran to the nearby safety of the small hills.

Behind them the fire still continued to rage as Sasha's past was consumed by the flames of magick.

*   *   *   *   *

Procel arose with the sun on a cold morning destined to be forever marked by sorrow. The sky was grey with smoke and ash; the last moving particles of Goodwin City, the capital of the world. He stood up, but hesitated in making his way up the small hill to gaze upon the ruins of his former home city. He glanced instead at the hill's peak to see with much surprise Sasha apparently staring out towards her home. He could not estimate how long she might have been standing there. He approached the still figure and stood alongside her. Procel exhaled deeply with a sigh upon witnessing the once magnificent capital, now no more than mere rubble with a few barely distinguishable ruined small houses scattered throughout the entire city.

But the guide was grateful for the presence of the dense smoke for it obscured the majority of the incredible destruction that had been wrought upon this region. To consider a city that had seen thousands of years, a settlement which had survived several wars, numerous storms; a city born in the ancient era of dreamtime when such chaos was unthinkable, and was now obliterated overnight.

"It's all gone, all of it...there's nothing left." She gasped and Procel laid a gentle hand on her shoulder.

"Come away, Sasha. There's nothing you can do; nothing anybody can possibly do. We must concentrate our energy and efforts on the creator of this madness."

The now massively decreased population of the capital were beginning to rise as the travellers descended the hill. The knight and the old man greeted them first, the elderly teacher displaying the warm smile of the friendly tutor. Vail however appeared to show no emotion whatsoever. He seemed to be an individual who took every hardship life could possibly bestow in his stride and cared little for its outcome. Procel also noticed with much interest that the people who remained appeared to be gathering rapidly around him. Primus stepped forward and grabbed hold of Sasha's arm to lead her away, leaving the guide to face the huge knight and his multitude alone.

"Well, Procel Sanicle, I believe you have an interesting story to tell us." The Chief of Guards boomed to the guide who was still taken aback by the overwhelming authority of the voice.

Procel sighed as he glanced around at the disappearing figures of Sasha and the old teacher, while the huge soldier waited impatiently for him.

*   *   *   *   *

Primus Rief groaned as his bones creaked upon sitting down on the rough ground. Sasha sat down alongside him and smiled at her old tutor and friend.

"You must leave here," he uttered as he faced her. "Take this." He handed her an envelope. "It is a letter to the Commander of the Knights Order and training school on Race Island. It contains an explicit order for the officer to receive you. It was written and signed by the Chief of

Guards of Goodwin City himself; Vali Balder. His command is that the Order is to escort you with its entire military force to the city Ketherin to await fresh orders."

"I don't understand." Sasha interjected, unsure of her role in this whole affair of battle strategy.

"The Ketherin Mountains will hide the great army which is going to shortly gather there for the battle. You are going to travel to Race Island instead of Vali himself for he is intending to raise another force here and the general populace will acknowledge him much quicker than you."

"That I do understand." She sighed, realising again her own lack of worth in this land.

"Do not worry," he smiled. "You have the easy job."

"I will leave with Procel and Amon Rusheus immediately." She replied and rose to her feet.

"Wait!" The old teacher cried out.

She re-sat and gazed fixedly at him in curiosity and puzzlement. "What is it?"

"The past." Primus responded simply.

She stared at him in blank wonder. He silently replied by opening the leather bag he had so carefully carried out of the burning castle. It revealed three large leather-bound books. One bore the name of her late father. Sasha recognised it as his personal magickal notebook; his grimoire.

"His life's work." Primus stated in explanation.

The other two volumes were the twinned books of reference to general black magick to which he constantly referred. She opened the primary grimoire to find abstract diagrams concerning the art of sorcery and spells written in the Old Speech.

"One day, all three would have been yours. You now receive them earlier than expected," he sighed. "Go to the front of his personal grimoire."

She quickly flipped back the pages until the front cover revealed itself once more. To her astonishment, an envelope fell out onto her lap. Her surprise was not directed at the discovery of the envelope itself, but at the name present on the front; Sasha Elise Goodwin, in her father's writing. She threw a glance to her old teacher in wonder and puzzlement, but he only smiled lightly in silent reply.

"It is not a will," Primus retorted flatly. "I believe he long ago foresaw this catastrophe which has befallen our city and knew there would be little to pass on."

A solitary tear of sorrow and regret fell from her right eye and landed on the medallion around her neck, giving off a glint of golden light.

He reached over and upon touching it, smiled. "I thought you might have it."

"What is it, this medallion?" She asked as he grasped hold of the gold object. "What does it mean?"

"It is not for me to say," he retorted. "I believe the answer lies in the envelope."

She stared fixedly at him in further wonder and hesitantly began to open the sealed envelope. To no great surprise, she found its contents to be that of a letter. She suddenly felt a shiver of excitement run through her at the thought of this being the revelation to the secret she had been searching for. She checked the end of the letter to see the familiar signature of her late father accompanying the seal of the Society of Mages; the seal which could not be forged. The paper itself felt new to the touch, but the writing however was old, the words fading. He had obviously written this a long time ago. It appeared he had indeed foreseen this event many years ago as her old teacher had mentioned.

The letter began in a morbid fashion as one might expect from someone expecting death in the near future. But as she read, she slowly began to notice another side to her father, revealing the past filled with what she previously believed would be foreign emotions. As the words of revelation began to unfold, tears ran down her face. She saw into the heart and soul of a dead man she had never really knew or attempted to understand. Her lifetime of hatred for all forms of magick had previously barred any possible entry.

I can see so clearly now the final grains of sand in the time-glass of my life begin to fall away to reveal events so horrible they do not bear description where Soren squirms in final triumph. I cannot begin to relate to you of the hardships you now must face and the bitter fact that I will not be there for you. But I will tell you this: You must be strong; stronger than you have ever been in your life, and to believe in yourself. Don't forget for a moment who you are, and although you probably will deny it, you have all the powers of a mage which you have inherited from me.

Hopefully you will have my medallion in your possession. I will now solve its riddle if you

have not already guessed as to its solution. The inscription simply explains that you can succeed where I have failed. The dark serpent of magick lives and breathes deep within your veins as it runs in my own, but I always suspected that it is stronger within you. It is said that when a power is inherited, it automatically doubles in size. By all the gods, for your sake, I hope it does. Use the art wisely. Never abuse or reject it, but look upon it as your greatest asset and most deadly of weapons. The fate of the entire nation may rest in your capable hands, Sasha. You have come far, but the game is not yet over. But whatever may occur, both I and your mother would have been very proud of you.
Segal Goodwin, High-Lord and Mage.

Sasha finally rose to her feet and began to wipe the tears from her eyes and face. "We must now part, my teacher. The road is long and time is indeed short."

The old man also painfully rose and smiled. "Go, Sasha Goodwin. May the wind of destiny blow you to victory."

She left the old tutor and soon found Procel amongst a large crowd revealing past events.

After several moments had passed, the massive Chief of Guards turned to greet her. "Welcome, High-Lord." He boomed to Sasha's surprise.

"I ride with the remainder of the army here to gather all the forces I can muster to Ketherin where I expect to see you and the Knights Order there shortly."

Sasha nodded in reply and two horses were quickly fetched. "A third beast for our fellow traveller Amon Rusheus." Sasha commanded the squire and Vali stepped forward once again.

"Your friend the guide will ride no more this day, but will rather lead our weary departed city-companions to their final rest in the Dreamworld." He stated quietly and so saying, lobbed an object which Procel caught.

In his hand was the medal for best guide from Valerian. He also noticed that it was stained with soot and dried blood.

"Another falls." Sasha groaned and turned her horse towards the wind and the distant harbour town Narew.

Procel before leaving turned to Vali and saluted the huge knight in admiration and respect. He wondered whether he would gaze again upon his face. Out of the original seven-member company, only two now remained. Procel sighed and turned to follow Sasha Goodwin on her path to victory or oblivion.

CHAPTER EIGHTEEN

The road to the harbour town Narew appeared insanely long. The midday sun beat down, flaying the skin from their unprotected necks and any other exposed parts, driving the sweat in rivulets off their weary bodies. But longing expectation gave way to relief as they finally sighted the large town situated on the coastline, with The Great Sea seemingly stretching into blue infinity. With some hesitation they entered the unguarded settlement gates, the populace within appeared to show none of the visible anxiety which was so overwhelmingly evident in other towns with talk of war in the air. Perhaps they did not know, or simply did not care, Sasha pondered. But she was nevertheless grateful for such ignorance or apathy, for this would prevent any possible impediment in their path when they obtained transport across the sea to Race Island. However, children began to dance gaily around the legs of the newcomers' horses and continued to do so until the travellers began their descent down the main road leading to the quay.

From her vantage point at the top of the hill, it seemed that Sasha could see the whole world. Before them stretched The Great Sea, its waters to be seen in every conceivable direction, except from behind. The brine appeared to have no visible end or limit. She fixedly observed the rays of the bright midday sun gleam on its clear surface as if in a trance and create a blinding glare which reflected in her own blue eyes. Procel glanced at her and smiled briefly. For the first time, he actually began to notice her beauty and his thoughts diverted to that of Ace.

How foolish the crazy mountaineer had been. Hell, he cursed, he even began to wonder if the man was still alive. But he was too fine a swordsman to be dead. Such a notion was absurd. Knowing Ace, he was more likely to be spending his time being drunk and whoring. Idiot!

His mind drifted once again, and he remembered back to his childhood when four innocent children played in the corridors of Goodwin Castle. How big it had seemed in their young eyes! Hell, as an adult, it still appeared huge, or at least it had before it all came toppling down. Life had been so simple then, not so complex and brutal as it is now. Just four children; himself, Ace, Sasha and Myru. Myru his cousin, and friend to all, but no matter how hard she and the guide had tried, they could never match the bond of companionship between Sasha and Ace. Two childhood friends he always believed would eventually marry, but now firmly and regretfully believed such an event would never take place before his eyes. Now Myru dead and Ace possibly also. But he knew if he were truly alive, he would make an appearance in the forthcoming battle. Ace would never dream of missing such a fight. Who knows, Procel laughed, perhaps I might just meet up with the old joker once more.

The quay boasted two long piers stretching like stone-fingers into the sea, possessing many a boat anchored. The travellers rode slowly along one pier and Sasha ventured ahead of Procel towards the smaller of two nearby trawlers where a single fat middle-aged man was in the process of sweeping excess water from his deck. The boat did indeed seem more akin to a fishing trawler than a passenger-boat. But the obese Captain rapidly begged to differ as his hungry pocket quickly devoured several of Sasha's gold coins. The horses and riders rode nervously onto the deck as it accepted their weight with a low groan of protest. They dismounted as Procel examined their ferry. It had no underdeck, but possessed only the small deckhouse. Procel hoped no storms were expected, or they could be in trouble. The ferryman then casted off and unfurled the sails, bestowing sudden life to the motionless craft.

It was a three day journey to Race Island, a tiny land in the middle of nowhere, isolated by water. It was an island populated almost entirely by dwarfs, elves and the knights. Both the races of the dwarfs and the elves had fled long ago to the desolate island in the search for refuge from the hostile prejudiced outside world, while the knights trained their squires and students there because of the adequate harshness of the land. If a trainee knight could survive there, he was ready for virtually anything. Both the desolation of the land and the legendary bitterness of the other races for outsiders bothered Procel. He hoped this was not a pointless voyage into a land filled with danger at every turn.

*   *   *   *   *

Late on the third day, they sighted land. Their very first view of the island was that of the giant Race Mountains rising high at the coastline and stretching far inland, robbing them of any visible sight of the land beyond these majestic towering mounds. The waves of the violent tide crashed frequently against the rocks of the beach, sending great sheets of frothy water high into the air. Beaching here was an impossibility. Procel sighed in frustration with the uncomfortable knowledge that it was yet a further three days journey to the island's bay where they could beach with the Knights Order situated nearby.

Procel settled down at the trawler's bow and lazily admired the barren flora of Race Island where desolation was the norm. His eyes slowly began to close as sleep consumed his consciousness.

The next three days passed like their predecessors and the boredom had now become actually painful. Procel woke from his slumber to the foreign sounds of excited voices. Only hunger and thirst had broken his sleep before this due to the boredom. He hesitantly raised his weary body off the hard wooden floor of the deck and gazed out towards the sea to see the now all too familiar coastline. But this time, they were actually going in to beach. And they were not alone. A meeting company of at least twenty knights on horseback were present on a long stone pier which led to a well-worn path stretching inland. The garrison at the town had obviously seen their arrival from afar.

The boat sluggishly approached the quay, but the heavily armoured soldiers appeared impassive to this movement. The trawler slowly drew alongside the pier and Procel threw the heavy thick mooring-rope to a waiting knight who quickly affixed it to a nearby stump on the edge. The tide was out and thus forced the oversized ferryman to attach a wide ramp from his boat to the pier, creating a slight slope. Procel led one of the timid horses up the stable ramp on foot whilst the ferryman began to tie down his sails. Sasha however on the other hand, remained on the boat, motionless, watching these actions and observing the likewise unmoving waiting knights. They were truly impressive. Giant broadswords were strapped to their left hip and each brandished a long lance in their outstretched right hand, bar the knight at the rear who instead possessed a standard bearing their coat of arms; two swords criss-crossed below a golden castle. They reminded her of her old friend and protector, Jual Dittany from Grieve who had given his life to save hers. Another pointless death of a once precious friend by Soren's hands which she vowed would someday be avenged.

Finally both beasts stood on the pier, and Procel remounted as Sasha approached the nearest soldier. However, he turned away and a second knight, the largest of all, dismounted and stood before her. The boatman in reply removed the ramp and quickly began to unfurl the sails. The armoured soldier before Sasha stood at a proud six foot-three and his armour like the others had been waxed and shined to a blinding glare. Another knight behind him carried his lance for the moment.

"Sasha, daughter of Goodwin?" He asked hoarsely and she nodded in silent reply. "A messenger arrived earlier to inform us of your impending arrival. I have orders to escort you to our town."

The soldier then returned to his horse without any further comment. He then turned about and began to ride slowly down the pier towards the road. The other knights quickly followed in pairs. Six however remained motionless at the rear behind the two travellers until they began to follow the departing military company on the worn path.

Only a few hours passed before they sighted the knights' town, if it could actually be called such. Large rectangular two-storey shaped barracks populated the town, while hundreds of horses surrounded the training camp, segregated by wooden fences. Procel let his gaze drift however from the town to the coast and gasped in speechless amazement. Twenty-five long-ships stood out at sea. Each bore three masts with four sails tied down and each could carry a hundred knights, their horses and provisions. They were impressive even from the distance.

The company itself stood atop a small hill, below them the town, its walls ablaze with activity. Populated within those walls were some five thousand men; the most highly trained and armed soldiers in the known world. Procel now knew why the elves and dwarves who also occupied the island, made no false move. The knights could crush them easily. They began their descent and soon entered the heavily guarded town-gates. The knights dismounted and the two travellers followed suit. They were then led by the lieutenant who had earlier addressed Sasha to the largest of all the buildings to be found in the camp. The knight quickly entered via a small entrance in the front wall of the structure and marched rapidly down a dimly-lit corridor inside the dusty building, with both Sasha and Procel following closely behind him. There were little windows to be seen at either side of the dark bleak corridor as they walked towards its end. At the end of the long hall was a plain wooden table behind which sat a middle-aged knight seemingly unaware of their steady approach. He appeared to be writing on a faded manuscript. No other piece of furniture or sign of life was to be easily seen apart from the seated soldier. The only sounds present being the echoes of the marching feet of the escort knight with the travellers walking in contrast, much more quietly and timidly behind him. But as they drew to a halt before the table, the seated knight ceased his scribbling and rose to his feet. The soldier was one of the largest and most impressive of men that Procel had ever seen. His height was easily that of at least six foot-five displaying a broad chest and bulging muscle-bound arms barely contained within his shining armour. The hard metal shone brightly below a handsome face which possessed a greying beard to match a short moustache of the same colour with grey straight hair flowing down to touch his shoulders. His face however bore the expression of evidence of witness to awesome battles too numerous to mention.

The guard halted four feet from the table. His feet thudded together in salute, his arms hung straight at his sides. "Sire," he boomed, "Sasha, daughter of Goodwin."

This appeared to be the entrance for Sasha and she was quick to seize the opportunity, moving forward in front of the lieutenant. The knight with this sudden action, turned about and rapidly marched back down the corridor and out of the dark building. The soldier at the table said nothing, but stared fixedly at Sasha. But she did not flinch or turn away from his piercing gaze. Instead she casually revealed the letter and dropped it on the table. Still staring at Sasha, the silent man reached over and grasped hold of the object. He instantly opened it and read it. Upon finishing, he let the notice fall to the table.

"So!" He declared. "It appears we have a mother of a battle on our hands."

He walked slowly around the table and leaned against its edge, facing the travellers, but also towering over both of them. Sasha found it all very uncomfortable and intrusive.

"Commander Deale King of the Knights' garrison and training camp here on Race Island, at your service." He bowed slightly to Sasha upon speaking.

Sasha however was quick to respond. "Sasha Elise Goodwin, only child of the late Segal Goodwin, mage and leader of the Society of Mages and Goodwin City."

"The letter bears the seal which cannot be forged and the signature of my only superior; Vali Balder. I am thus bound to obey," he stated, and then paused. "But I would anyway. My knights tire of practice. They seek blood and honour in battle." He bowed again to Sasha's surprise in respect. "Although I am bound to obey this summons, let it be known that I am not your servant. You will follow my lead." At this, Sasha was momentarily taken aback. "I will see you are well catered for. We sail with the morning tide; two hours after dawn. It is a day's journey from here to the harbour town Jorum. Half of the entire garrison will sail tomorrow with the ships returning for the other remaining two and a half thousand knights. The first group will then ride towards the city of Ketherin and arrive there with luck in a further five days' time and remain there for a further seven," he stated, and then paused again before continuing to speak. "That is all, you may now leave."

The commander then turned away and proceeded to shuffle and sort out abstract papers on his undecorated table. Sasha and Procel began to return back down the bleak corridor. But just as they approached the exit, the shut door suddenly flew open to reveal the lieutenant knight. He escorted the travellers this time to a large tent where inside stood a bare small table, two accompanying chairs, and two beds.

"A meal shall be served shortly and then I advise you to get some sleep. We sail early tomorrow." He declared before leaving the two travellers.

They sat and looked at each other wearily.

"They don't talk much, do they?" Procel said and Sasha smiled in reply.

"But they are highly organised."

"And highly armed," Procel interjected. "Did you see their long-ships? Magnificent!"

Sasha nodded in silent reply and began to toy with the medallion which hung heavy around her neck. Within a short while they were served roasted rabbit with an array of vegetables which they quickly devoured. The travellers then slept until they were abruptly woken early the following morning by the lieutenant.

"We sail in half an hour." He said and left as quickly as he had entered.

Sasha did not stop to ponder on whether she might ever see the knight again. They then dressed and left the tent to find the town outside once again ablaze with activity. But perhaps more so than what they had witnessed yesterday. Also there appeared to be less of the usual amount of soldiers present in the area surrounding them. Procel turned to the coast and instantly saw the reason. Protruding from the calm water were the impressive twenty-five long-ships. But this time they were alive with busy activity. Already twenty had cast off and were in the process of leaving the bay. The remaining five were currently also preparing to do so. They were waiting for the remaining soldiers already present on the pier preparing to depart for the long-ships via small rowing boats. The two travellers were part of these remaining passengers. They ran down to the quay where a waiting knight quickly escorted them on board a rowing-boat. Within a few minutes, they were aboard the finest craft Procel had ever seen. The three masts seemed to stretch as far as the eye could see into the very sky above them displaying mighty sails as large and as vast as a dragon's wings. Procel could feel beneath him the power of the awesome craft as if it were alive. It seemed to breathe and rejoice in its own magnificence. The ship then cast off and Procel watched in silence as unarmoured squires unfurled the sails above his head. All around on the deck were busy soldiers and Procel could hear the clamour of uneasy horses below deck.

Soon all twenty-five ships had left the bay and had steadily begun their short voyage to the mainland. Procel spent the remainder of the day studying and admiring the long-ship in all its great detail, while Sasha chatted to Commander Deale King. The following dawn revealed the coastline of the mainland and the harbour town Jorum. The idle populace crowded and gathered around the quay in awe. They were gazing upon something that had not been witnessed in over fifty years, all twenty-five long-ships loaded with knights sailing in to port.

The ships drew in and moored. The knights with both their supplies and what meagre possessions they had disembarked and rode into town. Excited children danced around the horses' legs, occasionally blocking the company's path. Within the hour however, all two and a half thousand men minus the ship's crew had departed from the town and had begun their long journey south-west to the city Ketherin. The voyage was to be unbroken; the army planned not to halt at any town that might lie in its path.

Sasha glanced behind her to see the snake-like silver chain of armoured soldiers moving through the land. She rode at the front with Procel and the commander who talked unceasingly about the proposed battle-plans to her while the guide half-listened. The knights behind him travelled in pairs or in threes in tight formation. Deale revealed that Soren in his blind over-confidence would not suspect this foreign movement so near to his home city. Procel wondered if this was the truth, he did not believe the Magus could be so easily fooled.

*   *   *   *   *

The following five days passed tediously slow, camping at night with sentries all around, riding without break by day. Eventually they sighted the city Ketherin. Sasha was the first to let out an audible sigh of relief. She had lost five travelling friends, her home, her best friend and a father to reach this place. She hoped it would all be worth it. Great excitement was already evident in the city as it quickly became aware of the presence of the massive armoured movement as they approached.

The two and a half thousand strong force did not enter the actual city itself, but made their camp a few hundred yards from the gates. They would only consider entering the city itself when extra supplies were required.

Sasha and Procel then gave their farewell for the present moment to the army for they would seek accommodation instead within the city-walls. There was of yet no sign of Vali Balder, but messengers had reported that he was approaching with a force in excess of fifteen thousand men which planned to amass at the city in three days. Sasha and the guide wearily entered the city. She glanced momentarily behind to see the large company in the process of settling down for the night. Sentries had already been appointed and they stood out at the frontiers of the main army. She thought of Soren and wondered bleakly if it would be enough. She hoped for not only their own sakes but for the sake of the entire nation that it would be.

CHAPTER NINETEEN

The rolling mountains of Ketherin rose high above to the left of them. A fierce chill breeze blew down from the east from those stone giants, sending a piercing chill through the weary bones of the group of fifty travellers.

All but four of these walked carrying heavy baggage alongside mules bearing even heavier burdens. The occasional clang of metal against metal sent sudden shivers down the spine of the nervous fat man on horseback at the front of the company. Behind his plump form rode three mercenaries and almost fifty bearers supporting between them almost ten thousand swords. They had to stop quite regularly to rest because of the enormous weight whereupon the protective swordsmen quickly took up positions as sentries, wary for any foreign approaching movement towards their obese leader.

Though none dared make such a move. One of the bodyguards in particular was enough to terrify the largest of the bearers. He was huge in stature and brandished a massive two-handed broadsword which he strapped to his back. The other two were instead of a thin but shifty-looking character, one of which was a young tall man possessing long blonde hair carrying an impressive thin blade at his side. Earlier that same day the bearers had witnessed his incredible swordplay. Several armed bandits had suddenly attacked the company, and this man alone had struck down five within a few moments. From that moment hence, most of the fifty porters never let their eyes drift from this man, here was one to reckon with.

All three mercenaries were hidden under a thick brown cloak and hood which flowed down to their feet and which obscured their features, adding a further sense of mystery and foreboding to these protectors. Within a few hours they sighted the city Ketherin and the trader uttered a heavy sigh of relief. But as they began their approach, they abruptly halted. The merchant's eyes drifted to the company of soldiers amassing barely a few hundred yards from the city-gates. The bodyguards' gaze went to their obese leader in both curiosity and puzzlement. But he only shrugged in apparent apathy and they continued their path once again towards the city.

The travellers approached the surprisingly unguarded city-gates and entered without much notice from the settlements' occupants or the armoured force stationed nearby. The plump trader and his group left the main road and ventured down a side-lane. An entrance concealed from the main street revealed itself in the wall of a small two-storey building, hidden by the shadows created by the dark clouds which rolled overhead. All quickly entered the crumbling structure whereupon the bearers were seen to leave minus their heavy baggage one hour later, leading their now burden-less mules out of the city and once again back into the wilderness.

Not long after two of the bodyguards also departed from the concealed establishment and entered the main road. The two still wore their cloaks, but none of the occasional passing citizen happened to pay any heed. The larger of the two mercenaries turned to his much smaller companion, a bulge protruding from the cloak on his back due to the over-sized blade strapped to his back and over his shoulder.

A few moments later, they turned off the main street and entered a tavern. Above their heads swung in the light breeze an odd sign displaying the image of a single eye, similar to that of a cat, but too large and scaly to be that of a feline. The tavern bore the name The Dragon's Eye. No other symbol identified the inn; just a huge grotesque eye. But the tavern was well known in the city for both its liquor and resulting fights. It was thus both loved and extremely popular in the city. But dusk was fast approaching and the sky was already transforming from blue to a dark-grey as it heralded the inevitable night. Inside the building was a single giant chamber almost filled to complete unbreathable capacity with people of every possible nature and description. The smaller of the two mercenaries smiled in some amusement as a well-built man in his early forties whom appeared to be quite drunk was in the process of attempting to talk to a young woman seated at the bar, displaying a slender form and long curly dark hair. She seemed to take no notice of the drunk's clumsy advances, but her seated friend rose to meet this foreign challenge. Both the female and her infuriated companion had their backs to the mercenaries, obscuring any possible view of their features. But all present could clearly see that a fight was about to break out. Both mercenaries smiled in silent satisfaction as the female's friend and probable lover suddenly struck the drunk in the face, his fist shattering the man's nose with an audible crack. The drunk fell backwards, crashing heavily to the floor. A companion of the fallen man quickly replaced his unconscious friend and struck the woman's saviour, breaking his nose and sending splatters of his blood onto the bar-table. The two then fell to the floor and began wrestling out their differences.

Another similar drunk ignored the two and approached the now defenceless woman, wrapping an arm around her shoulder. The smaller of the two mercenaries exhaled with a sigh of audible pleasure. The other larger mercenary laughed loudly as he realised what his friend had in mind. The current atmosphere in the inn was becoming increasingly tense. The room was ready to explode at the slightest spark and the smaller of the two travellers provided that medium. He strolled slowly and calmly to the standing drunk. The individual turned at the approaching foreign sound and the traveller picked him up by the collars of his jerkin, drawing him up until his feet no longer touched the ground, and both their faces met. The mercenary could clearly smell the drink off the man's breath and coughed.

The woman could not see her newly-appointed possible saviour for the traveller's hood still hid his face from view. He himself did not turn to look at her either for his full attention was focused entirely on the drunk. However, she let out a sharp cry of both shock and surprise as the mysterious traveller suddenly head-butted the man. The drunk's head went back with the blow and he screamed as the mercenary dropped his body to the floor. He crashed on top of his fallen companion and both let out a simultaneous groan of agony.

The room then broke into chaos. Across the chamber, the larger bodyguard ripped the brown cloak off himself to reveal a naked coloured torso and bulging muscle-bound arms. The very sight of him made men near him cry out in shock and awe as they gazed upon perhaps the largest individual they had ever seen. The swordsman did not hesitate, but simply picked up the nearest unfortunate man and flung him across the crowded room where he landed heavily upon two sitting men and broke the small table between them with his fall, scattering their drink-filled mugs to the floor. The men rose and instantly began arguing about who should kill the drunk before them. Screams of both pain and rage quickly joined the sounds of breaking tables, chairs and mugs still containing beer. The smaller of the two mercenaries bent down and picked up the drunk he had just struck and threw him onto the bar table. The man cried out as his head rebounded off the table with an audible thud and he collapsed again, falling back to the floor in a heap.

The general cries of pain and breakage were silenced by the sudden sound of a shrill, though all too-familiar whistle. The City Guards were on their way. Drunks ran in every direction in blind panic. They attempted to get past the giant mercenary who barred their exit, but in vain. However, he decided to let them go and they fled into the shadows of the dark alleys beyond the door.

"Karl," his companion shouted. "We have to get out of here."

The black mercenary responded by turning and fleeing into the street beyond. His smaller companion quickly followed suit. He did not bother to wait for any thanks from the still-sitting female who watched him flee without another word. She then began to help her embarrassed friend up off the floor, her voice a mixture of curiosity and nervous excitement. She somehow believed she had recognised the voice of her saviour. Both ran out of the ruined tavern and down the misty alley after the two travellers, as the distant sounds of armoured-feet echoed from the main street.

The rain began to fall heavily as the last of the able drunks started to flee down gloomy dark back streets to evade capture. They turned to see their saviours run down one of these, their distant forms barely recognisable in the misty darkness. They continued their pursuit as the City Guards now were close to approaching the almost deserted ravaged tavern. The large mercenary and his companion halted just outside a deserted condemned house and started to pant heavily in sheer exhaustion. The sweat was running off them as they hid in the darkness created by the alcove at the door of the building.

"I think we've lost them." Karl gasped.

"I hope you're right." His companion retorted and removed his hood.

He then began to brush back his hair with his left hand. Karl smiled lightly as he observed this act. He had none to brush. However, the smaller of the two individuals suddenly stared at his massive companion in wonder, for he had just unsheathed the giant blade from his back and stepped casually in front of his companion, facing the dark alley from which they had just left. The other swordsman now too heard the audible sounds of running approaching them.

"Karl, don't," he declared. "It won't do us any good if we kill some of the military-city scum."

The swordsman gazed down and his friend wondered if he was going to ignore the request. He appeared to hesitate, but then sheathed his broadsword. The other traveller relaxed slightly as he instead bared his muscles in preparation for a physical clash. But what finally approached them was not the familiar forms of the armoured guards, but a young dark-haired woman of some beauty and a young man. Neither were a match for Karl, so the mercenary relaxed. But he still barred the way to his weaker friend, lest trickery be foremost on their minds. The runners halted and gasped in awe at the size of the human obstacle before them. But then to the mercenary's complete surprise, the woman confidently stepped forward.

"Where is he?"

"Who?" Karl boomed, towering over her.

His attempts at intimidating her however were unsuccessful. She did not flinch, but rather on the contrary she instead stared fixedly into his hazel eyes, betraying no sign of fear. "Your friend."

Karl was impressed, but did not let it show. There was a sharp noise behind the large warrior as his companion stepped out of the shadows and Karl let out a low moan. The second swordsman stared at the woman under his brown hood for what seemed a lifetime, before his mouth fell open in shock and surprise.

"Sasha!" He cried out in complete disbelief and ran forward.

Karl frowned in confusion, but then memories of the woman's name came flooding back upon remembering the deluge of abstract mumblings that were his companion's drink-filled dreams. She said nothing at such an outburst, but then smiled broadly. They embraced and remained motionless for some time, body heat close as the heavy rain beat down onto their unprotected heads, Ace's hood strewn over his shoulder, discarded. Karl stared at Procel in curiosity, but did not let it show on his face. The hug broke and Ace smiled over Sasha's shoulder at his old friend the guide, but did not embrace him. It seemed that the old wound of suspicion still bled in Ace's mind.

"My eternal gratitude for taking care of her." Ace said, but Procel only shrugged his shoulders.

"It was I who was taken care of." He responded simply and smiled.

Sasha smiled lightly back at him, as the tears flowed freely without impediment down her cheeks both from sorrow and new found joy. She laughed in delight, but then suddenly her face became less jovial, as it took on a more serious and sober visage as she turned to face him. "The capital is gone," she declared flatly and Ace stared back at her in wonder. "Soren has destroyed my home and my father's work."

Ace turned to Karl in surprise, his shock reflected in the warrior's face. "What has happened since I left?"

"Not here." She retorted.

"I know of a place." Karl stated.

They all left the alley of reunion and followed the large mercenary to another tavern, a quieter one this time. Only two sober old men occupied the inn and were in no hurry to pester strangers. They sat and told each other tales; tales of the bloody past and the dark future, deaths of past friends and loss of homes, and the approaching battle. They reflected on this being the last stage of their long journey and the truth of insanity which lay behind the plans of Soren, his seemingly eternal power and inevitable triumph which lay resting on their graves.

*   *   *   *   *

Sasha wearily stretched her aching body and gently placed both of her hands to her temples, shaking her head with an audible groan. Her mouth felt as dry as the desert and her head ached with a steady dull-throbbing sensation which was gradually spreading down through the remainder of her body. It appeared the demon that is drink had triumphed once again. She glanced around the chamber until her eyes finally focused on the other five beds separated from her own. Two seemed to be unoccupied, but the others betrayed the hidden shapes of the guide Procel, Ace and the large black warrior. Sasha could only marvel in speechless wonder and amazement at how the bed managed to support the huge man's bulk. All three had their blankets drawn up over their heads, hiding their faces. Except for the rhythmical rise and fall of their chests, they made no other sign of life. They were otherwise perfectly motionless and lifeless.

The door flew open to reveal a gaunt thin man in his early thirties possessing auburn hair and beard. He was quite small in stature, but the dozen or so daggers strapped to his waist gave him weight and strength. Though apart from these, he appeared to carry no other weapon. He stared fixedly at Sasha for a few heart-stopping moments in a cold emotionless fashion that scared her, before turning and approaching Ace. Upon reaching his bed, he suddenly kicked the edge of the bedpost. The previously silent occupant gave a groan in reply before silence resumed. The sleeper had not awoken. The knife-thrower responded by sharply kicking the bed again and to his satisfaction, heard a curse manifest itself from beneath the covers.

"Out of your bed, sword-man," Genot growled. "The boss wishes to see you."

Ace slowly raised his aching head from beneath the blankets and stared hatefully at the small mercenary before him. "What the hell does he want?"

The blade-thrower only shrugged in reply.

"Give me ten minutes."

"Five, sword-man!" Genot snapped. "And bring that other bastard with you."

A sudden movement across the room occurred as blankets were discarded and thrown onto the floor from a particular bed in an instant. Karl arose from the bed and made for the knife-thrower. However, Genot managed to reach the door quicker than Karl and disappeared through it. Karl stopped at the door to see his prey flee down the stairs and disappear from sight as he fled down the corridor below them. The black warrior gazed outside for several moments in silence before he turned and walked towards Ace. Ace smiled as he approached.

"I know," Ace grinned. "I know."

Karl growled in anger and flexed his muscles in frustration. Ace began to move out of the comfortable bed and groaned again as his feet touched the cold floor. He glanced over at Sasha and smiled. But he finally rose from the all-too-welcoming bedcovers and quickly dressed. Ace and his large companion then left, and Sasha in their absence got out of bed herself. She walked over to the window and gazed out at the outside world. From this height, she could see right over the city walls to the camp where the knights had already begun to rise and were in the process of donning their metal skin. Here were men who had sworn an oath to protect and serve the people of the land in the name of honour and die if necessary for that sake.

Sasha sighed as she pondered on how many of these proud men would fall before all of this was over. It was all such a waste; such a pointless waste. Below, Ace and Karl had entered the familiar dining room where Genot and the trader sat and dined alone, as usual. The fat merchant turned to his personal protector as soon as he had entered the chamber.

"Who the hell are they?" He screamed, pointing to the ceiling.

Ace momentarily flinched and grimaced at the sound of such a loud tone of voice on such tender ears. "Friends." He responded quietly.

"How nice," Demur Galingale retorted sarcastically. "I want them out."

"They'll leave tomorrow."

"They'll leave now!" The merchant exploded.

"I can't do that." Ace answered flatly, and the trader stared at him in disbelief.

"Did you hear what I said?"

Ace did not reply. He only stared emotionlessly at his angry employer, betraying no sign of fear. Genot reached down for a knife, but a sudden hand from the trader on his arm relaxed him. The merchant could actually feel the great tension present in the room. He knew Ace could kill both he and the knife-thrower with little effort. He was also aware that the black swordsman was on the side of Ace and even if by some chance Genot actually managed to dispatch Ace, he would not have time enough to get Karl, and the warrior would finish them both without thinking twice.

"All right, all right!" Demur shouted. "They can stay one more night. But no more than that, agreed?"

Ace nodded and relaxed as he also felt his companion behind him do the same.

"Now, sit and eat."

*   *   *   *   *

Procel, Sasha, Ace and Karl left the house one hour later carrying the heavy baggage of arms the bearers had brought to the city the day before. They then departed from the city via the main gates and approached the knights' encampment. Several armoured soldiers marched out to meet them and collect their load. The travellers then returned to the house of the merchant with a dozen soldiers accompanying them.

After several trips, the guards were soon carrying out the remaining loads to their camp. The commander appeared and smiled briefly at Sasha before approaching the merchant. Money rapidly changed hands in the shape of a pouch of gold coins. The commander then quickly left to return to his camp. The merchant smiled broadly and chuckled happily to himself in satisfaction. War was indeed very profitable. Inside the giant baggage were almost ten thousand blades meant for the men Vali Balder was bringing. The remaining swords the former Chief of Guards would obtain from the city Ketherin itself where at this very moment weapons were being collected in earnest.

Sasha watched Commander Deale King leave before she too left with Procel to find some food in the city. Ace and Karl followed after them as the merchant stared on, observing them in silence. He gazed upon them again when they returned in the pitch darkness of the night, all quite drunk. He watched from the top window of his bedroom and sighed before returning to bed. He reminded himself to sort out this little troublesome affair first thing come morning. But sleep consumed his conscious thoughts, and he slept a dreamless slumber.

*　　*　　*　　*　　*

The weary travellers awoke not with the rising dawn, but just after noon to the sudden sounds of noisy commotion from outside of the house. Ace, Sasha and Procel ran to the window as Procel pointed to the distant Ketherin Mountains. From over the summit of a faraway mound came a mass of horsemen carrying what appeared to be lances. Sasha looked across to the knights' encampment which was alive with great excitement. The second half of the army from Race Island was approaching. The two and a half thousand horsemen began to march steadily down the mountainside in pairs towards the camp. There seemed to be no visible end to this line of soldiers and Sasha soon grew weary of watching the procession. She noticed however that one man in particular stood out from the mass of men at the camp. She deduced that this was Commander Deale King, coming out to greet his knights as they began to dismount upon arrival at the encampment.

Ace turned about as Karl approached and gazed out at the distant sight over his head.

"We need to talk." The man said and Ace nodded silently in reply.

Sasha watched them leave in curiosity. She knew that Ace had an unwritten agreement with the merchant, but he did not relate anything more on the subject. He had refused all the attempts on her part to persuade him to tell her about the earlier argument with the trader. She knew something was wrong, trouble was afoot. Below, the dining room door opened as Ace and Karl entered. As was to be expected, the chamber was empty. However, Genot suddenly entered via a side door and began cleaning up the morning meals' leftovers. He seemed oblivious to their presence.

Ace reckoned he was just ignoring them. He turned towards him and grabbed hold of the left sleeve of his jerkin. "Where's the merchant?" Ace growled.

Genot sneered in reply. "The boss is outside."

The two travellers left the knife-thrower and approached the main door, but halted abruptly as Demur opened the door and entered the room. They almost physically collided with the merchant.

"Are they gone?" He growled.

"Just leaving." Ace retorted.

"Good."

"And so are we." Ace declared in a sharp tone.

The merchant stopped and stared first at Ace, and then at Karl. He realised from their emotionless expressions that it was no jest. He had expected this, and thus to Ace and Karl, he appeared to show no sign of surprise. He only shrugged in apparent apathy and calmly walked past them. Ace thought he heard the man utter goodbye just before he left the room.

Karl stared at Ace and then burst out laughing. "Come on, let's get the hell out of here." The mercenary declared, and calmly strolling over to where his former co-employee Genot was scrubbing the dining table, pushed the knife-thrower across the furniture where he landed heavily on his right shoulder with a loud groan, much to Ace's amusement. "See you later, weasel," Karl grinned. "Try not to get yourself killed without us, that would be such a waste to humanity."

The four travellers left the house barely a few minutes later while Genot watched them leave from the open doorway. He smiled as he observed their departure, despite his aching shoulder. He was now the head and only bodyguard now Ace was gone, and he relished the thought. He sneered briefly before slamming the door shut.

The travellers quickly departed from the city for the last time and approached the now swelling knights' encampment. Five thousand soldiers now crowded the barren region just outside the city and racks upon racks of swords were being placed everywhere the eye gazed alongside lances. The commander noticed their arrival and went out to greet them. Within a few moments they were inside his personal tent where the only possessions to be seen were a small humble bed and an oak table on which various maps had been strewn.

Deale King was momentarily taken aback by Karl's incredible size even though he was a large man himself. He virtually ignored Ace and Procel for his full attention was focused on Sasha. "Vali will arrive here before nightfall," he stated to her surprise; she did not expect the former Chief of Guards to get here so quickly. "We have then only one week to arm and train his some fifteen thousand inexperienced men. It will be an awesome task, but I believe we can pull it off."

Sasha gasped in astonishment. Fifteen thousand men, she considered. Quite a number. But will it be enough? She had heard little of anything else he had said, but nodded silently in reply, all the same. Only a few brief minutes had passed before he finished his statement and they left his tent towards the one already pitched and ready for them. They then waited for the coming of the night. But the darkness came painfully slow, as if mocking their mental plight. However, just before dusk, a sudden shout was heard which was acknowledged by the entire camp. Vali Balder and his army were seen to be approaching.

Sasha ran out to greet them, but was taken aback by the strange sight which filled her vision. What appeared to be a giant mass of farmers and farm-labourers approached; one quarter of which were on horseback, the remainder sadly on foot. None seemed to bear weapons of any kind whatsoever. They rapidly began to fill the entire area such was the large quantity of them. Vali and his few remaining personal knights however could be easily distinguished from amongst the rabble. He went forward to meet his deputy, Commander Deale King and the two made for his tent. In his absence, the knights from the garrison on Race Island began to slowly crowd around their strange untrained allies in wonder and despair. Sasha ran after the two leaders, but neither Ace nor the guide Procel did follow. Karl was nowhere to be seen. The three entered the tent simultaneously as Deale began to speak, the quiver in his voice betraying his nervousness. Vali nodded to Sasha at her entrance, but she did not salute him back in reply. Something was preying on her mind.

She turned to face the former Chief of Guards, her face distinctly full of worry. "There are no soldiers from the towns among your army."

His face in reply lowered in anger and shame. "They did not wish to fight. They believe in their own individual strength and that they can stand alone against the Magus. Damn arrogant fools!"

Deale uttered an abrupt cough of intrusion to halt their conversation, bringing them back to the matter at hand. Both gruffly apologised as he began to talk. Finally after almost two hours, they eventually agreed on one definite plan of action which Deale began to explain further to Sasha when the former Chief of Guards had left.

"There is a small forest situated between Soren City and the town Samhai where we will be able to construct a battering-ram for the city gates of this new 'capital.' A dozen of my men with shields will protect about ten of the largest farmers carrying the ram. It is absolutely imperative the gates are opened quickly. Once down, all of Vali's force will charge in with two thousand of my men on foot accompanying them. Shortly afterwards, I will give the signal for the remaining three thousand knights on horseback with lances down to charge into Soren's unaware force inside. We hold nothing back in reserve," he stated firmly. "If Soren manages to stop us taking the front half of the city almost immediately, he will turn about and finish us. Once we do take the first half, four dozen of my elite crossbow company with special diamond-headed bolts will instantly take their position, and fire on the dragons," he paused for breath. "Soren is a coward at heart. He will remain inside his major tower, overseeing the battle from there. His castle is protected from the dragons' fiery breath by magick, he cares not if the entire city and all its occupants are incinerated in the process in attempting to destroy us. The bolts will have to strike the foul beasts' throats and eyes as soon as they approach lest they rain fire down upon us and cause widespread panic. The populace of the city will take up arms against us in the foolish belief that Soren will protect them with his magick. But the horrible truth is that he will rather conserve it to strike at us, if we manage to succeed in defeating his army. What is also worrying is that Soren is bound to have something up his sleeve; something we haven't seen, and will only discover at the battle. But we also have something to our advantage. The dragons' mating season approaches. Most of the beasts will already have left the city for their home; the great Cavern, and will not return for a fortnight."

Sasha let out a light laugh at such irony. To think the madman had gone to such trouble to obtain the creatures, and now they were of no use to him.

Deale again began to speak. "That is why we must be ready to leave for the city in one week. Seven days are all we can afford to train those men of Vali's."

Sasha uncontrollably yawned wearily at the end of the commander's speech and he smiled.

"Sorry I couldn't leave it till the morning, I will have little time to spare for such idle conversation later, for I will have to divert all my energy to the overseeing of the training and preparation for the coming battle. So, finally I will bid you goodnight Sasha Goodwin, and leave you in the care of my knights."

So saying, he escorted her out of his tent. She walked back to her own tent and explained the plans to the other three travellers who absorbed the knowledge before sleep claimed them.

*	*	*	*	*

The following seven days were filled with the familiar clanging of metal against metal and resulting grunts of exertion as Vali Balder's giant army of farmers and peasants trained. Many was the time that Sasha saw a man stumble or even miss a strike against a shield. Vali in silent reply put his head in his hands in bleak despair. He laughed bitterly at the thought of this rabble going against the highly trained forces of Soren. But it was all he had. These inexperienced, but courageous men came from towns and cities as far away as Heale and Colewort. But without the knights from Race Island, they would really have nothing.

Nevertheless, these were proud people before him, and the fact that they offered their very lives made them gain Vali's respect. He vowed that he would give them his all.

Time passed and the city Ketherin in its entirety came out onto the plains to bid farewell to the departing army on their path to battle. Sasha wondered if the populace really knew the gravity of their situation. Probably not.

All four companions rode at the front of the marching army alongside the two commanders. The two armoured leaders did not speak once on the long journey, but stared instead at the long road ahead in apparently silent contemplation of the coming battle. Both knew well that many of their men would perish in five days' time, and who would care or miss their lives?

Ace and Karl however chatted unceasingly, only breaking the perpetual conversation to occasionally smile at Sasha. She herself did not stop to ponder on whether Ace would die. She had lost too many dear friends already; too many to bear thinking about. She instead followed suit, staring in boredom at the long road ahead, the only sounds that of Ace talking and the endless rhythmic marching of heavy armoured feet behind her; marching towards their unmarked graves and into the soon to be forgotten pages of a history book; pages that would be stained with a legacy of lost lives on a bloody field of desolation.

CHAPTER TWENTY

A cold nocturnal breeze gave birth to a piercing whistling scream as it forced its way through the open window of the tower and into the chamber within, challenging the presence of its single occupant. The lone swordsman turned instinctively at the sound and moved to close the shutters. But he suddenly jumped back as a dark shadow flew in via the open entrance. Though startled, he instinctively drew his blade and searched for the intruder around the room. A shadow fell over the table which betrayed the creature's presence and Ortolan slowly crept towards it, sword at the ready. However as he approached, he frowned as the light revealed a black raven resting calmly on the table. It squawked at the approaching swordsman as he drew alongside the table. He then noticed a small silver container attached to its right leg. The assassin carefully removed it and the bird again took flight and disappeared through the window and into the night. He watched the beast leave before seizing the opportunity to close the shutters, and returning to the table whereupon lay the mysterious container. The tiny silver cap easily came off to reveal a small piece of parchment within. To no great surprise, he found it to be from Soren.

I believe that trouble is brewing in my land. My spies tell me there is even talk of war! This particular time would be the most favourable opportunity for the pathetic rabble to organise a rebellion against their great master, since the majority of my dragons have already left for the great Cavern to mate. The calling which comes once a year is far greater than any magickal command which even I could give for them to obey me.

I therefore order you to begin gathering the forces of Tamerindes at dawn two days from now and march towards the capital; Soren City. I will organise my own army out of the population here. Whom I cannot bribe or threaten, I will kill. They will side with me, one way or another, that I promise you.

That wandering senile old fool Vali Balder of Goodwin will not raise much of an army against me. However, what gives me concern is the Knights' garrison on Race Island. They have in excess of five thousand highly trained soldiers whom will surely rise against me.

I expect the attack to commence at any time during the next fortnight, if it will come at all.

I require your presence there, Ortolan. Don't disappoint me.

The Magus Soren, Supreme High-Lord.

Ortolan screamed in rage and flung the note into the blazing fire where it was quickly consumed. He had been expecting this moment for a long time with no great joy, and now finally it was here. At least he considered, it meant an end to this frustrating boredom.

He began to play with the large ring on his finger which Soren had given him and pondered on how he was supposed to command the senseless force within this city. *I'm a lackey, that's what I am.*

I wasn't hired for my skill in swordplay, but to simply command a bunch of freaks! He considered his position and decided that he would leave shortly after the battle. He would go somewhere where even Soren would not find him.

He turned to the window and opened the shutters, A sudden chill breeze struck his warm face and he flinched. He let his gaze fall down to the dark city below and could hear the distant shuffling of feet and low groans of a population not human, but rather something much darker; much more evil. But the distance meant he could not actually see them, and he was thankful for that. There would be time enough when he would have to gaze upon their gruesome features. He sighed as he began to wonder again how he was going to lead such an unholy army, anyone of which would kill him as they marched, but for the Magus' ring of protection. Ortolan groaned as he pondered on how the hell he managed to get himself into this job.

*   *   *   *   *

The clump of bushes shook violently as a small white rabbit darted out into the open clearing. The timid beast shook the early morning dew from its fur and glanced all around before venturing across the wide clearing to where a small plant lay. The creature quickly began to devour the growth, but then suddenly halted and raised its head in alarm. It gazed over to a small break in the treeline where the feared outside world lay. From this gap came a crowd of men crashing through the undergrowth towards the rabbit.

The animal fled back to its original hiding place to safely observe the strangers. A dozen men entered the clearing and began to inspect some of the nearby trees. The largest of the intruders revealed a double-edged axe and started to hack away at a tree. The tree in return shook with the blows and the rabbit instantly fled back to its warren. Curiosity had given way to terror.

The tree soon fell with a mighty crash and broke smaller trees below it as it fell. A second farmer took over and began to cut the tree twelve feet away from the original cut. The tree measured a foot in diameter and required eight men to carry it onto their shoulders and out of the woods.

Shortly afterwards, a farmer standing at six foot five with bulging muscles placed a giant cauldron over a blazing fire upon which wood was constantly added to maintain the heat. After three hours had passed, the same farmers now carried the fallen tree to the smith who then began to pour silver coloured molten metal over the first cut until it covered the bare bark. The tree was then slowly lowered to the ground to allow the metal to cool and solidify.

Commander Deale King soon arrived to inspect the battering ram and nodded in gruff satisfaction. It was a crude job due to the unsuitable smithing environment, but it would have to do. Time was in short supply. The officer began to wonder how long this small forest would hide the army from the many eyes of the Magus as they prepared themselves for their possible death on the battlefield. They would attack at first light in an attempt to catch the city unaware. It was imperative that the gates fell quickly before the settlement's populace could organise itself properly to rebuke the assault.

He glanced across to see Sasha observing her friends Ace and Karl train, the clanging sound of their swords quite audible. Nearby, his fellow knights also trained, but some just sat motionless in silence considering their fate while sharpening their giant blades.

The commander approached Sasha and smiled. "Worried?"

"A little." She responded with a sigh.

"Your friend Procel tells me that you knew the knight Jual Dittany well."

She nodded in reply as he sat down alongside her on the shortgrass. Both in silence continued to watch Ace and Karl now playfully wrestle, Karl winning easily every time.

"He was of course trained on Race Island, as you would have guessed," Deale said quietly. "He was also a good friend. I hear he died bravely."

"He died saving my life." Sasha responded, her face staring at the ground.

He nodded. "It was the way he would have wanted to die, he was like that."

An approaching messenger interrupted their conversation for the commander's presence was urgently required by Vali Balder. Deale gave his farewell and followed the messenger back towards the main centre of the camp. He passed by Ace, but did not glance at either he or Karl. Procel however noticed Sasha's change of mood and sat down next to her as she retold the short conversation with the commander and the guide smiled in likewise remembrance of departed friends. They turned their sight to the camp where the knights and farmers trained, preparing themselves for their death.

*   *   *   *   *

The camp that night required no sentries for very few knights or farmers could sleep for constant anxiety. The dawn for them came painfully slow, but it eventually did rise and with it came great activity. Their destination Soren City lay barely one hour's journey away, but the knights all the same were on their horses in a few moments. The farmers were far slower, but they nevertheless gathered around the soldiers in excitement and nervousness.

Deale King awaited the command to march from his superior Vali Balder, and it was quickly given. The soldiers moved off in tight formation, the farmers walking in disorganised bunches behind the guards. Within the hour however, they had travelled around the wood and sighted the capital. Two thousand knights dismounted. The remaining three thousand soldiers on horseback would stay with Vali Balder in hiding on the edge of the forest facing the city. They would wait for the signal to ride later into battle. The other knights now moved to the front of the largely peasant army of thirteen thousand farmers and disregarded their lances. They drew their swords instead, the chosen and preferred weapon for close combat.

Suddenly eight farmers carrying the ram with its crude metal head broke through the front group of knights and were followed closely behind by two dozen soldiers bearing shields. Commander Deale King who led this first assault ran on ahead towards the massive barred double gates of Soren

City. All sighed in relief upon seeing no sentries on the battlements. Surprise was crucial. So far it seemed they had this advantage. They carefully examined their huge objective.

The walls of the city stood at thirty feet, the gate itself at twenty. A turret of forty feet stood at both sides of the gates. The double doors were imposing; composed of thick steel and heavily barred on the inside. The farmers bearing the ram now silently approached as the mass of the army behind them drew ever closer to the city. The knights at the front now revealed ladders and makeshift ropes. As the farmers lifted the ram to their waists, ladders were quietly propped up against the walls. A young agile knight climbed up one of the twelve ladders and peeked in over the wall to see several of the guards now beginning to awake inside. As he let his gaze fall over the battlements, he noticed a further two dozen walking around the inside of the battlements.

It would be an impossible task to storm them without alerting others and open the gates from the inside. The soldiers would be massacred before getting the chance. Several knights would climb up the ladders instead and attack the men on the battlements, thus acting as a diversion for the farmers attacking the gates with the ram. A movement caused the knight on the ladder to glance below to see two more fellow soldiers now joining him on the ladder, swords drawn. Brief inspection of the other ladders revealed a similar scene, some of the knights carrying ropes to hang from the walls for their companions waiting below.

Everybody present became motionless, waiting for the order to attack. The farmers at the gates stood still, the ram heavy in their hands. All stared towards the main part of the army which had now gathered around the city gates in a mass of bodies. All looked to their commander and leader; Deale King, his armoured fist raised high into the air. The long awaited battle of battles was finally about to commence.

Suddenly the officer's arm fell, striking action into the motionless watchers. The leading knights on the ladders quickly scrambled up the final few steps and climbed onto the battlements, blades at the ready. They were however almost immediately spotted by awakening guards. But almost three dozen knights stood on the battlements before the city's bells rang out in alarm at this intrusion. These bells were joined by a louder foreign sound, that being an almighty crash as the battering-ram struck the gates. This violent noise continued to ring out every five seconds, the doors shaking with each blow. The entire population of the city was now in complete panic as guards and mercenaries searched frantically for misplaced weapons. The populace of the capital hesitated to consider their position and entertain their choices. They pondered on the money already received for the battle ahead, or the decision to throw it away and simply flee. But all knew with dire certainty that the Magus would find them and death would be a blessing when he was finished torturing such traitors.

Thus only one visible path lay open to them. The populace screamed their combined battle cry to the god of war before running towards the battlements to where their armoured intruders lay. One broke from the main group and screamed his rage and hatred at a nearby knight as he attacked the soldier with an axe, but the guard calmly replied by cutting short his scream and his throat with one swift movement of his blade. The man fell back and the soldier now turned his attention to others who quickly replaced the dead bandit.

By this time over fifty knights had entered the city and armed farmers now had begun to appear also on the battlements. One such large farmer possessed a six foot staff which he used to great efficiency, as he smashed heads without a second thought. But he was quickly dispatched from behind by a bearded mercenary who planted an axe into the farmer's head until it reached his shoulders, his head splitting wide open, scattering blood and brains onto the battlements.

Mercenary archers appeared at the turrets overlooking the gates and instantly began to fire on the farmers carrying the ram. The knights in reply raised their shields to protect them, but one labourer was killed by an arrow through the throat. Another farmer quickly replaced him as cracks now began to appear in the city gates. Screams of rage were quickly joined by cries of pain from within the settlement by both knight and mercenary alike. The knights were beginning to suffer heavy losses from inside the city walls. Although they were better trained and armed than their opponents, they were outnumbered and were soon forced to retreat back towards the city walls. Mercenaries on the battlements had already begun to push off ladders, but paid for their actions with their lives as farmers with bows picked them off. Commander Deale King groaned in frustration as he saw his knights driven back on the battlements, and then cursed even louder upon seeing bandits on the walls approach the gates with boiling oil for the knights and farmers with the ram down below. The city's occupants had quickly realised that the gates were their weakest point. Suddenly one of the huge doors of the city gates fell off its hinges and slanted inwards at an awkward angle, still firmly attached to its one remaining twin. The farmers instantly dropped the ram and proceeded to push the doors open, the shattered one dragging heavily across the ground, cutting deep groves in the dirt.

These intruders were rapidly joined by more soldiers and farmers who quite literally pushed the gates in with their combined body weight as all feverishly attempted to gain entrance into the city. In a matter of a few minutes, thousands of farmers and soldiers had entered the settlement. They charged down the main street to spread through the smaller alleys, searching for the enemy. But from seemingly out of nowhere came the population of the capital, brandishing swords and axes. They came from out of dark alleys, houses and shops and charged towards their intruders, screaming their ear-splitting battle cry. Near on twenty thousand men came from the city and ran towards Deale's army.

They met in the centre of the main street with a dreadful clash of blades and bodies. Swords quickly removed heads from shoulders and stomachs were split open by farmers attacking mercenaries. Grievous wounds were carried out by both sides, most being fatal. Observing all this from the safety of the woods lay the former Chief of Guards, Vali Balder. He gave a piercing scream and three thousand knights on horseback left the forest and charged towards the city. They descended upon the settlement in a flash flood of metal and flesh.

There was a great roar of approval from within the city as soldiers and farmers gave way to the attacking horsemen. The knights on horseback with lances down, level with the horses charged into the city, cutting men down everywhere. A lone mercenary near the broken gates watched with speechless astonishment as his opponent; a small farm labourer, stepped aside from their private battle. The hired killer watched his enemy calmly walk away, and still in transfixed surprise turned towards the shattered city gates. His wonder at this incident suddenly ended, as did his life as a knight's lance was driven through his face. Other members of the city's population met with similar fates, or even worse. Slowly, the mercenaries and bandits were driven back. Ladders on the city walls were replaced and a massive black warrior appeared at the summit of one to climb onto the battlements. A small bandit gave a shrill cry of shock and horror as this huge fighter suddenly appeared next to him. This mysterious individual picked the bandit up off the ground with little effort and flung him across the battlements into another mercenary. Both fell to the ground below with a crash.

However, near the coloured fighter a farmer was struck down from behind by a middle-aged bandit. Karl turned and embraced the man from behind in a bear hug and squeezed with all his strength, crushing his ribs. The mercenary let out a short cry before collapsing lifeless at the warrior's feet.

Across the battlements, another smaller individual appeared at the summit of a ladder and glanced into the city. A passing mercenary halted as he noticed this vulnerable intruder and swung his axe towards the man's unprotected head. Ace quickly climbed up the final few steps and jumped onto the battlements. He ducked the weapon which passed over his shoulders before turning to face his cowardly opponent. Ace replied by striking the man squarely in the face with his right fist before stopping to draw his blade. His sword then instantly swung, cutting off the axeman's head with a single movement, leaving a stump spewing a fountain of thick blood over the ground. Ace then turned to help Sasha up from the same ladder and then Procel. Karl returned and they split into two groups; Sasha with Karl who decided to leave the battlements and entered the courtyard below, while Ace and Procel remained on the battlements. They began to help knights and the peasants up from the ladders.

Procel smiled as Commander Deale King climbed up from a ladder. His face was awash with the blood of his enemies and his once spotless armour bore deep scars of combat. He and two escort knights then proceeded to run down the battlement steps to the city below as Procel turned to cut down a wandering bandit.

Ace turned to glance briefly down below into the courtyard to see Karl protecting Sasha, his massive broadsword cutting down at least three mercenaries with every swing. Sasha covered his back, her small blade striking out at the less courageous warriors who would not take the dark swordsman on face to face. Suddenly a shrill inhuman cry filled the city for a moment, drowning out the sounds of battle. What little remained of Soren's hired army fled at this strange scream and disappeared from view within moments, fleeing back into the settlement via houses and shops. Both knights and farmers alike stared at each other in speechless wonder and curiosity. Deale King appeared from amongst them and began to shout out sharp orders. A dozen knights armed with crossbows appeared and were rapidly followed close behind by a further three dozen. Ace judged by their clean appearance they had probably not been in battle, but were rather kept back safely in reserve for this particular moment. They proceeded to kneel in an organised fashion in front of the remaining army and aimed skywards.

Ace stared on in wonder as everybody stood motionless. With no live enemies around to fight, the entire city had become deathly quiet. The main street and square, the battlements and the entire region surrounding the shattered city gates were littered with the dead and the dying; farmer, knight and mercenary alike were strewn unceremoniously around the area. But none checked for dead or injured companions, nobody dared move in this eerie silence.

The calm was shattered as one knight gave a sharp cry of alarm. From out of the clouds came five large bodies; dragons, their massive wings spread fully apart as they dived down towards the army. Their giant fang filled mouths agape in a silent scream, preparing to spit fire down on their vulnerable victims. Farmers began to flee in every direction in blind panic as horses bolted. But the knights remained motionless. To them, fear in the face of thine enemy was cowardice, and would mean a serious loss of honour.

The beasts brought their wings in alongside their bellies to pick up speed, commencing their death-dive. Once again, Deale King stood alone from his army, his arm raised to the sky. Near him stood Vali Balder, bleeding heavily from a deep wound in his left arm. Deale's arm fell and the four dozen kneeling soldiers fired in unison. The sky was filled with crossbolts. Many missed, several struck, but they were only glancing blows against such strong tough flanks. However, a few reached their targets; eyes were punctured and throats pierced. The five massive creatures fell from the sky to crash heavily down onto houses, tearing them down with a dreadful crash. The knights quickly reloaded and fired into the injured beasts' throats at close range, killing them almost instantly, their shrill death-cries burning deep into the minds and memories of their murderers where they would reside for the remainder of their days. Now once again the eerie silence reigned. Timid farmers slowly returned, glancing fearfully around. But the dragons were dead and there were none to replace them in the city. Everybody again stood motionless, seemingly afraid to speak aloud or even dare breathe the incredible obvious truth. But then one lone soldier suddenly cried out and soon he was joined by many others, all screaming in triumph. Farmers turned to embrace knights and Ace smiled at Sasha down below with Karl. Procel laid a friendly hand on his shoulder and Ace hugged him and laughed.

The war was over. They had won.

But from the other half of the city abruptly arose a shrill unholy inhuman cry which shattered the cries of triumph and ended the joyful embraces. A new army began to emerge into the main street from the other side of the settlement and farmers began to flee the city in droves. Swords fell not only from farmers' hands but also from the hands of knights to crash onto the ground in complete shock, terror and despair. For no human army came towards them, but rather an unholy mass of stumbling magickally-created mutants of nature. No fighter could summon the strength to strike the weaponless monsters down. Those that remained in the city were rooted to the spot in speechless horror.

These were tales told to them as children to encourage nightmares. Nobody expected them to become flesh; to become a dark reality. No training on Race Island, no matter how harsh, could have prepared the knights for this scene from hell. This was the ace of Soren's that Deale feared. Creatures half-human, half-animal swept through the army of soldiers and farmers. Some possessed no head, others displaying several arms which protruded at grotesque odd angles to their foul-smelling bodies. All smelt heavily of death and decay; the scent of rotting flesh. Speechless knights stood motionless as creatures bearing two distorted legs, one arm and only half a face tore out throats with only its teeth for a weapon. The commander tried in vain to spur his troops into action. But the war was lost. The mercenaries had returned and Ace was again fighting them on the battlements. Procel had disappeared. Ace struck down a small bandit before running up the short stairs leading to a turret overlooking the broken city gates.

"Sasha, get the hell out of here," he roared as the foul creatures approached her and the black mercenary. "Karl, get her out of here!"

Ace watched in horrified fascination as both knights and farmers were cut down by creatures bearing no weapon bar their teeth. He forced his gaze away from the hellish scene; he could not bear to look upon the army's bitter destruction. His attention was diverted instead to the sudden arrival of a lone mysterious newcomer who emerged from amongst the midst of the monstrous army of mutants. Ace gasped in both awe and astonishment as the black-cloaked stranger proceeded to cut down men everywhere he went, one blow for each farmer or knight, each strike fatal. They fell like flies before him, even those who had overcome their fear and were brave enough to fight. The stranger was approaching the battlements and Ace prepared himself. Suddenly Deale King moved in front of the mysterious swordsman's path and barred his way to the battlement-stairs.

"Try me on for size, stranger!" The commander boomed and drew his blade.

Ortolan sneered at the knight. Deale swung his sword towards his opponent's head in reply, but the mercenary easily defended off the blow and struck at Deale's legs, meaning to cut them from under him. However, the officer simply brought his sword down and blocked the strike. But he too late realised his mistake; the attack was but a decoy; an old swordsman's trick. He cursed his foolishness. The stranger's speed bordered on the fantastic. Ortolan swung up towards the commander's right shoulder and as Deale blocked it, for he had no choice but to defend the blow, he knew he had left himself open. Ortolan moved his blade up further, turned it and then cut across, removing the officer's head cleanly from his shoulders. Deale King stood headless momentarily before the armoured body fell in a heap. A second knight moved in front of Ortolan, but was struck down almost instantly. The assassin ran quickly up the battlements as Ace struck down a nearby mercenary to reach him. The two swordsmen found themselves confronting each other. High above, the sun beat down relentlessly on the two silent figures standing on the battlements of the capital city of the world. Here stood the greatest swordsmen of their era. On this fateful day, one would fall.

Ortolan, thinking Ace a common farmer, moved to strike him down quickly and with little effort, but Ace just easily blocked the blow. The assassin tried again, and again, each strike defended by this apparent stranger. The mercenary hesitated, this individual before him possessed a skill and speed to almost match his own. This was no common knight or farmer.

"Who the hell are you?" Ortolan roared.

But Ace just laughed in reply.

"They call me Ortolan; The Dark Swordsman."

Ace nodded in respect to a fellow master of the art. "I have heard of you. They call me Ace."

Ortolan's eyebrows raised in surprise. "And indeed I have heard of you. You fought well in the battle of Colewort City five years ago. Your skill is of quite a high repute."

Ace nodded again.

"In another time and place, we could have been friends, you and I." The assassin said quietly.

"But that time and place does not exist." Ace retorted sharply as the fight resumed.

Blows were struck and blocked by both swordsmen until Ace drew the first blood, cutting Ortolan's right arm with a downward slash of his blade. The master swordsman quickly returned the gift as he struck a slight blow to Ace's right thigh. Ace clenched his teeth with the pain and drove his opponent slowly back towards the turret in order to corner the mercenary. Both were now however quite weary. Ortolan struck and drove Ace back across the battlements in reply. Both blades met at the hilt and Ortolan spun his sword around Ace's, removing the weapon deftly from Ace's hand and flipped it up over his head. It landed on the battlement floor, but well out of Ace's reach.

Ortolan smiled. "You fought well, Ace," then his voice took on a cold tone. "But now the game is over."

Ace prepared himself for the death-blow as he sneered at the master swordsman in a last act of defiance. But as the assassin raised his blade, Procel appeared and jumped in between them, sword drawn. His sudden appearance took both swordsmen by complete surprise. Ace surmised that Procel had all along been watching the battle safely from afar. There was no doubt in Ace's mind that Procel had just saved his life, but for how long remained to be seen.

Ortolan was momentarily caught off guard. Ace would have used this rare opportunity and killed the assassin had he a blade, but Procel was no swordsman. Ortolan easily blocked the guide's feeble attempt at striking him down. He knocked the blade effortlessly from Procel's unsteady hand and with one swift motion, ran him through the chest. Procel fell to his knees as Ace cried out in shock.

Ortolan moved to remove his blade from Procel, but found the metal to be lodged in Procel's ribs. He pulled with all his strength, but could not dislodge the weapon.

Procel weakly removed his dagger from its scabbard at his hip, and to Ortolan's utter astonishment, shoved the small blade into the mercenary's stomach. The master swordsman fell back and his sword came out of Procel as Ortolan now clutched at the knife protruding from his stomach in pain and disbelief.

Ace rose in time to catch his old friend as he began to fall and laid him gently onto the battlement floor. Everywhere Ace looked there was blood. Ace screamed as this old familiar scene revisited him; first Elisa and now Procel. The guide smiled up at him through a face wracked with pain and Ace held him close.

"It's time to say goodbye, old friend."

"Don't try to talk." Ace said as he began to weep.

"Don't cry for me, Ace. Another you have deserted before needs you more than I."

"I'm sorry Procel, so sorry," Ace whispered. "I always knew in the back of my mind that there was really nothing going on between you and Sasha."

Procel smiled. "You old fool, Ace. I could never come between you and her. She was always yours, as I was always your friend."

Ace held him close as the guide sighed and moved no more. He laid him gently once more down onto the battlements, before rising to his feet and retrieved his sword. Ace knelt before Procel once more just as a shadow passed over him. There was a crash of heavy metal as a bloodstained dagger fell onto the battlement floor near Ace. Ace stood instantly as Ortolan faced him once again.

"My last act will be your death." The assassin said weakly.

"I admit you are the better swordsman, Ortolan. But my friend's sacrifice has given me the advantage. You will die here." Ace retorted, no trace of emotion to be found in the cold tone of his voice.

Ortolan for the first time in his long fighting career carried his sword in both hands. He was unsteady on his feet and occasionally a hand went to his stomach in an attempt to halt the unceasing flow of lifeforce seeping steadily from the wound. Ace acted quickly, striking towards Ortolan's head and then to his legs. The master assassin blocked both, but then Ace appeared to stumble. In his nervous haste to finish the fight, Ortolan moved in, but too late realised he had fallen for an old sword-playing trick. Ace side-stepped out of danger as his blade ran the assassin through the chest and pierced his black heart. The commander of the town Tamerindes grunted and fell to his knees. Ace deftly removed the weapon as Ortolan fell off the battlements to crash into the courtyard below. Ace had defeated the greatest swordsman in the known world, but it was a bitter victory.

He ran down the stone battlement stairs to the main street to where a few brave knights were still struggling against the inhuman army from Tamerindes, apparently unaware of their human master's demise. Ace soon found Sasha with Karl, alone by the city gates. The black warrior had been struck across the head and was unconscious. Ace and Sasha together began to drag him slowly out of the city as Vali Balder sounded the retreat.

The two travellers left the warrior in the care of the few dozen remaining knights undercover in the woods, and began making their way back to the city. Vali watched them go in disbelief.

Sasha turned and faced him. "There is still one person left to die."

"You can't go back in there." Vali Balder declared.

"It is time to finish the game." She retorted before following Ace towards the capital.

The army of mutants had begun to return towards Tamerindes, their task accomplished; their prey fled. Few mercenaries were to be seen, since the foul creatures would feed on them just as quickly as it did on their enemies, finding it difficult to distinguish between friend and foe. In the confusion, the travellers managed to enter the city unseen and entered a narrow alley. Night was fast approaching as they crouched down behind the ruins of a house to watch the monsters amble slowly past, oblivious to their presence. Sasha abruptly frowned and stared at Ace, he back in wonder and puzzlement. He knew before she had even to ask what was festering in her troubled mind.

"Where's Procel?" She stuttered and Ace's head dropped in silent grief. She grabbed his shoulders roughly. "Where is he?"

Ace realised she was becoming hysterical and could reveal their position to the mutants. He grabbed her face in his hands and held her close. "He's gone." He breathed softly into her ear.

She appeared not to hear, but stared vacantly over his shoulder. She felt as if Procel was still out there, maybe in the woods, safe and well. But truth and reason slowly crept in and she burst into tears as he held her tight.

"No, not another one, not another one..." He heard her mutter until she said no more.

He held her close and time seemed to become meaningless, until the realisation of their dangerous situation brought them back to reality. He rose to his feet and helped her up. "Let's go," he said quietly. "Let's find and finish the bastard." As he grasped hold of her hand tightly.

They ran into the darkening street towards the centre of the city and the castle where resided the creator of this madness.

CHAPTER TWENTY-ONE

The travellers used the darkness of the night to their advantage to hide their passing into the city centre. There were few enough remaining of the population to light fires, but not enough to detect the travellers' presence in the shadows. What few there was did not bother to blockade the gaping vulnerable city entrance, for they considered their enemies dead and in this they were almost right. The Magus, Sasha considered would be currently laughing in triumph over the corpses. He might still get the opportunity to gloat over two more. She pondered on the futility of entering his castle; what could they possibly do to stop him? Such thoughts were however furthest from the mind of Ace. Too many good men and friends had died this day for him to even decide giving up.

All considerations were stripped from their minds by absolute fear and awe as the street opened out to reveal a massive dark structure stretching high into the clouds. Twelve-foot high black iron gates barred their entrance ahead to Soren Castle; a fortress composed of seven towers, the largest of these in the centre where the Magus himself most probably resided. The fences easily dwarfed the city gates and Sasha cried out in despair. They could not batter these down. She turned to Ace in frustration when an ominous creaking noise ended such thoughts. Before their astonished faces, the huge impassable black gates began to open with no visible force commanding this action. They continued to open until they had reached their limit.

A large company of knights could ride through this gap, not just two lone intruders.

Ace stared at her in silent dread. Both were fully aware of the meaning of this. They hesitated before entering, the courtyard ahead hidden by darkness. But above, the Moon Goddess was out of hiding to show their destination; the centre tower. Ace could not believe this was really happening. Both he and Sasha entered the small courtyard with trepidation and approached the double doors into the actual castle itself. To no great surprise, they found them to be wide open, and as they entered, Ace thought he heard a shrill laugh manifest itself from far above; an unholy sound from the very depths of the night. They both knew this was Soren's doing. The Magus was deliberately allowing them entrance, confident of no possible danger.

The double doors behind them creaked shut with a loud crash. Both briefly glanced at each other in nervousness. In front of them, several doors lined a gloomy hallway. No furniture or decorations were to be seen. One entrance however lay slightly ajar to reveal an incandescent glow from the other side. They crept cautiously towards the door and Ace drew his sword, stepping in front of Sasha. He peeked inside, but it was devoid of life, human or otherwise. A spiral staircase stretched upwards as far as the eye could see was all that adorned the chamber. A large gold inscribed sign on the door read High Tower.

They entered the room and began slowly and cautiously to climb the staircase, Ace first, sword drawn. The unceasing climbing however rapidly began to drain their strength for it seemed to stretch on forever into the tower. Soon they could not see the ground below and to no great surprise, the door below had also closed, shutting out any possible chance of escape. The Magus, they realised had full intention of taking their lives and ending the Goodwin line. Ace had to laugh at the thought that he was actually allowing himself to go freely to his own death.

Far above in the distance, a light became apparent and beckoned them on towards it. They had no choice but to go on towards that radiance, there was now nowhere left to go. They could not possibly turn back, that opportunity was long gone. Eventually they arrived at the top of the almighty staircase and Ace was the first to sigh in relief as his tired feet placed themselves on that top step. They both now took the grateful opportunity to rest momentarily, their eyes focused fixedly ahead where a single giant door stood open to reveal part of an incredibly huge study where shelves upon shelves of books and ancient volumes lined the walls. There was no other visible entrance into the room; this door before them was also the exit.

Ace again grasped Sasha's hand tightly in his and she smiled at him before they together stepped into their apparent oblivion. They entered the chamber and turned to their right as the door suddenly closed, barring off their exit to the stairs and the outside world. The square-shaped chamber before them where the Magus rarely left and carried out his plans for world domination and destruction gave out an uncomfortable aura towards the travellers.

Sasha gasped in terror as the shadows at the other side of the room seemed to hide a figure sitting behind a broad table littered with manuscripts and leather-bound volumes. Two tall slender candles on the table flickered into sudden life to reveal the form of a well-built man in his early forties. A black robe flowed from his shoulders to cover most of his torso and over the seat to hover just above the floor. The Magus displayed a thinning crop of brown hair with no facial hair. He was handsome, though his face bore the scars of forbidden dark knowledge and the sights of past awesome times. But he had not changed since Sasha saw him last at the Cavern, yet he was still as impressive and fearful now as he was then, even more so up close.

The mage did not speak at first, but stared at his invited intruders without any distinct sign of emotion. Sasha and Ace also did not speak; Ace in stunned wonder and awe, Sasha in speechless dread. Yet still she managed to sneer at him; the brutal murderer of her father and friends.

"I believed you dead, Sasha Goodwin," the Arch Sorcerer boomed. "I congratulate you on reaching this far, but here it must end."

Ace still held his sword as his eyes fell all around the room, searching for hidden guards and sentries.

Soren noticed this action. "No bodyguards, human or otherwise line these walls, swordsman. I have no need of them. All I require lies in this room."

Ace could only sneer in reply while Sasha played with her father's gold medallion in nervousness.

"I oversaw and directed the battle from here," he continued. "I saw you kill my servant

Ortolan after he disposed of that pathetic guide of yours."

Ace roared in anger. "Yes, I'll bet you felt real safe and cosy in here, you miserable coward!"

But Soren only laughed. "Your meaningless insults inflict no wounds, swordsman." Then his voice took on a colder tone as he turned to Sasha. "The game is over Sasha, you die now."

The Magus rose to his feet and his cloak flowed all around his tall frame as the great serpent of magick began to arise within him. Ace jumped in front of Sasha and prepared to attack the Arch Mage. But Soren just calmly raised a hand and Ace was hit by a terrific invisible force which blew him across the chamber to crash heavily against the wall where he remained, stunned.

Sasha was however geared into life by this action and raised without thinking both of her hands directly in front of herself as she cried out. "Abrah Doea!"

Soren stopped to watch in surprise as a strange wind began to blow harshly through the chamber from no observable source and scattered books and various volumes to the floor. But other than this, the magickal wind caused no real damage to the room or injury to the Magus himself and he burst into shrill laughter. Sasha began to sway, unsteady on her feet.

"It appears I was right," the mage sneered. "You do have some of the powers of your father, but not enough to harm me. Now for your life."

He raised his hand again and it became ablaze with a glowing green brilliance. Sasha removed the medallion from around her neck and suddenly flung it at the Magus in anger, but he ducked the missile and it landed instead with a loud clang behind him. He laughed momentarily before resuming his death spell. However, he halted and Sasha who had been preparing herself to join her father in the Afterlife stopped and stared at the Magus in wonder and curiosity. A faint whispering noise appeared to be coming from behind the mage as if several people were talking rapidly in a low voice. Soren turned around, though could see nothing. But he then frowned as his attention turned to the actual source of the mysterious sound. Lying on the ground not five feet from the mage was Sasha's medallion, though a couple of links of the gold chain appeared to have fallen on a thick black volume.

The Magus stared at the tome in silent fascination as he recognised the book as the one he had stolen from the demon all that time ago. But he remembered that he had actually returned the book to Choronzon. So what was it doing here? He barely heard Sasha mumble behind him a command in magick, but ignored it for his full attention was on the volume. The Magus could only stare fixedly in speechless fascination as both the book and the medallion before his very eyes seemed to melt; the pages of the book dissolving and fusing with the medallion to form a golden blackish pool of liquid on the floor of his great study. It slowly began to darken in colour until it became similar in likeness to that of black mud. Suddenly dark dense fumes began to rise from the small pool into the air.

Soren coughed for the fumes were thick and stank heavily of the foul stench of decay and death. But this action was beginning to falter in life as if it required something further to maintain its strength.

The fumes began to disperse as the peculiar item on the ground rapidly and strangely began to die.

During all this odd activity, Sasha was feeling quite ill. It was as if something had taken over her mind and was commanding these actions. She again raised her hands and pointed them at the black pool. "Now, father. Use your powers, flow through me and charge this medallion!"

Soren turned back to her in terror as the ancient prophecy he had read many years before came flooding back to him. Segal Goodwin will cause your ruin, he remembered. He believed that if he killed the man, this event would never take place. He did not reckon on his rival somehow living on through his daughter. He began to resume the death spell in panic, but it was too late. The words of the incantation died on his lips as he turned back to the pool. The fumes again rose, with greater vigour this time into a thick smoke above the pool until suddenly a frightening bodiless face appeared from out of the smog. It hovered in the centre of the smoke and slowly gathered strength until the face became more distinct. Both Sasha and the Magus now stared in speechless horror. It was an all too familiar face to Soren; an inhuman face, that of a giant ram's head displaying huge curled horns. The top half of its torso now came into view; a naked hairless body with deathly-pale arms ending in gaunt claw-like hands which lay crisscrossed against its chest.

Soren stared fixedly at the demon in shock and disbelief as it smiled broadly back in reply, revealing sharp fangs stained with dark blood.

"I have returned, mage!" It roared and the whole chamber shook such was the strength of its voice.

"How?" Soren cried out.

"Let's just say that an old friend of yours over here made a bargain with me, the deal being your soul and I was only too happy to oblige, if I acted quickly and saved Sasha's life."

"Who, who is this old friend?" The mage stuttered.

As if in reply, a second face suddenly appeared in the dense smoke over the right shoulder of the demon. Soren let out a low moan as the familiar visage of Segal Goodwin appeared. The deceased ruler laughed at the Magus before turning to Sasha and smiled.

"Only you, my Sasha could complete the deal. Only you could form the spiritual bridge for Choronzon to cross and claim his reward."

Sasha could only stare at her dead father in shock. Soren fired a fireball from his outstretched hand into the smoke in panic, but it simply disintegrated upon contact with the black cloud. The Magus suddenly felt his feet sliding uncontrollably towards the magick smog. Sasha could only stare on in speechless astonishment at what was taking place. His hands flayed out in blind panic, striking books and scattering them to the floor as he attempted to halt this action, but in vain. His hands went out to Sasha in a plea for help, but she was rooted to the spot in fear and fascination at the incredible scene before her. The Magus Soren for all his vast powers, was completely helpless.

The mage's back still faced the cloud as he continued to slide on his heels until he was only a few inches away from the black smoke. The gaunt skeleton-like arms of the demon unfurled and embraced the sorcerer who let out a scream of sheer terror in response to its touch.

Soren turned once more to Sasha. "This cannot be. I am the Magus, I am High-Lord. I am…a god!"

Then to her astonishment, it seemed the mage's legs had liquefied as they incredibly began to sink down into the black pool until they had completely disappeared. His waist soon followed as the demon did the same, still locked in a tight embrace with the Magus, lest his prey escape. Sasha's father had already vanished. Soren was screaming perpetually now at the top of his voice as the demon was laughing. The two then appeared to dissolve into the very floor of the giant chamber until neither remained. Soren was gone. The thick smoke cleared as it too faded into the black pool which had given it birth, which itself seemed to shrink and dry up. It vanished before her very eyes. The book and the medallion were nowhere to be seen. Sasha was left alone in the room except for an unconscious swordsman in the far corner.

Several minutes had passed before Sasha left that spot and woke Ace who was generally unharmed, save a bump on the side of his head. They left the chamber of magick and slowly made their way down the long spiral staircase and ran quickly out of the castle where the owner no longer reigned or resided. They fled from the city to the woods where the few remaining knights and farmers cheered in welcome and triumph at their news of victory.

The following morning the two remaining travellers of the original seven person company gazed upon the capital city of the world in weariness, but also in jubilation. Their mission complete, however at the great price of warriors and friends who had given their lives for the ideal of freedom and for this day; a day free of any kind of magickal domination.

"Yes," Sasha declared. "It is the beginning of a new era." As she grasped Ace's hand tightly and he held her close; closer than he had ever held her in his entire life, and promised he would never let go.

EPILOGUE

The lamenting and burials went on all day. Loose earth and limestone abounded everywhere, waiting to be returned together with rotting flesh. Gradually the smell of death began to lift from the streets and ruins of Soren City. Life was once more returning.

The cracked sign upon the city gates displaying the settlement's name had been removed and renamed Libertas; freedom. It had not been named Goodwin for the people did not wish to be reminded of he or his vanquished enemy. However, the transfer of title appeared to be the only positive change. Dead dragons still lay decaying in the main street, their incredible bulk restricting removal.

The city's original population of mercenaries and bandits had apparently deserted their crumbling homes, fearing reprisal in this abattoir of a settlement. But unknown to them, fewer than four hundred out of five thousand knights remained. They considered it unwise to return to Race Island, lest their enemies on the island discover their true size and massacre them. The few thousand remaining farmers had quickly left for home to their houses and their fields, never to return. Sasha watched as endless processions of knights carried their fallen companions to their mass graves. She glanced briefly to her right to see two such soldiers dragging the headless body of their commander out towards the plains where lay the burial plots. Deale King was not deserving of such a cruel death, this simple task was all they could do to honour his courage and memory.

Three long days of lamenting passed before the city could bear to witness such antithesis; a wedding of their new ruler and a great swordsman who bonded their love and lives at the shattered entrance to the city. Sasha was made leader of the city, but real power rested on the shoulders of Vali Balder. The Chief of Guards was once more in control. The dark castle of the Magus overshadowed the gathering, as if showing its great distaste. Vali sighed in relief in the certain knowledge that the dragons would not return to the capital. Their servitude ended with the life of their master, they were free.

Following the ceremony the soldiers present half-listened as Sasha promised great changes and the dawning of a new era. But the proud knights only cheered in reply when Vali offered his allegiance.

Night came quickly and the soldiers eventually rested, weary of rebuilding and endless burials. In their exhaustion, they noticed not the passing of a lone stranger in the shadows, hidden under a long dark robe. The intruder slipped past knights deep in slumber and ran through the city until it reached the castle of the Magus. The gates still stood open, offering safe passage to the tower, but it seemed to have lost not much of its malevolent aura. The intruder entered the foreboding courtyard with trepidation and opened the two doors leading to the familiar corridor of doors and the entrances to each of the towers. Inside had been placed earlier two large barrels of mead and the stranger smashed them open with a small hand-axe. Liquid spewed everywhere, across the hall and in under the doors. The stranger left, only to return a few moments later with a lit torch, its bright flame flickering wildly in the cold breezy night air. The dark cloaked intruder then threw the torch in and it landed, instantly igniting the floor and blazing into sudden fiery life with a passion. The walls of the corridor soon followed as the heat quickly became fierce. The stranger swiftly then left the castle and glanced back at a distance to admire its handiwork. A breeze came up the main street and blew violently across the face of the intruder, momentarily revealing shoulder-length wavy dark hair upon a tall graceful form. The stranger then turned away and left the scene of the crime, the castle now completely engulfed in flames. No knight seemed to have seen the great fire, as if they did not care.

The dawn revealed only black ruins, still smoking. The huge gates however still stood, a last eerie testament to the mage Soren and the madness left in his wake.

www.ingramcontent.com/pod-product-compliance
Lightning Source LLC
Chambersburg PA
CBHW061019120726
47910CB00006B/2014